skyfisher

skyfisher

A NOVEL

DAN DOWHAL

Blue Butterfly Books
THINK FREE, BE FREE

Blue Butterfly Book Publishing Inc.
2583 Lakeshore Boulevard West, Toronto, Ontario, Canada M8V 1G3
Tel 416-255-3930   Fax 416-252-8291   www.bluebutterflybooks.ca

Complete ordering information for Blue Butterfly titles can be found at: www.bluebutterflybooks.ca

First edition, soft cover, 2010

Library and Archives Canada Cataloguing in Publication

Dowhal, Dan, 1954 –
  Skyfisher : a novel / Dan Dowhal.

ISBN 978-1-926577-06-7

  I. Title.

PS8607.O98744S59 2010   C813'.6   C2010-903242-X

Printed and bound in Canada by Transcontinental-Métrolitho

The text paper in this book, Enviro 100 from Cascades, contains 100 per cent post-consumer recycled fibre, is processed chlorine free, and is manufactured using energy from biogas recovered from a municipal landfill site.

Mixed Sources
Product group from well-managed
forests, controlled sources and
recycled wood or fiber
www.fsc.org Cert no. SW-COC-000952
© 1996 Forest Stewardship Council
FSC

Blue Butterfly Books thanks book buyers for their support in the marketplace.

To Bo,

my own private voice from on high.

Whether you're a follower of Phasmatia, or a non-believer, you need to read this. It's time everyone knew the truth about the Church, and its evil leader, Sky Fisher. I realize I'm taking on one of the world's most powerful institutions, not to mention bucking one of the fastest-growing trends of modern times. Trust me, I wouldn't do it if I had a choice, and I may very well pay for it with my life. Please, just read it, and you'll understand.

For starters, don't believe what it says in their Sacred Text, or what you see depicted on the walls of the Phasmatian temples. The Universal Spirit did *not* enter Sky Fisher as he stood on the top of Mount Skylight, purified after seven days of fasting and meditation. I should know. I was there. Or, more accurately, I wasn't there... but neither was Fisher.

No, the closest thing to a divine epiphany actually took place in a trailer a hundred-odd miles away, where Fisher and I, and Stan Shiu, may the *real* God have mercy on his soul, were wrapping up a whopper of a weekend binge. Fisher suffered from the worst constipation I've ever seen in any living creature and was struggling in the washroom when his revelation arrived. As that cosmic conspiracy of the bowels finally relented and delivered forth a raisin of a turd that even a gerbil would be ashamed of,

Fisher screamed out, "I've got it!" You won't find *that* in your
Sacred Text. Holy shit indeed.

Don't get me wrong. I'm not trying to belittle Fisher's role in
the whole Phasmatian phenomenon—none of it would have happened without him. Take that weekend in the trailer, for example.
Stan and I did brainstorm key pieces of the scheme at different
points during our bender, but I mean, we were just blueskying
wild-ass ideas in between shots of vodka and hits from the bong.
Fisher was the one who had the fire in his belly to actually make
something happen. It was Fisher who took the ball and ran with
it—all the way to the end zone, and well beyond that, I'd say.
Still, he couldn't have done it without our help.

Most importantly, Fisher actually came up with the money,
including pouring every bit of spare cash he possessed, and
could beg, borrow, and steal, into bringing the Phasmatians into
reality. The rest, as they say, is history (also religion, politics,
sociology, economics, science…) and by now hardly anyone in
the civilized world hasn't been steamrolled in some way by the
Phasmatian juggernaut.

Certainly things would have been different if Fisher and the
Phasmatian religion hadn't ended up becoming The Next Big
Thing. I doubt Stan would have risen up and got himself killed
if Fisher hadn't become the global icon he is now. I don't blame
poor Stan. I mean, you can't pick up a magazine, or turn on the
TV, without Fisher's beneficent smile beaming down on you, and
it's tough to keep your mouth shut under those circumstances,
not from jealousy of Fisher's enormous wealth and success, but
because he's a fraud, a felon, and one supreme asshole—and a
constipated one at that.

But I guess Fisher's holding all the cards now, and I'm the
one scared shitless to leave this hiding place. The odds are when
the Phasmatian monks track me down I'll be as dead as Stan.
So, I suppose that's why I'm writing this—part revenge, part
penance. If by some miracle (a real, old-fashioned one, not the

scams Fisher peddles) I manage to get this onto the Net, and if it's not deleted, and if some politician who's not under the Phasmatian thumb has the balls to launch an investigation, then maybe it will have been worth dying for. I'm no martyr, and I'm not ashamed to admit I don't want to die, but if I've got to go, I'd sure love to take Sky Fisher down with me.

Sorry. I'm rambling. As a writer (even a hack advertising copy-writer) I should know better. Let me lay some of the foundation down for you, so you understand where I'm coming from—and more importantly, why you should believe me.

I first met Sky Fisher—born Louis Skyler Fisher—at Warren & McCaul, the ad agency where we both worked. The fact that Fisher was once a high-powered Madison Avenue account exec-utive seems to have been conveniently edited from the official record—I guess they don't want you to even suspect how he schemed to concoct the whole Phasmatian thing. The Sacred Text portrays him as a sort of wandering mystic who was called to Mount Skylight to receive The Universal Spirit. (I don't have a copy of the Text here, so I'm going strictly from memory, but then I *did* practically write the thing.) So let me tell you that Fisher was an ad man, and a damned good one. You probably recall some of the campaigns he came up with in his time: Preter-Comm, Sashu, UtiliMotion, RoboXen, Borealex. Remember that beer commercial that had every joker in North America going around screaming, "Where's your head at?" That was his too.

In hindsight, Stan and I should probably have been suspi-cious when Fisher started chumming around with us. I mean, he was a good half-dozen levels above us on the organization chart and tended to move in different circles from the rest of us lowly grunts. I think now that it was Stan he was targeting all along, and I just sort of fell into it. Stan was, after all, Warren

& McCaul's alpha geek, and had engineered all of their biggest
and coolest client web sites. Not that he ever got the credit he
really deserved, even when the agency spun off some of the software he developed and made themselves a tidy sum, of which
Stan got zilch.

But Fisher was a smooth talker, and a consummate flatterer,
and Stan and I ate it up. Drank it up too, all on Fisher's tab. A
lot of Asians have a genetically low tolerance to alcohol, but not
Stan Shiu. I guess that's why he and I had hit it off. We were
both partyers (some would call us drunks), and Macbeth's, over
on East 29th Street, was our regular hangout. (Damn, I could
use a drink now. Maybe when I figure out where to upload this
file, I'll find a liquor store.)

Anyway, one night, apparently out of the blue, Fisher bumped
into us at the bar.

"Stan! Brad! Fancy meeting you here, dudes. Can I buy you
a drink? What are those, vodka martinis? How about doubles?"
He pushed his way to the front of the crowd and waved a plati-
num card at Bill, the bartender. "Good sir. A round for my
esteemed colleagues here, if you will, and keep them coming."
Stan and I exchanged a look like we'd just won the New York
State Lottery.

It's not like we all didn't know each other, of course. A lot of
Fisher's accounts included a web component, so we had worked
under him before. He would have been familiar with the work
Stan and I did. Even so, face-to-face contact had amounted to
little more than a dozen of us minions sitting around a boardroom table while Fisher did all the talking. Now, here he was
in the flesh, not only casually calling us by our first names, but
wanting to party with us too.

Fisher played it real cool at first, sticking to innocuous con-
versational topics. He had probably been drinking with us practically every night for two weeks before he started picking our
brains. I remember him pouncing on the news that some trendy

social networking site, which had grown to thirty-odd million users in only a few years, had recently sold for $2 billion.

"The two guys that started it are, like, twenty-four years old now," Fisher said, shaking his head in awe. "I tell you guys, the internet is the place to be ... that's the twenty-first century gold rush."

"C'mon, Lou," said Stan (he was still Lou to us in those days— Sky Fisher came later). "You're doing alright. You're making six figures and the scuttlebutt has it you're in line for VP."

"Chump change," said Fisher. "These guys are making millions ... billions, even. It's not the technology per se. Shit, Stan, a world-class guru like you could set up something in your sleep, right?" I remember Stan smiling giddily, like a debutante who's just been told she's the most gorgeous girl at the ball. "It's just coming up with the right idea."

"The good ideas are all taken," I piped in, swirling the ice in my empty glass so Fisher would take the hint.

"Bullshit!" Fisher said, but he did fetch fresh drinks, and afterwards he proposed a toast. "Here's to finding a killer idea, and to the three advertising geniuses that can make it happen—concept, content, and execution."

I excused myself after that. (By then I was already starting to notice that Fisher's use of the bathroom was, to put it mildly, eccentric. I could never figure out how so much food and booze went in, and so little came out.)

When I came back, Stan and Fisher had their heads busily together, babbling about eBay and Google and YouTube, and were ignoring everything else around them, even the hot blonde admin assistant from W&M who was practically sticking her huge tits into Fisher's back, trying to get his attention. I tried unsuccessfully to flirt with her, but she knew I was just a lowly copy writer and had her sights set on bigger game. That should have been one of my first clues as to just how driven Fisher was. In any ad agency, rank has its privileges, and there were plenty of sweet young things trying to get his attention, but he stuck to our trio, and stayed on topic. Now, of course, he has his harem of Phasmatian nuns, but that's another story.

When I poked my head back into the huddle, Fisher was saying, "What we should do is go away this weekend ... you know, like in the country some place ... stock up on booze and weed, and have a serious brainstorming session."

I certainly didn't know I was about to make history—it just sounded like a party, and the fact Fisher was including us in his weekend plans was not lost on me either—so I quickly said I was up for it, and that's when Stan, eager to please, suggested his folks' place.

"They own some land in the Adirondacks ... and there's a trailer on it," he told us. "There's plenty of room for the three of us. It would be perfect."

Now, Stan and I had known each other for over three years, and that was the first I was hearing of the availability of a country retreat, but at the time I took it in stride. I can see now it was an indication of how he was being seduced by Fisher. You could say it was also the first step on the path that led to Stan's death ... and maybe mine.

Damn, that just sent a shiver down my spine, or perhaps it's just the cold outside. I guess I'm pretty worn out from the trip here—three hundred miles on a motorcycle, dressed up as The Grim Reaper for part of the trip. Okay, I know that begs an explanation, and I'll do that tomorrow. Right now, I'm going to shut down my laptop and get some sleep.

Article updated Saturday 1 November 10:08

Reading back over things, I see that I've neglected to introduce myself. It's only relevant in the context that you know I'm not just some guy slamming the Phasmatians because I don't agree with their theology. Actually, I do agree with most of it, except for the part about Sky Fisher's divine powers, which are all made-up bullshit, and I should know, because I helped make it up. So, for the record, my name is Brad Evans, I'm thirty-six years old and was born in Poughkeepsie, New York. I have a Bachelor's degree in Communications from Columbia and, as I mentioned earlier, I worked as a copywriter at Warren & McCaul, where Sky Fisher was once an executive bigwig.

I say "worked" (past tense) because yesterday I left my desk and, without telling a soul, got out of New York for good. By now, all my co-workers know I've disappeared, and since a good many of them are anointed Phasmatians, that means Sky Fisher and his hit squad now know I'm missing too. Yesterday was also Hallowe'en, and it was the reason I picked that particular moment to leave (well, that and the knowledge I'd be dead inside of twenty-four hours if I didn't). There are traffic cameras everywhere these days, and I know, even if you don't, that the Phasmatians can pretty much gain access to any of them, so what other day of the year can you drive around with a mask and costume on, and not attract attention?

Since the car I typically use, or what's left of it, is lying in a police auto forensics lab, I purchased a used motorcycle for my escape, paying cash and using a fake name. The guy in Soho I bought it from (you've got to love New Yorkers) didn't even blink when I put on my black robes and skeleton mask before driving away. I'd chatted him up while I was looking over the bike, just to be sure he didn't have Phasmatian leanings, and I'm reasonably confident I got out of Manhattan without being spotted. Oh yeah, and as a diversion, because I guarantee they're tracking it, I couriered my cellphone to Buffalo—at the firm's expense. Look at me, a regular junior spy. Funny how quickly you can pick things up when your ass is on the line.

I ditched the costume, and even crudely spray-painted the bike black, once it was dark. I then took a roundabout route getting here, staying off the major highways and sticking to country roads. I'd left the office with just my omnipresent shoulder bag, trying not to attract suspicion. Since I hadn't brought any supplies, I stopped in White Plains to buy as much food as I could carry on the back of a bike, plus some warm clothes (again, all paid in cash), before heading north, here to Stan Shiu's trailer.

The irony is not lost on me that this is the very place my troubles began, over five years ago, but aside from the fact I have nowhere else to go, I don't think Sky Fisher would ever guess that I'd come here, even if he was managing the search for me himself instead of delegating it to his monkish Death Squad, which I doubt. Of course, if I'm wrong, then I'm a dead man, and more importantly, you'll never read this.

The last time I was here, though, things were certainly different. We all took off early on Friday afternoon and loaded up for a heavy-duty weekend of drunken, stoned revelry. But even on the drive up, Fisher's agenda was obvious. He was totally focused on coming up with a way of striking it rich on the internet, and soon we were passing around ideas as freely as we were passing the weed.

I don't know why I keep coming back to Fisher's colossal constipation, but it's the thing I remember most about the weekend. Sure, there are vague recollections of the ideas we kicked around before stumbling upon the Phasmatian thing (although it didn't have a name in the beginning). I remember we analyzed in excruciating detail the history and anatomy of all the sites that had really made it, from Amazon to Yahoo, and I kept harping on two things. The first was that we had chosen for our brainstorming a location with no internet connection. The second was that the niches had all been filled, so we weren't going to find an angle that millions of greedy, slobbering wannabes hadn't already explored. What can I say? I got wasted fast, and stayed that way until Sunday afternoon.

But the fact that Fisher didn't have the same basic bathroom urges as Stan and I soon entered the conversation, and that's when Fisher confided he had a genetic condition that affected his bowel movements.

"What? Are you saying you don't have to shit?" Stan exclaimed. (I'm not sure whether he was incredulous or impressed.)

"Of course not...everyone has to shit," Fisher replied, "but it takes a long time...like a lot of little tiny turds that I have to work hard to force out. I envy those guys that have their one regular, monumental crap every day. They don't appreciate what they've got."

So, that was it. We sat around, poured our way through a forty-pounder-plus of vodka and a case of beer apiece, smoked our stupid heads off on some killer shit Stan had gotten hold of, stuffed our faces (the trailer's small kitchen is remarkably efficient), and worked our way towards The Big Idea. In between, Fisher would regularly adjourn to the crapper and unsuccessfully try to force something out, usually quite vocally.

One thing did impress me. I distinctly recall, despite the massive amounts of recreational neurostimulants we ingested, how masterfully Fisher facilitated our little brainstorming session. I could see how he had risen to where he was in the firm. I mean, there were only the three of us, and we were totally wasted, and yet somehow Fisher kept his eye on the objective and managed to get us to contribute. Even me, or actually, *especially* me. Stan, despite his peerless knowledge of the esoteric technologies that drove everything webby, did not exactly have a depth of creative new ideas of his own, at least beyond new ways to write code and integrate systems.

I, on the other hand, and to the surprise of all of us, soon proved to be a gold mine of bright ideas, despite my initial it's-all-been-done, you-can't-get-there-from-here negativism. It's not really surprising. I was, after all, the only staff copywriter in the Interactive Division of Warren & McCaul, and lived, ate, and breathed the web, soaking up as much as I could (mainly to make up for my lack of formal technical training.) Although things are a little hazy, since it was Day Two of non-stop substance abuse when it happened, I'm pretty sure I came up with at least the germ of the final idea.

But don't think for a moment I'm trying to steal credit from Fisher (even if I wanted to take on that much bad karma). I'll admit right here and now the man is a genius—just a seriously twisted one. I may have pointed the way to the Promised Land, but it was Fisher who actually led us there. Even if he did do it from the toilet.

We all knew it would be time to head back to Manhattan soon, and I think this created a sense of urgency among us, especially Fisher. We had by this time agreed on all the characteristics our new web site needed to have in order to lure people in and keep them coming back, having mashed together all the best ideas that were already out there. Stan had even started to sketch out wireframe diagrams of how everything would work, especially the slick behind-the-scenes software that would secretly track users and record every aspect of their preferences and activities. But although we had a good handle on what the web site *did*, we were still searching for what it *was*.

I get pretty mouthy when I'm high, and I clearly recall my words were flowing. Fisher was back on the can, although he had left the door open so he could hear what we were saying, and by now we were used to his grunts and groans.

"It has to be a place where people come voluntarily to get something that's missing in their everyday lives," I babbled, "a sense of something bigger than themselves, something..." I swear I was on the verge of saying "spiritual" when Fisher screamed, "I've got it," and we distinctly heard the tiny plop of something finally dropping into the toilet bowl. (Maybe, having worked so hard to get it out, Fisher was reluctant to flush away his handiwork, or more likely it was because he was in such a hurry to get back out and tell us his idea, but when I went in there later to pee, I spotted that tiny, pathetic little peanut of shit floating around and I laughed out loud.)

"I've got it, I've really got it," Fisher was yelling when he burst out, and there was this wild-eyed look of utter joy on his face. "It should be a new religion!"

I remember Stan's eyebrows clamped down in concentration like he was doing advanced calculus in his head, but I immediately lapsed into my cynical know-it-all persona.

"Come off it ... there's already a thousand different church web sites out there," I protested, "and not one of them is in the same league as, say, a Facebook."

"That's because they're bricks-and-mortar religions with a supplementary web presence," Fisher insisted. "What we have to do is come up with a religion specifically for the internet." He obviously read our skepticism and reflexively launched into his adman's pitch. "Look, everything you hear about these days is how people are becoming disconnected from one another. Hell, that's exactly why these social networking sites have become so damned popular. Well, think about it. Nothing's eroded more in our modern technological society than the role of traditional religion. But the fundamental mystery of all mysteries, the purpose of our existence and what happens after we die, hasn't changed. I mean, isn't that why religion started in the first place?"

"More like to give an elite priesthood a hold on the masses," I said, but the look on Fisher's face spoke volumes.

"Works for me," he whispered.

Stan still didn't get it. "But if religions that have been around for thousands of years can't do it anymore, how can we?" he asked.

"Well, except for radical Islam," I said. "It's spreading like wildfire."

"Spreading into the socio-economic vacuum of the world's oppressed and disenfranchised," Fisher agreed. "Which just proves my point." He turned to Stan. "But to answer your question, our particular religion will succeed because we'll design it from scratch, and tailor it specifically for the web. Take it from me, Stan, I can sell stuff to people who don't even want it. Well, here we have billions of aching souls who are screaming out for something to fill their inner voids. I say we give it to them."

"Religion isn't a soft drink or a pair of jeans," I countered, my most recent hit off the bong making me feel smug about my special insight into the universe. I was pleased to see Fisher suddenly clamp his mouth down on the next glib argument that was just about to springboard off his tongue, in order to ponder my statement more fully.

To my chagrin, he smiled after a few seconds and replied, "You're wrong. Marketing is marketing. Period. People don't pay a couple hundred dollars for a pair of jeans because of the quality of the stitching done in a Vietnamese sweatshop—they're buying the designer label. And a soft drink doesn't make it big because of the flavor of the sugar-laced artificial crap they stick in the can, it's about brand ... it's about *image*."

"That's right," said Stan. "They buy stuff because it's cool, especially the kids." He seemed to realize exactly what he had just said and that made him frown. "Whoa. Weren't you saying that teens are the key target market if we're going to make it big on the web? How the hell do we make religion cool to teenagers?"

But Fisher instantly had the answer. "By making it uncool to their parents ... by making it seditious and shocking."

I was still skeptical. "I don't know. I can see how something might spread virally among the kids once it gets rolling, and then among the wannabe-young-again adults if it gets big enough, but we still have to have some kind of hook or angle to get it off the ground in the first place. Sure, we can build a slick web site, and offer a personalized experience, and provide chat rooms where people can meet and message each other. But if the kids come and all they see is a bunch of weird-ass religious mumbo jumbo, what's going to make them want to stick around?"

"That's where we come in, boys. We just have to apply the basic principles of advertising. First of all, we have to attract attention. Maybe seed some media articles, and round up a few celebrity endorsements. Geez, just look what Madonna has done for the Cabbalists. Rule two is to stimulate interest. Maybe we create something that's like a big online multiplayer game, but instead of some shoot-'em-up fantasy world where people waste one another, we'll have it as a spiritual place where people *save* one another."

"Sure, and instead of points you win karma to be redeemed in the next lifetime," I cut in. Once again, I was trying to be sarcastic but, God forgive me, apparently I was being brilliant.

Fisher beamed. "That's fantastic. It's what'll keep people coming back again and again. And we can have characters in the game who are online counselors, either human or computer-generated, to offer advice and guidance to troubled teens." He turned to Stan. "Wasn't that you who was telling me about all the artificial intelligence software they're building into games today?"

Stan nodded. "In fact, I've got some old classmates who were bragging to me online just the other day about some of the cool AI shit they're developing. I bet I could get my hands on the code we'd need, at least to make a good start. Everything else would have to be custom, of course." You could just see how excited Stan was getting at the prospect of a unique technological challenge to sink his nerdy teeth into. I half expected him to whip out his laptop and start programming on the spot.

Fisher was pretty excited too. "We have *so* nailed it. This will work... it will really work. Man, we're going to be rich!" He held up his hand for a round of high fives, and Stan eagerly obliged. As for me, I saw this scary look of pure power lust on Fisher's face—a look I would become only too familiar with (strictly behind closed doors, of course) in the years to come—and I desperately began searching for some dark cloud to spread over Fisher's sparkling silver lining.

"Something like that is going to cost a fortune to do right," I objected. "There's only so much we can do by ourselves in our spare time." Yes, I did say "we" because somewhere in the course of the weekend Fisher had sucked me in too, despite my constant harping over the details. Or maybe it was just the smell of greed in the air.

"You're absolutely right," Fisher said, "but I for one am willing to put every cent I've got into it, and we'll beg, steal, or borrow the rest somehow. This is just too big an opportunity to let go by." He eyed us both with a look that would make a viper pale. "How much money can you guys put together?"

Stan and I exchanged sheepish looks. After all, we didn't make nearly the kind of coin Fisher did, and it's not cheap living (and living it up) in Manhattan. "I can scrape together a grand, maybe two," Stan said, and you could just see how he hated to let Fisher down.

I pulled out my wallet and looked inside. "I've got about sixty bucks." Okay, so I was being a bit of a wise ass, but I basically lived from paycheck to paycheck, and that was the point I was trying to make.

Fisher, however, barely blinked. He was eyeing my credit cards. "What kind of a limit do you have on your cards?" he asked. I guess he could read my reluctance, or more likely he had only been trying to make a point of his own, because he reached for the legal pad where we'd been jotting down ideas over the weekend, turned to a fresh page, and began to scribble down numbers. "I've got about 75K in GICs, and another fifty in stocks. I'll liquidate those tomorrow. I can probably net fifteen after I trade in my Porsche for some shitbox in the next day or so. It'll take longer to arrange a second mortgage on my condo, but I figure I'll be able to borrow 200K or more on it."

He paused and fixed us with this flint-eyed look, and it didn't take a genius to understand how deadly serious he was. I wish I could tell you I wanted to opt out, but the truth is, there was this crazy tingling feeling running throughout my body, wholly discernible even through the residual haze of cannabis and ethanol, and I felt like the hottest chick in the bar had just walked right up to me and asked to screw me.

Stan was obviously feeling it too. "I can borrow 15K on my credit cards," he jumped in, "and I bet I can hit my parents up for 30K easy." With my meagre pledges added (I felt like I should be signing something in blood), we soon had almost $400,000 tallied on the pad, and spent the rest of the day, until it was time to return home, figuring out how to spend it.

Now, you're probably noticing two things. One is that I confess openly to having materially contributed to the Phasmatian genesis—I won't call it the "conspiracy" because, at the time, it was just a tiny, helpless fetus compared to the evil beast it eventually became. The second thing is that Stan and I combined only bankrolled a tiny percentage of the initial venture. But though Fisher was by far the major stockholder, he never held it over us, at least in the beginning, and treated us as equals, even if he did have a natural tendency to boss us around.

Pardon the interruption. I've just returned to writing this after a bit of a scare. I heard a sound outside and (oh, aren't I the brave one) went to investigate, a shovel in hand as my only weapon. There was a rustling in the bush nearby, and for a fleeting instant I was convinced they had found me. I was contemplating jumping back on the bike and making a run for it, when out walks this deer, a big eight-point buck, cocky as hell. It just stood there eyeing me for a minute until the sound of distant gunfire reminded us both it was deer season, and the buck bolted. Poor critter. I know just how he feels. God, I wish I had a rifle.

So, I was talking about how we three pooled together our money and got to work building the web site. Well, Stan got to work on the physical site, while Fisher and I started fleshing out the idea. Hold on, I'm skipping details. I should mention (and this just proves how driven he was) that upon returning to work on Monday morning, Fisher immediately quit his job. He hadn't told me he planned to do it, but word spread around Warren & McCaul like wildfire. Of course, the scuttlebutt was that he had jumped to another agency, and apparently old man McCaul himself had

Fisher up in his office for two hours trying to bribe and cajole him to stay, before calling security to escort him to the door.

Although the three of us had just pledged to mortgage ourselves to the hilt for our communal scheme, I had assumed we were only going to work on it in our spare time. Fisher's resignation surprised and unnerved me. It's not that I didn't have some degree of deep-rooted greedy hope concerning our idea, like you do when you buy a lottery ticket, it's just that I lacked any real faith it was actually going to pay off. In that regard I felt I was only being realistic.

Sure, I was ready to go into hock for the project, but somewhere in the back of my mind I had already projected the whole affair into an interesting barroom yarn I'd be telling in a year or two (always, in my fantasy version, with a rapt audience of secretarial hotties hanging on my every word) about how I had been a partner in this bold but quixotic scheme with Fisher that almost made us rich. However, after a recuperative period of belt tightening, I fully expected to be back in the black (or as close to it as a habitual spendthrift like me could expect to be), and leading the same old merry life as an advertising wage slave. I hadn't pledged my full-time, undivided commitment to the plan. Or had I?

Around lunch time, I went looking for Stan to see where he stood on things. Frankly, I was looking forward to the opportunity to get him alone—I had already noticed how he behaved quite differently whenever Fisher was around. In the old days, before Fisher joined our little twosome, I had considered myself to be the de facto leader, through a combination of my writer's gift of the gab and Stan's pliant, introverted nature.

I was relieved to see Stan was in his office, hammering away at the keyboard. I closed the door behind me, and sat down on the edge of his desk.

Excitement was written all over his face. "Did you hear about

Lou?" he asked right away (even in those days he was the only person I knew who called Fisher by his real first name). "Man, this is really going to happen."

"Did Fisher tell you he was going to quit his job?"

Stan hesitated for a second, and appeared to be considering his words carefully. "Um, no ... " His face turned beet red, and I instantly knew he was lying—a first in our relationship—although with Stan it wasn't a hard read.

"What the fuck, Stan?" I protested. "I thought we were all in this together."

That did it, and he relented. "Sorry, dude, but Lou said not to tell *anyone*. He didn't exactly say he was going to quit, but he phoned me first thing this morning and told me the powers-that-be were going to be asking the system administrator for copies of all his recent emails, and wanted to know if I could erase any trace of messages between the three of us ... you know, when we were emailing back and forth last week about 'our private web site project' and 'nailing down that idea that'll make us all rich.' So, I kind of knew he was going. It's standard practice around here to audit emails when someone leaves the company ... they want to make sure someone's not trying to poach clients."

I was speechless, as much from the revelation that my emails might be monitored (even though that should not come as a surprise to anyone who works for a big company) as from the idea that Fisher and Stan were keeping things from me.

"Were you able to do it?" I asked. "I mean, did you delete our messages?" My real motivation was concern that my job could be in jeopardy if Warren & McCaul tied me to the departing Fisher.

The ear-to-ear grin on Stan's face gave me the answer before he spoke. He laughed. "Piece of cake. The security around here's a joke. Pretty smart of Lou to think of it, though ... we don't want anyone stealing our idea." Then he lowered his voice to a whisper, complementing the atmosphere of paranoia that was starting to spread over me. "So, are we going to quit too?" He was like a little boy asking permission to go outside and play.

I wanted to slap him on the head and say, *Are you crazy? This is just some harebrained scheme we've been sucked into, and we'd be idiots to throw away our good jobs.* But I didn't. I could lie to you and say I was only trying to spare Stan's feelings, but the truth is, even if it was at some subconscious level, I had subjugated my will to Fisher's. I would do whatever he told me to do.

"Let's wait until we hear from Fisher," I replied.

I wish I had paid more attention the last time Stan had us up here to the trailer. The main power just kicked out (again, my first thought was they had found me) and I'm writing this on my laptop's battery reserves. I know there are solar panels on the roof, and a fair-sized propane tank attached to the side of the trailer, but I have no idea how full it is, or what my status is energy-wise. There are a few hours of daylight left, so I'd better try to figure things out while I can see what I'm doing.

Man, I'm an idiot. It didn't even register with me that I wasn't on the grid anymore, and had to conserve my power. I was so cold when I got here two nights ago that I turned on the electric heaters, and ran them all night and all through the next day ... until I drained the trailer's batteries. It's taken a while to recharge them from the solar panels, and during that time I've taken stock of things. I appear to have about half a tank of propane, which I'm only going to use for cooking and hot water, so that will last me for weeks. And I've stocked up on firewood for the little wood stove that does a dandy job heating the trailer, although I had to wake up a few times during the night to keep it stoked. If I'm frugal, the solar panels will provide all the juice I need for powering my laptop, for lights, and for running the fridge.

When I went looking for the cause of my power outage yesterday, I found labels and notes in Stan's handwriting in the battery bay, including one on a circuit-breaker that said: HEATERS—HIGH POWER CONSUMPTION. USE SPARINGLY. That's so typical of Stan: to provide that kind of detailed instruction, even though his folks could barely read English. Or maybe it was just his way of reaching out from beyond the grave to help out his technologically-challenged buddy Brad. God, I miss Stan.

***

Back to the task at hand. I was writing earlier about how Fisher
quit his job the very next day after we hatched our internet
scheme, and how Stan and I were waiting to hear from him.
Around 3 p.m. I got a text message from Fisher saying to meet
him at Macbeth's after work.

When Stan and I showed up, Fisher was ensconced at a corner booth, scribbling away alternately in three different hard-
covered note pads. He quickly spotted us and earnestly waved
us over, before I even had a chance to order a drink from the bar.

I'll never forget the unsettling expression on Fisher's face.
He'd always had this somewhat superior look about him (not
unusual for a top gun in a major ad agency, I suppose), but
now his lips seemed twisted in a self-satisfied smirk, as if everything that was going to pass from them was undiluted wisdom.
I admittedly have the advantage of hindsight as I write this, but
I mention it because it made such an impression on me at the
time. It's important, too, because you need to know Fisher is a
manipulative, two-faced bastard, and it's so easy to be taken in
by him. Maybe you're one of his followers, and as you read this,
you're fuming because the only look you associate with Fisher
(the one he struck for the cover when he made *Time*'s Man of the
Year, for example) is one of compassion and benevolence. Trust
me, he's been rehearsing that one in front of a mirror for years.

Stan and I slid into the booth, and Fisher began spouting a
detailed report of what he'd been up to all day, and wow, had he
ever been busy, especially when it came to making good on his
word to liquidate all his assets in order to accumulate working
capital for our venture.

"So, which one of you two am I moving in with?" he asked. A
lump appeared out of nowhere and took up residency dead center in the middle of my throat (and me without so much as a beer
to wash it down with.) I had a flashback to the time in college

when this chick I was screwing suddenly announced I'd knocked her up, and proceeded to begin taking control of my life. The pregnancy turned out to be a false call, and I dumped her immediately after learning the blessed news, but the conversation I was having with Fisher had the same your-ass-is-mine vibe.

Fortunately (for me, not for him) Stan jumped right in and eagerly volunteered to share his place, a rundown but spacious two-bedroom down in Tribeca. I could tell, however, that my reluctance did not go unnoticed on Fisher's part, even if he did not so much as murmur a single overt syllable of criticism or complaint. Neither did he press us about our own promised financial contributions, or insist that we had to quit our jobs too. He had the patience of a spider.

Once again, Stan was at the front of the line when it came to showing his loyalty. "I'll serve my two weeks' notice at work tomorrow," he volunteered, practically jumping up and down in his seat. "The best part is that I've got like a month's vacation coming to me, so there's a couple extra thousand bucks for the kitty." I'm convinced Fisher hesitated just long enough to be able to get a read on what I was going to say next, because the second I opened my mouth to jump on the bandwagon and say I was willing to quit too, he interrupted.

"I think you guys should hang on to your jobs," he said, surprising us both. I do remember, however, that it was Stan he locked his eyes on as he explained why. "This thing will take too long to come together if we just do it by ourselves. That's what the money is for ... to buy the talent we need."

"But I wanted to build this myself," Stan said. "I don't want someone else to have all the fun."

"And you *will* build it," Fisher said soothingly. "You say you've got a month's vacation coming, right? Well, how much work do you figure we can get done in that time ... I mean if we work around the clock, and only take time out for sleep and meals?"

We both puckered up our faces in contemplation. Stan was

clearly weighing the problem at hand. As for me, I was wondering what the hell I had gotten myself into, and was silently saying goodbye to life as I knew it. Little did I realize how true that really was.

"I can't code it all in a month," Stan finally concluded. "There's just way too much work for one programmer."

"You have to stop thinking like a worker bee," Fisher chided. "You're management now. Your job is to architect the system, especially those cool features we talked about the other day, and delegate the grunt work to others—maybe offshore to some bargain-basement coders in India or Russia." At this point he pulled out one of the notebooks he had in front of him and handed it to Stan. "I've allocated seventy per cent of the budget for the technical development ... that's like 300K. Figure out how many people you'll need on your team, and we'll hire them." Fisher flipped open the book to the first two pages, where he had sketched out everything we'd talked about over the past two days, using exquisitely rendered multi-color bubble diagrams and flowcharts. "I've started it off with the big picture ... you'll have to fill in the rest."

Stan was clearly impressed. (Diagrams will always do that for a geek.) "Yeah, yeah, I get it," he was saying, and immediately pulled out a pen and started to add notations of his own. "Of course, there are some parts I won't trust anyone else with," he commented as he worked, "but you're right. There's no reason someone else can't do the low-level shit."

I now understood that one of the other notebooks Fisher was fingering was meant for me, and I must admit I was dying to know what my role was going to be in the new order.

Fisher had read my mind. "As for you, Brad," he said, sliding over my black-bound notebook, "you need to write all the copy and scripts ... everything the users read, see, and do, from the first welcome messages they get when they log on, to the advanced religious dogma we'll be offering to the hard-core devotees. I don't see the actual wordsmithing as the hard part for a hot-shot writer like you, though—that's why I don't think you need to quit your job, especially given your financial situation."

Fisher's patronizing tone was rubbing me the wrong way, but I was so relieved to learn he wasn't expecting me to resign from my position at Warren & McCaul, I let his bossy attitude slide. When I started to flip through my own pages, however, most of which consisted of nothing more than a heading atop a blank page, I was suddenly struck by the enormity of the challenge facing me.

"You claim the writing per se is not going to be hard," I said, "but there's a hell of a lot of major blanks that need to be filled in."

"You got that right," Fisher agreed, with a condescending smirk, "and most of it's not the sort of stuff we can really trust a subcontractor with, is it? I mean, we're talking our most secret and sacred doctrines."

I think that was the very first time it actually hit home what we were truly attempting to do. I'd been thinking of our idea like it was going to be any other web-based diversion, albeit one in which I had a financial stake. Now, laid out in front of me in Fisher's ornate, design-school hand lettering, was an entire concocted belief system we were going to try to get people to buy into—literally.

"Don't worry," Fisher said, "we'll work out the details of our doctrine together. That's going to be my prime focus for the next month." He reached under his chair to haul out a knapsack, and began placing a pile of religious texts on the table. There were books on Christianity, Islam, Buddhism, Judaism, Hinduism, and Taoism, plus a number of other more general ones covering mysticism and mythology. "It's basic marketing, boys—you start by evaluating the competition. Our religion is going to have to be the real deal, providing all the answers for those confused, seeking souls that come to us. Oh yeah, and we're also going to need a cool name and a kick-ass logo."

He opened his own notebook and began to show off some of the ideas he'd been tinkering with. But no sooner had Stan and I leaned forward to peruse his handiwork when Fisher slammed the notebook shut in our faces. I flushed with anger, convinced this was some sort of power-tripping ploy on Fisher's part, and was just about to let the cocky bastard know what I thought of his arrogant mind-fucking games when someone spoke from over my shoulder.

"Hey you guys... is this some kind of going-away party? How come I wasn't invited?" a husky female voice said, and I turned to see Rita DeMarco, the hot chick from W&M's accounting department. She was accompanied by some skinny, pimply-faced young guy I didn't recognize, who was clearly devastated to have lost his monopoly on Rita's attention. She may have been addressing all three of us, but her eyes never wavered from Fisher.

In an odd reversal of roles, I was the one about to tell a chick to get lost, when Fisher put on his most seductive smile and motioned for the pair to join us. He nonchalantly swept up the religion texts, and all three of our notebooks, into his knapsack, and patted the seat next to him, which was promptly occupied by a giggling Rita. Her companion, instantly forgotten, had to fetch a seat and unhappily squeeze in between Stan and me.

"I was supposed to meet someone here, but he had to cancel," Fisher lied. "Brad and Stan just happened to run into me. Not much of a going-away party, really."

"Well let's see if we can do something about that," Rita purred, leaning closer to him.

Fisher smiled back. "Excellent idea." He turned to me. "Say, Brad... why don't you fetch us all some drinks?"

I was pretty pissed off at him, on so many levels—his condescending tone, the fact he was making me buy the round and, most of all, because he had this gorgeous babe hanging off of him—but, of course, I meekly complied. When I got back, Rita and Fisher had their heads so close together you wouldn't have been able to slip a piece of paper between them.

Stan, which was typical of the lovable galoot, had meanwhile already befriended Rita's estranged companion, and the two of them were going on about some sci-fi TV show I'd never heard of. I felt completely left out, so I headed over to the bar where I could at least chat up Bill, the bartender, given it was a Monday night and Macbeth's was dead. As I looked over, I saw Fisher reach down towards Rita's chest and pull up a crucifix she wore around her neck. As I watched him fondle the small gold cross between his fingers and whisper something seductively in her ear (no doubt about how he had something to offer her that Jesus didn't) I found myself shaking with violent jealousy, even though I barely knew Rita.

I mentioned earlier how Fisher had never previously shown any interest in women while the three of us were out carousing together, despite plenty of come-ons. Perhaps I had come to think of him as asexual, and this had helped me feel less threatened by Fisher—more like his equal. Now every ounce of competitive, pound-on-my-chest, primate belligerence came to the surface and I wanted to throttle the fucker. I think I could have done it. I had four inches and at least twenty pounds on him, and he looked like the sort of guy who had never been in a scrap in his life.

Would anything have changed if I'd acted on my violent impulse? I doubt it, unless I'd actually killed or maimed him. I won't play at revisionist history and claim I wish I'd performed that service on behalf of humanity, even if it meant going to jail. I'm too much of a wimp, and didn't even so much as hurl an audible insult Fisher's way. Instead, I sat at the bar, fumed in silence, and got progressively drunker ... until the rutting couple couldn't keep their hands off one another any longer, and practically ran out of the bar together.

With the gift of hindsight, I can see now that Rita was simply Fisher's way of rewarding himself for having taken a major step towards accomplishing his ultimate goals. This is not a man who gives up things easily, be it his secret thoughts, or his bodily secretions, but he has a megalomaniacal belief in his own destiny, and the unwavering sense of the intrinsic entitlement which that brings. Any sexual behavior I would subsequently see Fisher indulging in—and there would eventually be an epidemic of debauchery at the highest levels of his church—was simply a manifestation of his lust for power, reflecting a twisted, pathologically self-obsessed personality. I never saw so much as a glimmer of genuine affection for any of the legion of women he fucked. In fact, I seriously doubt that Sky Fisher has ever loved any living thing, despite his title as the Benign Wellspring of Universal Kindness (a title I invented, among others). And that, my friends, is the real skinny on the fat cat.

I thought I was done writing for the day, but the weather has turned nasty, and there's not much else to do in this trailer. All that stuff I wrote earlier about Fisher's eventual orgiastic lifestyle spawned vivid remembrances of the sexual scraps that came my way (at least for a little while) and made me horny, so I knocked off to masturbate and take a nap.

When I woke up, it was snowing, and I went out into the surrounding bush to gather some more firewood before the stuff got too deep. I doubt if a few inches of snow would deter any Phasmatian death monks from coming to get me, and the odds are it would in fact be easier for them to sneak up on me, but somehow that white blanket covering everything makes me feel a little more secure here in my snug, warm little hideaway. My strategy to conserve energy seems to be working, so I'm going to spend the evening plugging away at my own version of Revelations.

The next night, the three of us got together at Stan's apartment, which would be our headquarters for the next several months. Fisher had already converted the living room into an office, complete with a big whiteboard for sketching out ideas. Stan was hard at work, poking away at the keys of his computer, while Fisher and I began methodically to lay out the guts of Phasmatia.

I don't imagine any other person alive today can say he created an entire religion from scratch, certainly not one that would eventually rival the other major faiths on the planet—almost a billion card-carrying members at last count, and growing. Yes, as I've already told you, Fisher was the one who gets the lion's share of the credit (blame?) for directing the eventual outcome, but I confess freely (and, damn it, to some extent proudly) to having had the major role in crafting the dogmatic details.

We began by coming up with a name for our religion. Here, Fisher, as a marketing expert, was in his element, even though our budget didn't allow for high-priced brand consultants and focus groups. He stood in front of the whiteboard, writing down and crossing out possible candidate names, and you would have thought he was in a boardroom full of a dozen high-powered clients, not a cluttered apartment with two lowly accomplices. We must have poured through a thousand possible ideas, always cross-indexing them against trademarks and registered web domains, before settling on "Phasmatia," derived from *phasmatis*, Latin for "spirit." I'm positive, especially seeing as I studied Latin for four years in high school, that I'm the one who originally uttered the word. Fisher blessed it, added the more feminine "a" ending, which also made it unique, and proclaimed it his idea. I kept quiet. *Homines libenter quod volunt credunt.* Men freely believe what they want to.

Next, we drafted God into our cause. I was adamant, and Fisher readily concurred, that it was necessary to have a supreme deity at the core of all things. He was hell bent at first, however, to give Him/Her/It a unique name, physical incarnation, and personality, arguing that this would give our religion a uniquely recognizable spin.

I disagreed, feeling this would work against us, and became quite vocal on the subject. "You're crazy!" I remember shouting. "If you tell people, for example, that the universe is run by some giant purple dragon with a million legs, they'll just laugh at you."

"I was thinking more along the lines of a sentient galaxy," Fisher countered, and he rose to the whiteboard to again sketch out the stylized spiral symbol we had unanimously agreed earlier was the best of all the logos he had come up with. He was quite proud of it, I could tell as he doodled it over and over again—and judging by the number of people who now wear that symbol around their necks, it seems it was indeed a brilliant piece of design.

"But the universe has billions of galaxies," I said. "Are you saying that it's our own galaxy that's alive? Are they supposed to worship the Milky Way then? And doesn't that technically mean there just might be a pantheon of competitors out there? Not to mention the possibility of a higher intelligence that created those galaxies."

"What do you suggest, then, an old man with a beard?" Fisher shot back sarcastically.

"But why have anything corporeal at all? Isn't it better to keep it vague? ... some nebulous, but benign, all-pervading intelligent force transcending space and time ... "

"A Universal Spirit! I like that."

"Well, it's hardly an original concept," I admitted, "but maybe that's a good thing. It would sound familiar."

Fisher was already ahead of me. "No, no, you're right. That would work in our favor. We don't necessarily try to compete directly with the other religions. Rather than condemn them as false ideologies, we endorse them as facets of the same great ultimate truth. That would make it harder for them to slam us."

Stan meanwhile hadn't so much as murmured a single syllable for the past hour—he was concentrating so hard on his

programming that we had forgotten all about him. But suddenly
he lifted up his head from the keyboard and inquired, "How do
I code that?"

"What do you mean?" Fisher asked.

"Well, our web site is supposed to be a place where people
come to worship, right? If God, or The Universal Spirit, or
whatever you want to call it, is this invisible cosmic force, what
exactly then do our users *see*?"

That had Fisher backsliding. "He raises a good point. If our
religion is going to be an immersive online experience, maybe we
should have some visible representation of the deity ... you know,
something for the advanced practitioners to aspire towards. It
could still be ethereal ... say a sort of hovering, glowing, shifting
shape." He wasn't really sold on the idea, though, and (Lord
forgive me) turned to me for advice. "What do you think we
should do, Brad?"

I groaned. "Sure, that's fine ... if you want this to end up being
some kind of video game—*God Quest: The Battle for Your Immortal
Soul*—and frankly, with our budget, it'll be a lame-ass game compared to the multi-million-dollar titles the big boys are cranking
out." I went over to the stack of religion texts and spilled them
over the table. "Don't you get it? All of these religions do. God
needs to be invisible. That's why they call it faith. As soon as you
start depicting your deity as some hokey special effect, you open
yourself up to the critics who'll claim you stole the idea from Star
Trek. Not to mention, if you're trying to convince people this is
the real deal, they'll want to see God in real life."

It has dawned on me more than once that the whole thing
likely would have fizzled if I hadn't been so brilliant with my
ideas. Yes, Fisher ultimately brought it all to market and, like I
said, he was an advertising genius, but I personally don't believe
Phasmatia would have worked without the real spiritual substance I gave it.

Stan, however, was still having trouble visualizing the virtual world he was being asked to build. "But if they don't see God, then what's in it for them?"

"You don't come to the church, synagogue, or temple actually expecting to see God," I pointed out, "yet they've been packing them in for millennia."

Fisher jumped right in. Give him credit, he always caught on quickly. "Geez, Brad, you're right. How could I have been so stupid? Of course we can't let them *see* God... that would ruin everything. It has to be the ultimate tease—the payoff you never have to deliver..."

"Until the next lifetime, that is," I interjected with a smirk.

He smiled too, and turned to Stan. "What they'll see are the priests, and a beautiful church, where they can acquire their own personal pew. And they'll come to get the answers they seek— guidance for their everyday problems, answers to the great mysteries of life, and, most importantly, they'll come to buy their way into a happy afterlife."

Fisher was back in control. He began scrolling through his cellphone's address book. "We'll need to hire someone first rate to design the Church space and furniture," he explained, "and a big-name fashion house for the priests' robes." He turned to me. "We're going to need a creation myth, and a treatise on the fundamental nature of the human soul in relation to The Universal Spirit."

Now there's something a writer doesn't hear every day, I told myself, but before I could bitch about the heavy demands suddenly being made of me, Fisher was on the phone, even though it was past 11 p.m., busily making arrangements.

It was a slack time for me at work, and with Stan taking a month's vacation, there were few distractions. As long as I appeared busy at my computer screen, the powers-that-be let me be, and I surreptitiously got most of the writing Fisher demanded of me done on the job. Stan had warned me that my computer could be monitored by management, so I worked from a portable flash drive, and was very careful about what files I stored on the firm's network drives. And, if they ever checked up on what web sites I was browsing, all they would have found was a predilection for comparative religion—pretty squeaky clean compared to all the porn and online games the rest of the company was secretly into.

In the evenings, after work, I would stop off on my way down to Tribeca and grab supper for the three of us. My arrival, and the meal break it precipitated, became something of a cause for celebration for the hardworking shut-ins. Still, as welcome as they made me feel, I couldn't help but notice the bond that was strengthening daily between Stan and Fisher, who were, after all, spending virtually every waking hour together. I began to wonder if I had been purposely allowed to remain on the job, not for financial reasons, but to exorcise my former influence over Stan Shiu.

We fell into a groove, and it was really amazing how much we managed to accomplish in the first few weeks of development. Every night Fisher would critique the writings I brought home from the office, and then we would brainstorm and debate the next section in The Sacred Text. Steadily our dogma grew, and in hindsight, I have to say it was some of the best stuff I've ever written. And, with each day, my appreciation for Fisher's creative genius only increased. I also feel I impressed him too, not just with my ability to turn a phrase, but with the metaphysical depth and soulful insight I brought to the exercise.

One point of thorny debate that arose again, however, was over the degree of morality that we would espouse for our followers. It was the same problem we had wrestled with, right here in this trailer, on that seminal night. Fisher again brought up the goal to attract young people with the web site, and wanted to offer an edgy, anything-goes sort of doctrine.

"Nothing's going to turn a kid off more than a bunch of 'Thou shalt not' commandments," he insisted. "They're at the age where they want to cut loose ... to rebel against society."

To my own surprise, mine was the rather vocal dissenting opinion. Fisher may have bought that stack of religious research texts, but I'm the guy who actually read them.

"Every successful religion has a moral code at its heart," I said. "We have to do the same if we're going to be taken seriously."

"Come on, Brad, think outside the box," Fisher chastised me (it was one of his favorite put-down clichés). "We're going to be the *alternative* religion. People are lazy, greedy, horny, selfish hedonists by nature ... let's give them what they want."

"Come off it, you're preaching spiritual nihilism!"

"What's wrong with that?"

"Well, for starters, how are we going to stay in charge of things if there are no rules?"

"By being in control of the good times they'll be having. We'll be the ringmasters ... the pushers that regulate their next fun fix."

"Then why even try making it a religion? We'll be just another online entertainment site and, at the risk of sounding like a broken record, we just don't have enough money to compete with the dozens that are already succeeding out there."

Fisher screwed up his face and began tugging at his left eyebrow—a sign, as I had learned by then, that my argument had hit home. He sighed. "Then what do you suggest?"

"I don't think you're giving kids enough credit," I said. "Sure, they may be eager to break some laws, like the ones governing soft drugs and underage drinking, but overall I believe they're generally decent ... well, except for the screwed-up freakazoids that bring an automatic rifle to school and open fire in the cafeteria. Look, within their own social groups, there are codes they follow, and follow willingly. They don't typically rip one another off, or betray their friends."

"That's right," Stan chimed in, ungluing his eyes from the computer screen for the first time in hours. "Even the most successful social networking sites lay down firm rules their users have to follow. It's part of what prevents the bad apples from spoiling the experience for everyone. But, dammit, in order to program the logic, I need to know what those rules are going to be."

Now that I had the reins again, I plunged on. "Remember that religion is first and foremost about your immortal soul, and about earning your way into heaven, or achieving nirvana, or whatever we choose to call it. After all, without a payoff in the end, there's no real incentive to follow the rules or grant authority to the priests. We don't want free-thinking nonconformists. We want unquestioning, obedient sheep."

"It still sounds boring to me," Fisher said. I began to realize, despite the fact he's now become a bigger spiritual leader than the Pope and the Dalai Lama combined, that part of the reason Fisher didn't *get* it was that he lacked any fundamental beliefs of his own. He never talked about his own religious upbringing, nor revealed anything to do with his own childhood, but from the few unguarded comments he let slip during the time we worked closely together, I don't think he had ever truly believed in anything. Well, other than looking out for himself.

"Then let's put some fun into it," I suggested. "We'll tell them that partying hearty and having sex is beautiful, and not a sin."

"Within limits," Fisher said, with a smug grin, "as long as they don't harm others, or themselves." As I've said, he was a quick study.

The next few weeks are a bit of a blur, but based on what came out of them, I'd have to call that time the single most productive period of my life. I was surviving on a couple of hours of sleep a night, and pretty much writing non-stop the rest of the time. I'd get as much done at work each day as my Warren & McCaul duties allowed, and then I'd crank it up even more every evening, and on weekends, at Stan's apartment, where I had my own designated corner filled floor to ceiling with religion books. Often I just put down my head and slept there, with the Bible, or Koran, or Upanishads as my pillow.

Initially, Fisher would look over what I'd written and offer some token suggestions, but I guess he soon realized he had little of substance to contribute to the arcane minutiae, and let me plunge ahead on my own. Besides, he and Stan had plenty of work of their own as the web site moved closer to its big reveal.

Normally, my output isn't so good when I'm tired, but in this case I felt inspired and uplifted, despite the ongoing sleep deprivation. The stuff just seemed to write itself. Oh, and what beautiful words they were. Firstly, there was the metaphysics, and I personally feel I did a brilliant job walking the fine line between the novel and the familiar, so that the religion would seem new and exciting, but ring true in an archetypal way.

Any Phasmatians who are reading this will recognize it all, of course. Your body is merely a vessel and an incubator for your soul, which is a microcosmic manifestation of the great Universal Spirit—a positive and sentient all-pervading life force whose brightness counters the destructive darkness of intrinsic entropy. That's right, boys and girls, it's all about light versus dark. Now that's hardly original, I know, but I'm especially proud of the modern touches I added to bring that ancient plot line up to date.

I had roomed with a physics major during my first year at Columbia, and remember him going on and on about dark energy, the hot new topic in astrophysics. You can't see dark energy, and it's all purely hypothetical, but it always stuck in my mind that these physics geeks had nevertheless established that dark energy accounted for seventy-four per cent of the total mass-energy in the universe, and was propelling its accelerating expansion. So, dark energy became the bad guy in our dogma, and The Universal Spirit is the heroic cosmological force resisting it.

A piece of The Universal Spirit is within you. Like a fire that needs tending, your own spirit must be nurtured and fed. With cultivation (and the guidance of the Church, of course) your essence can achieve a divine state of spiritual energy that transcends space and time, and persists beyond the death of the body. But if you neglect your essence, or allow it to become besotted with negative energy, then it will shrivel to a state where, once your body can no longer sustain it, your spirit will be swallowed up and extinguished by the dark force.

That brings me to Part Deux, our moral code. In setting down these basic rules for a fit and healthy soul, I borrowed the best from Aquinas to Zoroaster, with choice bits of Aesop, Mark Twain, Nietzsche, Gandhi, and Tony Robbins thrown in for good measure. I'll be honest, there's absolutely nothing original there (other than the rewording, so I couldn't be accused of outright plagiarism). After all, how do you improve on "Do unto others as you would have them do unto you" or "Do the right thing"?

I think my only stroke of genius was to point out to the young adults, who were our prime audience, the shortcomings and hypocrisy of previous generations, so that the young would feel rebellious and revolutionary by being good. It wasn't much of a sell to convince them their parents had screwed up the planet, and were morally and socially impotent. Each new generation always feels like it's invented sex and drugs and rock 'n' roll. I just added virtue to the list.

So, out with greed, and destructiveness, and violence, and hypocrisy, and misogyny, and excess. Embrace creativity, and charity, and compassion, and tolerance, and patience, and love, and kindness. Yeah, yeah, I know. It's the same old litany of sins and virtues that have been preached for millennia, mixed with self-improvement clichés. What can I say? The classics never go out of style. But even though we were shamelessly ripping off ideas from just about every credo that ever existed, I felt it important to be fresh and inspirational. That's why (you're welcome) music and parties and consensual sex are formally endorsed. Just remember to protect the environment and meditate twice a day first.

Maybe I was merely responding to an aching and emptiness within myself, but I wanted to create something uplifting that would give people hope and make them want to be better, happier human beings. So, even if the trappings and mythology of Phasmatia are all pure fiction, I believe the fundamental code of personal conduct I created absolutely rings true. It is a distillation of everything that is fine and decent in the traditions of human spirituality, updated for the realities of our modern times. I guess what I'm really saying is that I hope this exposé doesn't cause a backlash amongst all of you who have believed and followed your faith. Yes, I want you to take down and punish that evil megalomaniacal monster, Sky Fisher, and his murderous inner circle, but that doesn't mean we have to undo the good that has come out of Phasmatia.

After we set down our fundamental doctrine, and despite all the inspirational prose I wrapped it in, we soon realized something was still lacking. Stan was doing a bang-up job putting together the web site, and Fisher had hired a bunch of hot-shot young game developers out of the New York Film School to build the virtual world where the worshippers would congregate, but when we started preliminary testing the responses we were getting were lukewarm. Everything looked beautiful, and the interaction and performance were smooth as silk, but the overall experience was boring.

That's when I saw a new side of Lou (soon to be Sky) Fisher, which I now know to be a much more accurate representation of his true nature. He went ballistic, and started blaming the two of us, but especially me, for the shortcomings.

"I should never have listened to a moron like you," he railed, sweeping papers and office supplies off the table and onto the floor, then kicking them around for good measure. "You're an incompetent hack." He came over to where I was sitting in an armchair, and leaned over right into my face, baring his teeth. "Thanks to you, everything is ruined, and I'm bankrupt."

"Fuck you!" I screamed back at him. "Don't you dare try to blame this on me!" I leapt to my feet to confront him.

"You're the one who said we should make it some lame, goody-two-shoes religion. Peace, love, and fucking understanding. Yeah, *right*."

"And you're supposed to be the marketing hot-shot that can sell sand to Arabs. Don't point your finger at me, asshole."

I don't know how long we stood there, toe to toe, trying to stare each other down. It was one of those pivotal moments that you examine in hindsight, and realize how dramatically different life could have been if you'd chosen to act differently. I should have just bitch-slapped the sucker, and walked out the door. If I had, the whole scheme would have died, Stan Shiu would still be alive, and I wouldn't be hiding in a trailer in the woods waiting to be murdered.

"Look, there's no point in freaking out," I finally said, choosing to try to defuse the situation. "Arguing will get us nowhere. I'm telling you, we're really close. It's just missing something... a hook of some sort. I don't know what it is yet, but we can solve the problem."

"I'll tell you what the problem is!" Fisher screamed, knocking over a chair and kicking the wall. "You're a useless drunk. Hacks like you are a dime a dozen. I don't know why I ever thought you had what it takes to do something... something *great*!"

Oddly enough, my blind rage had subsided by this point, and

his latest insults just bounced off me. I was suddenly determined to show him just what I could do. Now I look back and hate myself for it. Christ, where was my backbone? Why did I need so badly to impress a man who was berating and insulting me? It would be easy to lie and say I did it out of pride, or because I had already invested so much, emotionally and intellectually, in the venture. But it seems to me, what I really did was submit to Fisher's will—I caved in and wimped out in an act of blatant submission, as surely as if I'd lain down on the floor, rolled over, and exposed my throat to the snarling dominant male.

"Just get off my case for a while, and you'll see," I said. "I can fix it."

"Well, *I'm* not giving up, and so you sure as hell better not either," Fisher warned, needing to have the final word, even though he was, in essence, acquiescing to my demands. He turned to Stan. "And as for you, if you're such a genius, then come up with something nobody's ever done before instead of stealing other people's ideas." With that he went off to the bathroom for the next hour to grunt and curse and try to force out another one of his microscopic turds.

When he came out again, his anger seemed to be spent, and although the three of us scarcely exchanged a word the rest of the evening, we threw ourselves back into the work. I stayed up all night, and phoned in sick the next day, just so I could keep at it and figure out what was missing from our online religious experience.

The answer, when it finally came to me, arrived like a thunderbolt from the heavens. I had just been plowing though the pages of those religious texts again, but my revelation actually came as I was staring vacuously at the whole collective stack of books or, more accurately, at the titles on their spines.

"That's it!" I exclaimed. "I know what's missing. Ah, man, it's so simple." And I started laughing like a mad fool (which I probably am).

Fisher came running and looked at me angrily, hating to be left out for even a minute. "What? What? Tell me!"

"We need a *prophet*," I said proudly. I expected them both to see the light as brightly and profoundly as I did, but the look on their faces was one of annoyance and disappointment instead. Fisher cursed under his breath and went to walk away. I think he thought I was playing some kind of joke, and was trying to say we needed to find a fortune teller to divine our solution. I grabbed him by the arm and spun him around to face the pile of books.

"Here, look," I said. "What's this title say?"

"*A History of Christianity*," he read, the impatience virtually dripping from his words.

"And this one?"

"*Buddhism Explained*. What the fuck's your point, Brad?"

"Don't you get it? Those religions are named after a *human* who espoused them, not after the God being worshipped per se. Jesus, Buddha, Mohammed, Lao Tzu, Zarathustra—the great religions are as much cults of personality as they are about the actual doctrine. We need to offer our followers someone to actually *follow*."

Fisher gave that some thought. "What about the Jews?" he said finally. "That religion is named after the people themselves."

"Maybe so, but it preaches the Messiah will come and walk among them. And meanwhile they've had more prophets than you can shake a staff at—it's as much about Abraham, and Noah, and Moses, and Solomon, and Ezekiel as it is about God."

"So, what you're saying is our product needs a spokesperson," Fisher mused, and I could tell from his facial expression he had not only caught up to me, conceptually speaking, but had shot right by me.

I don't need to tell you who Fisher eventually arrived at as the figurehead for Phasmatia—he anointed himself—and I want to go on the record as saying I had no hand in that particular deci-

sion. In fact, I didn't even realize he was doing it at first. He went
back to our group of game developers and got them to build us
a new and very special avatar for our virtual temple. Meanwhile,
Stan jumped onto the logistics of how this new, key figure was
going to figure in the overall programming.

  I was more preoccupied with what to call our new character,
and how he (I refuse to capitalize it as "He," despite the con-
ventional usage) fit into our whole overriding sacred dogma. I
didn't want to name him explicitly, because I thought it would
work better if he was somewhat mysterious and nebulous. The
Prophet, The Messiah, and The Savior were already branded, so
to speak, and so I finally settled on The Chosen One.

  In all the test renderings the animators sent us, The Chosen
One was clothed in these amazingly beautiful shiny robes, and
wore an exquisite ornate headpiece, which Fisher explained
proudly had been conceived by a three-time Oscar-winning costume designer, and therefore had not come cheaply. Plus, the
figure was always shrouded in a backlit purple aura, so it was
hard to make out his face in any detail.

  It wasn't until I was doing some testing of our improved web
site that I found out what Fisher had done. In these trial runs, I
would register as a new user/worshipper, and try as objectively
as I could to put myself in the head of someone experiencing our
virtual world for the first time. On this occasion, I had signed
up as a seventeen-year-old cheerleader from Idaho named Cindy,
and was chatting with a couple of other like-minded online buddies who were complimenting me on my newly posted profile.

  Even though I knew both of the people I was apparently ex-
changing messages with were really synthetic characters generated by Stan's software (later, as our enrolment grew, there
would mostly be real participants), I played along as best I
could. And then one of the characters, who was supposed to be
a high school senior named Todd from Tacoma, Washington,
suddenly interrupted, acting all excited.

Hey wow!! Let's go check out the special gathering in the Great Hall. The Chosen One's going to be there himself!!! Todd typed.

Who's The Chosen One? I replied, playing along.

He's soooooo cool, my other new (and artificial) friend, Brittany from Texas, jumped in. *When I broke up with my boyfriend he like totally helped make me feel better. Come on, let's go see him.*

So I clicked on the appropriate icon, and a new window appeared on my computer screen showing the Great Hall. Even though I'd seen it dozens of times before, the space never failed to impress me (which is a good thing considering how much we'd paid for its virtual architecture). The scene showed hundreds of happy, good-looking kids around my (i.e. Cindy's) age gathered in front of a stage, where a rock band was playing. (If I'd been portraying a retiree from Florida, the crowd would have looked very different—more like the lawn bowling club from Sunset Acres, only happier and healthier.)

Make sure your sound's turned on, Brittany advised me, and so I obliged. My speakers were flooded with a catchy pop ditty as the band strutted their stuff on stage. The real me knew the band was a talented, but unknown, bunch of musicians from New Jersey recruited by Fisher, but I tried to stay in Cindy's naïve little mind and enjoy the experience, although also fully prepared to drop out the minute I felt we'd exceeded her short little teen attention span.

The song wrapped up, and the band simply faded away in a dancing whirl of smoke. (You've got to love virtual worlds, where the laws of physical reality can be suspended at will.) A resonating voice then came out of thin air, and my jaw dropped, because I recognized the speaker immediately.

"We can make life better," the voice—Fisher's voice—said, and despite my indignation and incredulity, I have to admit it was slick and soothing. "There is a great force all around us. The Universal Spirit of love and harmony." A shimmering glow appeared in mid-air and then solidified into the figure of The Chosen One, in all his costumed splendor, as he glided down to the stage. He had a beatific smile on his face, and I recognized instantly that Fisher had modeled the face after his own.

I spun in my seat, ready to launch a verbal tirade at Fisher, who earlier had been sitting and scribbling notes in Stan's armchair. But he was suddenly standing right there behind me. The smug sneer on his face was a far cry from the saintly smile of his virtual doppelganger.

He chuckled. "So, what do you think? Pretty fucking good, eh?" He leaned over me to turn up the volume on the speakers, so he could hear his own sermon better, and I had to resist the urge to grab him by the throat.

"Who the hell said you could be The Chosen One?"

"Hey, easy Brad," Fisher said patronizingly, "you were the one who insisted we needed a spiritual leader. I just figured it was too important to entrust to an outside actor. And then imagine the extra cost. On top of a repertoire of sermons, we're going to need thousands of hours of voice recordings to cover all the possible things The Chosen One can say to users one-on-one when he appears at appropriate times. If this thing catches on the way we hope, any actor we hire would have us over a barrel in the future."

"But why you?"

"Who else? Stan? Or *you?*" He had a point. Stan was an insecure introvert who habitually stumbled over his words if he talked anything other than technospeak. Although he was born an American, Cantonese had been his first language, and there was an oddity to his speech—not quite an accent, but something that made his English sound imperfect. As for me, I'm fine when communicating via my keyboard, but I'm no public speaker. My voice can get a little high-pitched and I have a tendency to forget what I was about to say, especially when I get flustered. Back at Columbia, my professors had discouraged me from any career choice that would entail appearing on camera.

Fisher, on the other hand, was an accomplished pitchman who made a living out of persuading people. His voice was a mellow baritone, and he had an actor's gift of controlling emphasis and cadence. I also recalled from his bio, which I'd once edited for the W&M corporate web site, that he was much in demand internationally as a speaker at conferences and symposia.

"Okay, I get it," I said, my voice instantly getting squeaky to prove his point, "but why does he *look* like you?"

Fisher shrugged. "He had to look like somebody, and this way we're covered in case we ever have to make the jump to the real world."

In case we ever have to make the jump to the real world. Those simple words, said so nonchalantly at the time, now speak volumes in hindsight. And, in truth, Fisher wasn't a bad-looking man. He had thick brown hair, a strong chin, piercing hazel eyes, and a dazzling smile that was a testament to the art and technology of cosmetic dentistry. He was a little on the short side, and that might explain his need to overachieve, but there is no shortage of successful height-challenged politicians and actors. I had no choice but to admit Fisher was perfect for the job.

Mind you, I should have heeded my own writing. I was, after all, the one that put down in The Sacred Text that we should not be deceived by the appearance of the vessel outside, for what's truly important is the quality and quantity of spirit burning inside. Amen. In Fisher's case, the glib tongue and photogenic smile hid a scheming, greedy, and power-hungry sociopath. And that, folks, is the bottom line on the top dog.

This is the first thing I've written in almost two days. The snow just kept falling and falling, and there's a good two feet of it on the ground now. I think I must also have come down with the twenty-four-hour flu or something, because yesterday I couldn't even find the strength to get out of bed to keep the wood stove burning. It's a good thing the Shius left behind a quality down-filled sleeping bag to keep my aching bones warm, though, because it was cold as hell in here when I woke up this morning.

There's an interesting phrase—cold as hell. The stereotypical Catholic hell is, of course, full of fire and brimstone, where damned souls burn in eternal agony. I purposely never chose to create a Phasmatian equivalent of hell. I figured that having your soul permanently extinguished at death should be enough of a deterrent for would-be sinners. If I had, though, and in keeping with our theme of the dark entropic menace pervading the universe, my hell would have been cold to your very miserable core.

But I've got it nice and toasty warm in here now, and the sun is shining brightly outside (even if that's because a large high-pressure front from Canada has parked its frigid Arctic air over top of us). I'm going to go and stock up on firewood, and make myself a nice bowl of (canned) stew before settling down to continue this chronicle.

Oh my God. They may have found me. At least, *someone* walked by here yesterday while I was passed out, and checked the place out. When I stepped outside to fetch some more wood, I saw footprints in the snow, leading right up to the window, where it looks like my visitor peeked into the trailer before circling around once and walking out again to the road. It's a good thing I'd thrown a tarp over my motorcycle when I first arrived, because it was well hidden under a mound of snow. Or buried, I should say. As excellent a choice as the bike may have been for escaping Manhattan, I don't think it'll get me very far in all this snow.

Of course, it might only have been a passing hunter, or a nosy neighbor. But if it *was* one of the Phasmatians, then it looks like the weather (and being under it) may have saved my life. The heavy snowfall would have covered my earlier tracks, plus, who-ever peeked into the trailer wouldn't have seen me huddled up top in the sleeping berth, and there would have been no lights on, or smoke coming from the chimney.

I'm not sure what to do next. My fresh tracks and the wood smoke from my fire are a dead giveaway if anyone comes back, but if I wanted to make an escape now, I'd have to walk out—not that I have anywhere to go. So, I guess I'll just stay here and hope my visitor doesn't come back. Meanwhile, even if I don't know yet how I'm actually going to get it distributed to anyone, I'm going to keep relating the truth behind Sky Fisher.

With the addition of The Chosen One as our cyberprophet, plus a few gigabytes of software revisions Stan had added to make the web site perfectly attuned to a visitor's profile and activities, Fisher felt it was time to open the doors of our virtual church to the public. Not only did he want to shake out any bugs our own internal testing may have missed, but he also wanted to amass a significant base of users before launching any full-scale media blitz.

That strategy made perfect sense to me and Stan, not that we really had a say in the matter. Although our respective program- ming and writing activities never seemed to end as we tweaked and fine-tuned the web site, we were now pretty much taking a back seat as Fisher assumed control. While we took him at his word that he could use his advertising genius to fan the flames of interest in our web site into a full-out internet conflagration that would make us all rich, that first initial spark was still vital. But I had more than a few doubts about Fisher's ability to make it a go. I've always had a fatalistic (some say pessimistic) view of life, and was fully expecting our scheme to fail.

By now, Stan had finished his month's vacation (which he had stretched out by an extra couple of weeks with some unpaid leave) and had returned to work at Warren & McCaul. Each night the two of us would take the subway down to Tribeca and rejoin Fisher at the apartment, although Stan would inevitably be working on his laptop computer the whole way, and I felt like our former closeness had disappeared. I guess the emotional (and financial) investment in the Phasmatian project weighed heavily on us, and had altered the nature of our relationship forever.

In the beginning, the faithful certainly did not come flocking to us. Each night, under a gaggle of aliases, we would log on to other social networking web sites and try to induce people to come check out our virtual church. The skepticism and resistance was palpable. It would have been easier to convince people that the Queen of England was secretly pregnant with an alien's baby.

Fisher had also hired a dozen college students to help us with our online solicitations, although he kept them as much in the dark about our project as possible. The students had some marginal success, but of everyone it was me who proved by far to be the most effective at making converts. My technique was simple. I pretended to be an attractive teenage girl, posting fake photos of myself I'd lifted off the web, and Photoshopped just enough so they wouldn't be recognizable. I'd drop subtle hints I might be promiscuous, and soon had the young bucks chatting with me—salivating and eating out of my hand. Then I'd leave, saying I was off to join my girlfriends on the Phasmatian site. *Voilà*! A few minutes later, one or two of the young males would inevitably show up there, having first dutifully registered in order to gain access.

We each kept tabs on our progress—sort of the equivalent of a salesman's call sheet—and my superior success rate soon became evident. A few nights after our soft launch I was watching over Fisher's shoulder as some guy flamed him after being told to go visit the Phasmatian site in order to seek salvation.

Fisher looked up at me sheepishly. "I don't have your knack at convincing them, and me a card-carrying master of persuasion."

I shrugged, although the act of surpassing Fisher at something always gave me a warm glow. "Your problem is that you're trying to grab them by their souls," I explained. "Me, I lead them by their dicks." I explained my technique to him.

Fisher's eyebrow shot up, and he spun in his chair. "Hey, Stan, did you hear that?"

Stan grunted acknowledgement from his computer without skipping a keystroke.

"Can you write a program to do the same thing Brad here is doing?" Fisher asked.

That brought Stan's fingers to a halt as he contemplated the challenge. "I dunno, Lou, it's not the same thing as when we're on our own server...you know, where we have total control over every single piece of the data being trafficked back and forth. I mean, Facebook, MySpace, Hi5, Twitter, Yahoo—each one of those sites is totally different, and we're strictly limited to what we can access via a browser."

Fisher said nothing. He understood Stan well enough by now to know the propeller on his head just needed to spin a few more times in order to start crunching out possible solutions. "Then again," Stan mused, "I could write a custom plug-in that would automatically cut and paste data to the chat from a special inferencing engine that's running in parallel under the covers." His face brightened as the light bulb over his head went on. "Yeah, yeah...that would do it, and of course we already have all the code for natural language processing and for simulating human dialog, including variations on dialect, age, gender, etc." He turned to us and tried to look stern, but you could just see how he was busting out with pride at his own cleverness. "Naturally, I would need an exact set of rules to follow."

"No problemo," said Fisher, jerking a thumb my way. "Brad'll write down the steps he follows...and while we're at it, let's see if we can figure out a way to make this work on women too. I don't want a congregation that's nothing but horny teenage males."

Fisher needn't have worried. We soon discovered lures and come-ons that worked even better on women, although unlike the one-track sex-obsessed minds of the boys, the algorithms Stan had to program for chicks were much more complex. They didn't follow boys into Phasmatia, for instance, but they did follow other girls. I think in general women are more spiritual than men, and that explains why today a majority of the Phasmatian priesthood and general membership are female. Of course, I like to think the gender-neutral and egalitarian dogma of The Sacred Text helped—the one place where my skills for writing ad copy really paid off. In fact, once we saw the groundswell of female supporters, we soon took to referring to The Universal Spirit as "She." That's why I find it so ironic that all my pro-feminist efforts only ended up helping to stock Sky Fisher's harem with willing sex-slaves.

Within a week we had launched the equivalent of a robot army, crawling all over the internet and creating an artificial buzz about the Phasmatian web site. Initially the growth, although steady, was still slow. The amount of time people were spending on the web site was sparse, and most dropped out and never returned. But then, shazam, things seemed to reach some kind of critical mass, and abruptly our popularity began to grow exponentially. I won't pretend to fully understand how exactly we caught on, even with the crystal-clear vision of hindsight. I mean, why *do* hula hoops and Texas Hold 'em Poker suddenly become international crazes, while other ideas, better designed or more intrinsically appealing, fall by the wayside? Naturally, Fisher was quick to puff up his chest and start pontificating about the psychology of viral marketing, but I know for a fact the bastard didn't really have a clue either.

Nor did we have time to start pondering and analyzing what had inexplicably gone right. Having caught the wave, all of a sudden we were being pulled along at breakneck speed on the ride of our lives. The demands on our time became huge. Stan was constantly debugging code, upgrading functionality, and expanding his racks of servers to keep up with the growing numbers of users. And I was now being asked a thousand questions by our burgeoning flock of cyberfollowers about the esoterica of the Phasmatian dogma. Well, usually not me specifically—the questions were being directed to our virtual priests (although I would regularly assume the role of a priest and wander amongst the faithful, so to speak, chatting directly with them.)

Stan's software was good—brilliant really—but in the end there are real limitations to so-called artificial intelligence. Don't misunderstand me, the behavior of our synthetic characters was more than adequate for staging canned rituals, and in simple meet-and-greet scenarios they were brilliant. I felt we even held up well when troubled people really started to open up their aching souls to us. The programmed responses weren't quite as sleazy as the old psychiatrists' trick of asking, "And how did that make you feel?" when someone has just admitted to wanting to screw their kid brother. Our replies were full of flowery Phasmatian platitudes, but were equally vague. When you're asking hard questions about the nature of the universe, the limitations of the programming became evident. I mean, cryptic answers like, "seek the shining light, and in its reflection you will find yourself," will only get you so far when someone has just asked, for example, where The Chosen One came from.

When I suggested to Stan that we needed to make the replies of our virtual priests and priestesses more specific and believable, I got an earful. He summarily acquainted me with the Turing Test, one of the holy grails of AI. If you're not familiar with it, you can Google it (as Stan rather testily made me do), but the bottom line is this: nobody has written a program yet that's good enough to dupe discerning users into thinking they're talking to a human instead of a computer.

"And here I thought you were a genius," I quipped to Stan, and was somewhat surprised at how flustered he became at my innocent (I thought) joking.

"Screw you," he spat back. "If I was that good, I sure as hell wouldn't be working for Warren & McCaul, would I?"

I had been able to tease Stan about stuff like that back in the day when we were carefree barflies, but now the interminable progression of long, stressful days had soured his mood...or else perhaps I'd touched a private nerve.

"Whoa, chill, dude...I was only pulling your leg," I said, giving him a big man-hug to show I cared. "Your code is fan-fucking-tastic. Most of the people out there haven't got a clue they're not talking to a real person...in fact, I think that's one of the reasons we've gotten as far as we have." Admittedly I said it to placate him, but I was being perfectly sincere. "If I understand that technobabble you just made me read, then what you've done here is, like, totally cutting edge. Hell, dude...you should publish a paper on the subject."

You could actually see Stan's scrawny chest puff up six inches with pride. He gave me a friendly punch in the arm, and for a brief instant it was just like old times. But then Fisher, that cosmic killjoy, who had been working away at his workstation yet eavesdropping the whole time, had to piss all over our parade. "Nobody's publishing any damned papers," he yelled, jumping to his feet and waving his arms like a cartoon dictator. "Do you want the whole world to know our secrets?"

"Hey, take it easy," I said. "It's not like we're doing anything illegal, is it? In fact, it might be a neat angle for your PR campaign."

"Don't tell me how to do my job," Fisher screamed. "The problem here is that you're not doing yours."

Chip away at a man's sleep long enough and he gets kind of crazy. I went off like a Roman candle. "What the hell are you talking about? I've been working my fucking ass off! I can't remember the last time I had more than a couple hours of sleep!" I guess in my mind I assumed Stan would be a natural ally, and so I pressed the offensive against the tyrannical Fisher. "Stan and I are both working two jobs, you know. What the hell do *you* do during the day?"

"A hell of a lot more than you," Fisher said, and from the spectacular shade of red his face was turning, I could tell he was really angry. "Yeah, you go off to your petty agency job, alright, but I'm the one who's put himself out there with absolutely everything on the line. Do you want to know what I do during the day? Well, I'll tell you … I bust my buns to keep coming up with the cash that's keeping this thing going, and it's ten times the money both of you have put up, combined." He came right up in my face, and as long as I live, I'll always remember his crazed, twisted-up expression, and the retched breath, which had a brimstone-like smell to it, not necessarily for any demonic reasons, but because he'd been living off nothing but black coffee, and probably hadn't been inside a bathroom to brush his teeth—or shit—in days. "It's not Stan's software that needs fixing, it's your religion." (Funny how, all of a sudden, it was *my* religion.) "Right now, you need to plug up the holes in the dogma … you need to give all those people the sort of details and answers they're clamoring for."

"He's right, Brad," Stan said from behind me, and I felt like I'd been kicked in the balls. The poor, brainwashed little prick was actually taking Fisher's side. Right then and there I was tempted to walk out on both of them—to quit the whole insane endeavor, and go find a decent meal, and get roaring drunk, or better yet (seeing as my credit cards were all maxed out anyway), to just go home and sleep for a week.

I sincerely doubt if my departure at that point would have stopped anything. By then, the huge Phasmatian snowball was already racing uncontrollably downhill, getting bigger by the second. It's a moot point anyway because, one more time, I threw up my hands and capitulated.

"What do I need to do?" I hated myself the second I saw the

smug self-satisfied smile ooze onto Fisher's face. But it was really Stan I was talking to, and together he and I figured out a way for me to essentially be in a thousand places at once. More accurately, what Stan created was a real-time pipeline for me directly into the knowledge base used by the virtual Phasmatian priesthood in its online conversations. I may be a professional wordsmith, but I quickly learned a whole slew of new words like *polysemy* and *ontology* and *semantic reasoning* that made my poor head hurt (even more).

But, since Stan is no longer here to roll his eyes and grumble if I oversimplify things, I'll explain it this way: What we did was collect all the key theological and liturgical questions that were being asked by our burgeoning mass of followers, and then, as quickly as I could, I would devise an answer for each of them, which was then instantly written into a database of possible responses and reused by the virtual priests and priestesses in our online world.

That was how The Chosen One came to stand on the top of Mount Skylight to receive the directive for Phasmatia directly from The Universal Spirit. By now, The Chosen One's identity had been revealed as Sky Fisher, since our worshippers had demanded in no small measure to know more details about their human savior. With his marketing savvy, Fisher had effected the name change to a much hipper-sounding and more mysterious Sky, a variant of his middle name, Skyler, but this was one of the few direct contributions he made to the theological content. He was far too busy making random "live" appearances on the web site, when not planning the next big step in the overall market-ing plan.

I suppose I shouldn't have been surprised that more people wanted to know what Sky Fisher ate for breakfast than about the virtues that would bring us closer to The Universal Spirit. We had created a religious superstar, and the masses have a bottom-less fascination for celebrity. (Just witness the state of today's television shows.) So, I spent a lot of time inventing little details about Fisher and his holy calling, although at the same time making sure we kept him suitably mysterious.

I purposely chose Mount Skylight as the site of his divine epiphany because I had hiked to its summit, back in my days as a Boy Scout, during a camping trip to Lake Tear-In-the-Clouds, source of the Hudson River. Aside from having a cool-sounding name, I remember having felt a sort of quiet rapture standing on its peak, and thought it would be a nice addition to the growing lore of Sky Fisher. (Besides, even though we were safeguarding Fisher's anonymity, I felt it prudent to place him somewhere believably local. Sure, the top of Mount Everest would have been much more dramatic, but the records would easily have demonstrated he'd never been there.)

The constant demands of the Phasmatian worshippers and the lack of sleep were taking their toll on me, and I constantly felt like I was inches away from a breakdown. Even when I did crash for a few hours, whatever dreams I managed to have were inevitably haunted by faceless people clamoring after me for answers.

Needless to say, my work at Warren & McCaul began to suffer, and finally one day I was called into my boss's office and warned that my job was on the line if I didn't pull up my socks. Given how far in debt I was, I couldn't afford to lose the income. That night I went back to Fisher and told him something needed to change.

"I can't keep this up any longer. I swear I'm about to lose it." I knew the others were working as hard as I was, and financially were in far deeper than me, so I thought it was an opportune time to talk about where the entire out-of-control venture was headed.

"This thing's grown too big for the three of us," I continued. "If it's going to work, then we're going to have to hire more people to help us out... talented people we can rely on. And that takes money." I remembered Fisher's frequent reminders about the disproportionate amount of his cash already invested in the venture, so I moved to preempt him. "You've poured the lion's share into this thing, Sky,"—we had already started using his new name by then—"so I'd be interested in knowing how you plan on keeping this going … and getting your money back." I turned to Stan. "How many users do we have now?"

"Over 250,000 and counting," he said, although his eyes never left Fisher's face.

I whistled. "A quarter million! Man, if we could only get, like, two bucks out of each one of them on average, we'd be back in the black in no time." I let that hang there, and waited for Fisher's response. I half expected him to take a temper tantrum of some sort, and to start blaming things on me, as per usual. Even with all the effort I'd put into the project at that point, I think part of me was hoping he'd push me too far this time, and finally compel me to quit.

Instead, he smiled benevolently at us (which, in some ways, was scarier than his angry outbursts) and nodded. "Yes, I agree totally. In fact, I've been giving all this very serious thought over the past couple of days, and I've already taken the next step." He went over to what had once been Stan's dining room table, but now had been expropriated as Fisher's personal desk, and pulled out a sheaf of papers. "Today I filed the forms to have us incorporated as a formal church. With that, I was able to open up a merchant account that lets us start taking donations online. If I'm not mistaken, Stan has almost finished writing the software to start passing around the virtual collection plate, so to speak." He looked directly at me with that self-satisfied, lopsided grin of his. "I'm pretty sure we can average better than two dollars a head."

This was not something we had discussed among ourselves … or that they'd talked about with me, at any rate. I snatched the papers from his hands and began to scan them quickly.

"Us...a formal church? We can do that? I know there are hundreds of weird-ass congregations out there, but how do we qualify? I mean, it's really just the three of us and a web site!"

"Ah, but we do have hundreds of thousands of worshippers. The Supreme Court has already set a precedent...I believe it related to recognizing the Wiccans." He shuffled around the papers on the table and found what he was looking for. "Ah, yes, here it is: *Members of the Church sincerely adhere to a fairly complex set of doctrines relating to the spiritual aspect of their lives, and in doing so they have ultimate concerns in much the same way as followers of more accepted religions. Their ceremonies and leadership structure, their rather elaborate set of articulated doctrine, their belief in the concept of another world, and their broad concern for improving the quality of life for others gives them at least some facial similarity to other more widely recognized religions.*"

Fisher was starting to get a glint in his eye that I had spotted once or twice in the past, and would become all too familiar with in the years to come. I call it his Almighty Look. "I've already talked to a lawyer friend of mine," Fisher continued, "and she's totally confident we can make an identical argument for Phasmatia. And, trust me, if the government resists, we'll get our followers to stage a massive protest they won't be able to ignore...plus, the publicity from it will guarantee tens of thousands of new recruits."

He went to take the papers back, and although he did it casually, I got the distinct feeling he was trying to hide something from me. I squeezed down and jerked the forms back to scrutinize their contents more closely. My own action was not performed as subtly as his, and must have betrayed my suspicion. Fisher's face squeezed into a frown, but he let me look. Maybe he thought I wouldn't get what he was doing, but I saw it immediately.

"Stan and I aren't listed here," I said. "We don't have an active interest."

"I know. It's for your own good, Brad. As a church—and, really, that's just another form of a charitable organization—none of the net profits are allowed to go to private shareholders. I know how hard up you are for cash... I wanted to make sure you were in a position to take out money freely, without it creating an issue about our tax-exempt status."

"Makes sense," Stan chimed in, and I could have walloped him. How could anyone so smart be so stupid? Sure, it made perfect sense—if you were standing in Fisher's shoes. Maybe Stan still worshipped the ground Fisher stood on, but I could see what the devious prick was up to.

"But you're the only one of us who's a director," I pointed out.

"Well, naturally, we have to make sure we keep control, don't we? And I'm already the official face of the Church anyway." He finally managed to slide the papers out from my fingers, and waved it casually in front of my face. "Honestly, Brad, all this means is we're able to start collecting money on the web site. That's the important thing, right? After all, you're the one that just stormed in here demanding an end to our current dilemma... well, here it is. Our troubles are over."

"And what about you, Sky? Aren't you worried about conflict of interest and fallout from the IRA when you start trying to get some of your own money back? I mean, you've got a couple hundred thousand invested in this."

"Closer to a half million... I cashed in my pension fund two weeks ago... but that's not the point. Hell, we'll be pretty much pouring every penny back into the Church anyway. But now we'll finally have the kind of money we need to hire staff and launch a proper marketing campaign. Oh, sure, we're starting to take off... but we can really make this baby *fly*!"

As he spoke, and got all worked up, I noticed something odd about his mannerisms. By nature, given his former position in the ad agency, he was a talented speaker. But now his style had changed somewhat, becoming more deliberate and theatrical.

There was something familiar about it, and it took a few minutes to sink in. He was starting to emulate the style of Sky Fisher, The Chosen One, from the online experience. The motions of that virtual character had been choreographed by the original crew of animators, and I seem to recall they'd actually put both a dancer and a magician in their motion-capture suit in order to come up with just the right hybrid body language. I never knew whether it was deliberate, or if Fisher had subconsciously picked up the habits from all the time he spent online shadowing his virtual alter ego, but now he was starting to speak and behave the same way.

I'm going to knock off the writing for today. Actually, I'm surprised I've gotten as much down as I have, given that I've been getting up every few minutes to look out the windows for anyone who might be trying to sneak up on me. I'm running low on firewood too, and it's going to be a lot harder to round some up with all the snow covering everything. Who would have expected this kind of weather in the first week of November, even in New York? I also need to inventory my food supply, and figure out what I'm going to do next.

Thank God for my Boy Scout training. Or, more precisely, thank God for Ernie Ronson, my old Eagle Scout leader in Pough-keepsie, who helped me earn my merit badge in camping. Ernie was an old-timer who had spent a lot of time up in the Yukon, not to mention a stint as an army ranger, and so took his survival skills very seriously. He taught us a lot of stuff beyond what was in the book. Yesterday, despite the absence of a saw (although I did find a small hatchet in the trailer's tool box), I managed to gather up a good supply of dry firewood, most of it from dead lower branches. Squaw wood, Ernie used to call it.

That small stuff burns up pretty quickly, though, and I stayed up all night feeding the fire. I couldn't sleep anyway, and just sat there with the hatchet in my hand, waiting for Death to come knocking on the door. I covered the windows with towels and sheets, if only to make me feel a little better. It's still bloody cold outside, but the silver lining is that it makes the snow crunchy, and therefore easier to hear someone walking up to the trailer.

My food's running out too—there's only enough left for a day or two, depending on how well I conserve my rations, which hasn't been very well so far, since a hot meal is one of the few luxuries available to me here in this hideout. Oh, well, I'll worry about that tomorrow. Today I want to get more of this story finished.

After Fisher set up a bank account for the Phasmatian Church and Stan implemented the online payment system, money began to trickle in, although not at the rate we had hoped for. I suppose we had counted on our followers to voluntarily send donations our way out of the pure goodness of their hearts, but most simply ignored the requests. In a real-world church, people know their neighbors are watching them when the collection plate goes around, but the anonymity of cyberspace seemed to work against us.

In fact, the very appearance of donation boxes in our virtual temples caused a certain degree of grousing from some of our devotees, and a slight slow-down in our membership growth rate. That instantly killed any plans we might have had to charge mandatory enrolment fees, or be more aggressive in our solicitations. Fortunately, there were many people out there who were genuinely moved by our spiritual message, and a number of these gave quite generously... not to mention wandered among the other users and enthusiastically spread the gospel.

Fisher and I realized the potential of this emerging class of hard-core believers almost simultaneously, although for different reasons. I badly needed to cut down on my workload, and saw them as potential trainees who could eventually take over for me in day-to-day interactions with needy users. Fisher, on the other hand, saw an opportunity to begin charging them fees for special privileges on the web site—especially access to The Chosen One.

In essence, these devoted believers became an emerging class of priests and priestesses who each paid the equivalent of a tuition fee to become indoctrinated in the hidden mysteries and rituals of Phasmatia. For Stan and me, it was out of the frying pan and into the fire in terms of the demands on our time, as we were now pressed into service to develop the content and programming for an online Phasmatian theological college.

To give the devil his due, Fisher was true to his word, and saw that Stan and I began to be financially compensated for all the time we spent working on the site. He also started to pay other people to help us, choosing the keenest and most loyal from among the growing Phasmatian priesthood, especially for interfacing with the public. There were also more and more Phasmatian lay workers, from cafeteria staff to administrative assistants, all working under iron-clad non-disclosure agreements.

I had no interest in becoming a paper-pushing administrator, so I was actually grateful that Fisher handled all the personnel matters himself, although, in hindsight, he was just making sure all the power lines emanated directly from him. One notable exception was the IT department, where Stan continued to micromanage his operation in exquisite detail, no matter how many people he had working for him.

It was a milestone in our rapid organizational growth when, before very long, we began to promote middle managers from within the priesthood. After toying with a variety of titles for these second- and third-level priests, I deferred to the granddaddy of ecumenical bureaucracies, the Catholic Church, and simply christened them bishops. I had no hand in their selection or management, and they reported directly to Fisher. Nevertheless, while he wrote their official job descriptions, I wrote all the divine jargon and rites surrounding them, making sure the bishops were also elevated in holy stature within the context of The Sacred Text.

They were elevated in other ways as well. When Fisher restructured the Church's hierarchy, the board of directors became a governing council of bishops, with Fisher naturally at the helm.

Again, being deprived of a formal seat at the boardroom table rankled me, but every time I grumbled, Fisher simply bought my silence with more money.

And I can honestly say I never saw Fisher take a dime for himself, and he was very open about every single expenditure he made. Mind you, Stan had access to all the online accounts anyway, so there was no point in trying to conceal anything from him. Although he was a trusting soul (too trusting) by nature, he did have a child's insatiable curiosity.

Not that Fisher actually needed to put money in his own pocket. Phasmatia was basically forking out for all of Fisher's needs. He didn't pay rent, and everything he ate and drank was expensed—legitimately, since he was constantly out schmoozing and hustling. Besides, he was devoting every waking hour to growing and running the Church, and so appeared to have little need for additional luxuries or diversions anyway.

We had long since outgrown Stan's apartment in Tribeca, and much to the relief of the neighbors (who had been complaining about the 24/7 traffic and noise for months) and the landlord (who had been threatening action over the extra power our servers and workstations were sucking up) the operation moved up to Hell's Kitchen and took over 10,000 square feet on the top floor of an old warehouse. The setup mostly resembled a call center, with dozens of neatly arrayed cubicles, each furnished with a computer and operator's headset, and staffed by three rotating shifts of Church employees.

The west end of the space became Fisher's private domain, and included a tiny loft-style apartment, which even afforded a glimpse of the Hudson River in the distance. When he wasn't out supervising the workers, Fisher would spend his time sequestered in his combination office-studio, from which he could communicate just as efficiently in either the real world or the virtual one.

Stan also had his own little corner of the kingdom, which

included the server farm and switching room from which the web site was hosted. Membership on the web site continued to grow steadily, but unlike the early days of the enterprise, when funds were scarce, Stan now had carte blanche to expand and upgrade as the technical needs demanded, plus a quartet of bright young subordinates eager to carry out his instructions. Not surprisingly (especially given that Fisher was paying him more than the cheapskates at Warren & McCaul) Stan finally resigned from his old job outright, and came to work full time for the Phasmatian Church.

The only one of us who didn't have a formally designated space in the new facility was me, although I was technically able to log on and work from any computer in the place. I stubbornly chose not to work in spare cubicles, though, and would typically set up in the boardroom with a laptop I had Stan acquire just for me and set up on the office's wireless network.

I sometimes wonder whether things might have been different if Fisher had offered me a throne beside his. As it stood, I was never even tempted to quit my day job, although I continued to come in to the Phasmatian offices most evenings and also to work weekends. Lord knows there was certainly still plenty for me to do, but that was only part of it. Despite a nagging suspicion that Fisher meant to cut me out of any long-term payoff from the scheme, I was now being compensated rather handsomely for my time, and inside a year had not only regained everything I had hocked and borrowed to help jump-start the project, but was now in fact sitting on the biggest nest egg I'd ever had in my life. Of course it helped that I wasn't pissing my money away at Macbeth's every night.

But it wasn't just the financial rewards. I have to admit it felt really good to be part of something substantive, and there was an infectious vibe among the Phasmatian workers, most of whom were young, eager believers who, get this, looked up to me. Even though I didn't have an official title (although I suppose I could have written one for myself, like The Keeper of the Word, or the All-Hallowed Fountain of Divine Answers) they could still clearly see I was someone of importance who moved freely among the highest circles (i.e. I chummed around with Stan, and could walk in on Fisher whenever I felt like it—he didn't have bodyguards in those days).

And, given that a good two-thirds of the workers in the Phasmatian office were female, my combination of status and mystery had its aphrodisiacal effect as well. I was soon grateful I'd had the forethought to make our religion non-repressive, sexually speaking, and in fact had included some overt ecstatic rituals within the doctrine. At the time I'd been thinking all that up, I was just being pragmatic—preaching abstinence and virginity to a prime user base of horny teenagers was just asking to be ignored—plus, I truly believed in my heart, which was where the core of our beliefs ultimately stemmed from anyway, that there is nothing sinful about recreational sex among consenting adults.

The first was Mae, a slightly chubby twenty-one-year-old brunette with a cute, earnest face, who started flirting with me during her breaks in the coffee room. It wasn't long before I'd asked her out for some late night drinks, and from there it was pretty much a beeline to the bed in my apartment. She was followed shortly thereafter by Angela, a short Italian chick with an incredible body. Her regular shift ran through the weekend, which is how we ended up hooking up—that, and the fact she seemed to think everything I said was hilarious. I should say Angela supplemented Mae, not followed her, since I was actually doing them both at the same time.

The funny thing is, my two gal pals found out about one another (as was bound to happen in a relatively small office) but they didn't make a fuss about it. Both were, in fact, not only willing, but eager to continue seeing me. At first, in my egotistical way, I assumed I was such a great catch for them that they were willing to share, rather than risk losing me altogether. So I broached the subject with Angela one Saturday night as we were taking a time-out between torrid bouts of lovemaking, and lay blissfully wrapped in each other's arms.

"Don't get me wrong, Ang," I explained. "I love that you and Mae are, like, you know, cool with the fact I'm seeing both of you. I'm just a little surprised, that's all. A lot of girls wouldn't be so, well, open minded."

Angela's head was on my chest, and she grabbed one of my hairs in her teeth, and gave it a little yank, just to show there was still some degree of inner conflict wafting beneath the surface. But then she giggled, and explained, "Well, it's like The Sacred Text says, isn't it? 'When we reach for the light, we must be careful of the shadow we cast.'"

It was somewhat odd having my own writing suddenly being quoted back at me, especially given that that particular piece of divine wisdom had been left purposely vague, as all good scripture should be to some extent.

"'Just as we seek light in the darkness, we must be careful not to darken the light,'" I completed the passage, knowing my ability to quote from The Text was a big turn-on for these girls.

"Exactly," she sighed. "So, Mae and I totally get the Phasmatian thing. Like, take me and you making love and just trying to be happy. It's so natural and beautiful, right? That's the light... but we always have to be careful not to let our bad emotions overshadow that light and darken it—you know, like being too possessive, or getting jealous and wanting to hurt someone." She must have suddenly realized who she was preaching to, because her face reddened, and she gave a self-deprecating little laugh. "But I don't have to tell *you* that, do I?"

"'Beware, lest thee offend The Universal Spirit, and diminish the light in thine own soul,'" I quoted, just to reinforce my superior position, but it was a real eye opener nonetheless to talk to someone who had glimpsed the immaculate beauty at the core of my message, and had bought into it as a personal credo. Mind you, the passage she had just quoted had also been meant as a warning against hypocrisy—among other things. I had always hated the way some radical Christian or Muslim sects had twisted messages of love and hope into something dark and destructive. So, the fact I was seducing this sweet, naïve young thing through my status as a founding defrauder did not exactly escape my conscience's notice.

It seemed to me I had also written something about false prophets and being your own leader, but I couldn't remember the exact words. "Just be careful about who you believe in, and make sure you're thinking for yourself," I whispered.

A scared expression came over Angela. Suddenly she looked all of twelve years old. "What do you mean? You're not talking about Phasmatia, are you?"

I swallowed hard. Part of me wanted to do the right thing and confess how the whole thing was made up. In that moment of unguarded tenderness, I felt ashamed that I was, in essence, lying to this innocent girl. (Well, maybe not so innocent. During our pillow-talk she confessed she'd once been a stripper, and heavily into snorting coke, before turning in her g-string and starting a search for spiritual salvation.)

It wasn't that I was opposed outright to lies of any sort, and in fact I had wrestled hard with the whole moral dilemma of truth versus untruth when I drafted The Sacred Text. After all, often a lie can be benign, or even a constructive thing. In the end I had sided with Mark Twain, who had once written: "There are 869 different forms of lying, but only one of them has been squarely forbidden. Thou shalt not bear false witness against thy neighbor." My version wasn't as colorful, and had come in the form of an aphorism from the lips of The Chosen One (although he had never really said it): "A lie is like a knife. It is not in and of itself evil. But do not use it to harm others, and careful lest you cut yourself."

I gave Angela a peck on the cheek. "No, of course not, sweetie. Trust The Universal Spirit to lead you to the light," I told her, and you could literally see the relief wash over her cute face. I'd like to say I did it because I didn't want to impede her personal quest to cleanse her soul of all stains and strive for illumination, but the reality is I was afraid she'd stop screwing me if she knew the truth.

As it turns out, I needn't have bothered. A few weeks later, just as I thought I had a shot at getting her and Mae into bed for a threesome, both of them abruptly stopped seeing me. I wasn't really in love with either girl, but their simultaneous rejection hurt nevertheless, and I wanted to know what had happened to change their feelings towards me so suddenly. Neither girl would return my calls, however, and when I managed to corner them at the office, they would offer nothing beyond terse, non-committal apologies.

Then, one Sunday morning as I came in uncharacteristically bright and early to get a jump on my work, I saw the pair of them coming out of Fisher's private apartment, along with a third girl from the day shift whose name I didn't know. Mae's eyes met mine, and the way she instantly looked away, and the red flush that painted itself on her cheeks, told me everything I needed to know.

I stormed into Fisher's apartment, and found him still lounging in his bed, his night's ministrations to his disciples having clearly worn him out. He heard me enter and opened one eye. "What the fuck are you doing in my bedroom?" he demanded.

"You just had to do it, didn't you? You just had to take them away from me."

He didn't play dumb, or try to deny it. Instead, he smiled patronizingly, as if some child had just done something amusing. "Technically, Brad ol' buddy, I didn't take anybody away from anyone," he said, sitting up in his bed and rubbing his eyes.

"Those gals are devout Phasmatians with real long-term potential. I figured getting close to me would help motivate them even more."

"Only doing what's good for the Church, is that it?"

"Listen, dude, people in stained glass houses shouldn't cast the first stone, especially if they're not free of sin. Pardon the mixed metaphor, I'm tired. But don't pretend you actually give a rat's ass about either of those girls beyond a roll in the hay. I think you'll find I care more about their welfare, especially their spiritual well-being, than you do."

I snorted. "Oh, please, save it for the flock. I helped concoct this scheme, remember? It's never been about anything but the money for you."

"Hey, I've got my life's savings tied up in this thing, and I'm still not taking a damned cent for myself—which is more than I can say about *you*." He softened his stance. "Listen, I know what it was all supposed to be about in the beginning, but we've got a lot of people believing in us now. I know it seems crazy, but I really think this is my destiny. It's like I was, you know ... "

"Chosen?" I said sarcastically.

"Well, why not? Maybe there really is some higher power out there pulling the strings, and this was all meant to be."

My mouth flapped open a few times, but I surprisingly had nothing to say about that.

The argument was evidently proving too much for him, and he collapsed back onto the bed. "Look, I don't want to fight with you, Brad. I really need your help for the next step ... I think it'll really be a quantum leap for the Church. I can't do it without you. If you want, I'll convince one of the girls to go back to you. Which one do you like? Mae? No, you prefer Angela, don't you?"

I spun on my heels and left, cursing him as I went. I didn't know why I felt it at the time, but the idea of having anything more to do with either woman repelled me. I think now that I didn't want to be intimate with anyone who had succumbed to

Fisher, subconsciously considering them corrupted in some way, as if they had become infected with the ugliness that festered inside of him.

My bursting in on him apparently had its impact on Fisher, too. No, he didn't stop dipping his wick into the pool of holy workers—quite the contrary, it only got worse. In fact, shortly thereafter Fisher collected his own permanent retinue of live-in female attendants. They wore form-hugging dresses and distinctive head scarves, and so I dubbed them Fisher's nuns, although celibacy was certainly not in their job description.

However, the next time I tried to walk directly into Fisher's private quarters, I was stopped by a scowling man-mountain of a personal bodyguard named Devon, the patriarch of what is now Fisher's legion of killer monks.

"You can't go in there," Devon told me, pulling back his shoulders so I could get a fuller appreciation of the mass and density of his pectoral muscles. I was more impressed with the large gold Phasmatian symbol he was wearing around his thick neck. It wasn't just a fashion statement—I could tell this man was taking it all very seriously.

"It's okay," I explained. "Sky will see me. You might say I'm one of the Phasmatian founding fathers. I've got important Church business. He's the one who sent for *me*."

"*Nobody* sees The Chosen One without an appointment," Devon persisted.

"Look, just go in there like a good boy, and tell him Brad's here to talk to him."

"The Chosen One is in private prayers. He can't be disturbed." From inside I could hear a woman's laughter, and I knew that whatever Fisher was doing with his privates, it wasn't prayer. Devon, however, didn't even blink.

"Fine," I said. "When he's done with his devotions, tell your master I dropped by to see him as requested." I went to pout in the boardroom. An hour later, Devon came in, and with a slight jerk of his head indicated I had been granted a private audience. He remained outside while I was admitted into the apartment, and there stood Fisher in front of a mirror, admiring his own gold Phasmatian pendant, worn over top of something that I could only describe as a cross between a tuxedo and a dress Star Fleet uniform.

"What do you think, Brad?" he asked. "I figured we needed special everyday outfits for the priesthood … something a little more contemporary than cassocks or robes."

"What the hell's with the goon outside?"

"Who, Devon? He's my personal assistant. Helps me manage my appointments."

That made me laugh. "You mean your personal doorman, don't you. He wouldn't let me in."

"Aw, c'mon Brad, I was in a meeting. After all, when it's said and done, this is a business, and we have to run things accordingly." Fisher was doing his damnedest to be convivial, and if I hadn't known him so well by then, I might have been taken in by it. But I knew it was only because he wanted something from me, and I didn't have to wait long to find out what it was.

"Say, listen Brad, remember how I was saying I was counting on your help for the next major step? Well, I want to publish The Sacred Text, you know, in hard copy. How long do you figure that would take?"

I shrugged. "Well, there's a good 200,000 words of content there now, but it's not exactly set up as a single cohesive volume. I mean, it's designed to be accessed in bits and pieces as you wander through the virtual environment, talk to priests, ask questions, and listen to The Chosen One's sermons. Why would you want to put it in a book?"

"Well, for starters, we could sell it. There's a huge demand from the followers, you know. But I also figure we could generate a lot of interest from the general public and encourage them to visit the web site." He pasted on his best crocodile smile, and the hairs instantly stood up on the back of my neck. "So, what do you think, Brad? Could we get it all done in, say, a week?"

"I guess it wouldn't be much for Stan to export out all the individual text files, although you'd have to verify that with him. But listen, Sky, even though I've tried to be thorough and consistent, there are still tons of holes in the doctrine. Naturally, I've been trying to fill them, especially when the users ask specific questions, but I have shitloads still to do. It's really still a work in progress."

"Christ, Brad, this is a religious book, not a novel. It doesn't have to hold together from start to finish ... just look at the Bible. People generally just read passages anyway, don't they? Just polish up the pieces that you figure need the most work and get it ready for press in a week."

"Why the rush?"

His phony smile morphed into something showing genuine delight. "I'm going to be on the Billy Reno Show," he said reverently.

I whistled. Billy Reno was the long-reigning king of late-night talk TV, and an appearance on his show meant serious exposure. That also explained the fancy new quasi-liturgical outfit Fisher had been trying on when I came in. "Alright," I said, "I'll get it done." And that's how I became a best-selling author, even if my name's not on the book, and it's the damned Phasmatian Church that gets all the royalties.

There was more than just ego driving my decision, however. As I've told you already, I honestly believe in the core message of the religion, and I welcomed the opportunity to expose more people to the message of hope and peace and self-betterment it espouses. In my own way, I thought I was making the world a better place.

The printed version of The Sacred Text landed at over a thousand pages, and it became necessary to indoctrinate Fisher, not only on all the new sections I pulled together at the last minute,

but on the overall writings in general. After all, if he was going to
be strolling around in public with the Phasmatian dogma under
his arm, he would need to be intimately acquainted with its contents. But despite the fact I spent dozens of hours cramming
and rehearsing with Fisher before his appearance on Billy Reno,
each meeting still meant gaining admission from the grim-faced
and imposing Devon (or, during those few hours a day when the
big bodyguard slept, from Spencer, an equally muscle-bound
and formidable-looking stand-in, who was rumored to be a former Green Beret).

Fisher's interview with Billy Reno was a hit, and I immediately
saw the wisdom of choosing that particular venue for exposing
Fisher to the public (even if part of me still railed at his grabbing the spotlight). Reno rarely put his guests on the hot seat,
and in this case it soon became evident that the host had himself
been on the Phasmatian web site on several occasions, and was
sympathetic to the cause. Also, Fisher was downright masterful,
radiating a beneficent calm, cleverly eluding any personal questions that hinted at him being an ordinary mortal, and quoting
the most entertaining and thought-provoking passages of The
Text as if the bastard had written them himself. It was The Soft
Sell at its finest, and got me wondering how Jesus or Siddhartha
would have fared in the television age.

Although I winced at the overt lies Fisher told, especially his
vivid fictional description of the revelatory mountaintop com-
munion with The Universal Spirit (which he told apologetically,
as if he was not worthy of that divinely imposed responsibility),
there was a part of me that was whooping with pride at what
I had accomplished. Hell, it was history in the making. I was
changing the world—and, I believed, for the better. Although
Fisher was the one sitting there in his charcoal-gray, futuristic
ecumenical uniform, watched by millions, I honestly felt like the

hand of God was reaching down and patting *me* on the head. I was filled with a feeling of rapture unlike anything I'd ever experienced before, as if possessed by the proverbial Holy Ghost. I didn't need public recognition—that could come in due time. I, Brad Evans, was bringing forth something profound and monumental for the betterment of humanity, and which might be talked about for millennia to come.

Oh, God. I'm terrified. There's definitely someone moving around outside the trailer. I don't know whether to hide here and fight it out, or to make a run for the woods. I'm going to try to find a place to hide my laptop, and hope maybe someone finds it later... in case I don't make it. Shit, I'm wasting time, but I wanted to write down what was happening. Please God, have mercy on my soul.

It's okay. It was just my neighbor, or rather the Shius' neighbor. His name is Andy van Vroonhoven, and he was out deer hunting when he spotted the smoke from my chimney. He found it odd, since the Shius typically only visit their property for a month or so in the height of summer. Or rather they used to. Apparently Mr. Shiu, Stan's father, has been suffering from a bad hip that has pretty much kept him laid up in their house in San Francisco lately. (Will he manage to get out to attend his son's funeral, I wonder, once the coroner is done with Stan's corpse, or what's left of it, and ships it home to the West Coast?)

A very likeable, old, plain-speaking rural character, Andy is, and his people have been around this part of the country for centuries. I invited him in for a cup of instant coffee and powdered milk, and we had a pleasant chat that ran on for hours. I don't think he was in too much of a hurry to go out traipsing through the shin-high snow again.

I told him my name was Jerry Porter, and said I was here working on a novel. Andy seemed genuinely delighted to meet a real writer (well, I am technically a best-selling author, aren't I?), but I couldn't help feeling bad about lying to him, even if it was done out of caution and an absence of malice. Something about my recent experiences has sensitized me to life's karmic currents.

Andy and his wife, Beatrix, are devout Protestants (I had to work the conversation around to that to see where spiritual loyalties resided) and he has little enthusiasm for the Phasmatians.

"Oh, I've read about them in the newspapers, and seen that Fisher guy on the TV," he told me, "but I just don't get what all the fuss is about."

As relieved as I was that Andy had no connection to Phasmatia, I actually felt a little hurt that he was dismissing all my hard work so summarily.

"It has millions and millions of converts, especially among the young, wired generation," I explained. I'll confess to feeling damned proud of that accomplishment. (I never understood why Pride was considered one of the Seven Deadly Sins, and I deliberately omitted it from Phasmatia's list of moral no-nos. To me the real sin is *excessive* pride—being conceited and arrogant. I see nothing wrong with taking satisfaction in a hard-earned accomplishment.)

"Yeah, I've read all about them people who are jumpin' on the bandwagon. And don't get me wrong ... anything that brings lost souls to God is okay in my books. But even though the trappings are different, it seems to me a lot of what those Phasmatians are saying ain't exactly new."

"It's the world's first great internet religion—that's new."

"Well, there you go. I've never even been on the internet," Andy replied. It almost seemed like he was bragging.

"It offers a new spirituality for our digital age. The old institutions are having a hard time hanging on to their followers ... and it's leaving a moral vacuum that Phasmatia is filling."

"So you're a practicin' Phasmatian, then?"

Somehow the question caught me by surprise. The obvious answer, given my hands-on role in its creation, and sincere belief in the spirit of the dogma, should have been, *Why, yes, I'm a*

devout Phasmatian. But, in fact, I had never personally under-
gone any Phasmatian baptismal rites, nor had I ever fallen down
to my knees (real or virtual) filled with The Universal Spirit. I
certainly did *not* acknowledge Sky Fisher as my messiah and
spiritual leader. "Well, let's just say I try to follow their teach-
ings, but I don't actually attend Church."

Andy chuckled. "Sounds like most of the Christians I know.
I certainly can't argue with you about shrinking congregations,
though. It's happened right here in this county. A couple of years
back we had to close the doors of our own church in town, after
pretty near a hundred and fifty years. Beatrix and I have joined
up with some Lutherans in a parish forty miles away … just to
have a place to worship. It's a real pity. Just ain't the same. Now
don't get me wrong … unlike some folks I could tell you about,
I truly believe it's what you do the other six days of the week,
not just Sunday, that makes you a good Christian. Still, I sure
do miss the smell and the feel of the old place, and seeing all my
neighbors around me."

The waning light outside caught Andy's attention and stirred
him from his thoughts. "Geez, will ya look at me. Jawin' away
the afternoon, and you with work to do." He rose to go. At the
door he turned and offered his hand.

"Say, Jerry. Do you like venison? Why not join me and Beatrix
up at the farm for dinner tonight? She'd love to have you … why
we both would, especially seein' as you're a new neighbor and
all, even if it is only for a short spell."

I happily accepted his invitation, and even walked him part
of the way home so I could get my bearings straight, which
wasn't hard once you found the well-worn trail connecting the
two properties. I could certainly use some company, not to mention a decent meal. More importantly, Andy will be able to give
me useful information about the towns in the vicinity. Knowing
what kind of facilities they have will help me plan my next step.

I feel like a new man this morning. Supper last night was hearty and scrumptious, and Beatrix hovered over me all evening, heaping extra helpings onto my plate, and constantly refilling my wine glass. I think she's been feeling a little lonely since the last of her kids moved away eight years ago, and welcomed the opportunity to lavish her hospitality on someone other than Andy. She's quite the rotund and ruddy ol' gal now, but you can still see that Beatrix was quite the looker in her time—a fact verified by the old albums I dutifully browsed. It touched me to see the way she and Andy doted on one another, even after forty years of marriage.

There was an awkward moment when she inquired after Stan (I had told Andy yesterday that it was Stan who had given me permission to use the trailer) and I finally had to break the news of his death. I didn't see the point of bringing up the nasty details of Stan's murder, and told them it was a car accident, which is, after all, what the official police verdict will say. I also told them it was Stan's death that had moved me to come to the trailer to write, and that I was doing it for him as well as myself. Well, it's the truth, isn't it?

Beatrix broke out into tears, and seconds later I was blub-
bering right along with her. For the past few days I've been self-
ishly worrying about my own hide, and in that cathartic moment
I was finally able to grieve openly for my friend. I do believe
my unabashed display of emotion only endeared me to the van
Vroonhovens that much more.

Andy drove me back to the trailer afterwards in his venerable
old farm truck, with a basketful of Beatrix's leftovers and other
goodies on my lap, and walked me to the door. He hesitated for
a minute, and took my hand with both of his. "If there's anything you need, you just come and ask, okay?" I had enough of
a measure of the man by that point to realize he was offering me
his friendship, and he did not take such matters lightly.

As he was walking back to the truck, he turned and asked,
"How long are you planning on staying, Jerry?"

I shrugged. "I don't know yet... depends on how far I get
with my writing, I suppose."

He nodded, as if that was the answer he was expecting, and
added, "Well, feel free to come take your meals with us anytime
you like. Beatrix gets tired of just looking at this grizzled old
face of mine all the time, I reckon. And if there's anything at all
you need, just follow the trail on over to our place."

I slept like the proverbial baby that night. The bellyful of
venison, yams, and pumpkin pie helped, I suppose, as did the
knowledge I had someone to turn to in a pinch. But I think the
best inducement to a good night's sleep was the .30-06 Reming-
ton deer rifle Andy had loaned me (under the pretext I was going
to try my hand at some hunting). I hugged that sucker all night
long like it was some hot babe, and dreamt of Stan and rounds
of drinks at Macbeth's.

So, now, with a fresh mug of coffee in front of me (real home-
ground coffee, not the powdered crap I've been drinking) I can

get back to my exposé, and have a newfound sense of optimism I can get it posted to the web, where it will be read.

After his appearance on the Billy Reno show, it was patently clear why Fisher had rushed to get The Sacred Text into print. Stan told me afterwards that his online store alone sold two million copies in a week, and that traffic to the web site quintupled. There had already been a number of stories in the mainstream media about the Phasmatians, which is how it had come to Billy Reno's attention, I imagine, but now the press coverage really exploded.

Fisher orchestrated his media exposure masterfully, and proved to be a gifted interview subject. He cleverly avoided commenting on controversial secular matters, was exquisitely vague about his own earthly origins, and flogged the seminal core of the Phasmatian doctrine so relentlessly that each piece broadcast or printed amounted to a free infomercial.

His first interview with *The New York Times* still stands out in my mind. Fisher was asked his opinion on the situation in the Middle East, specifically whether extremists in the Jewish or Muslim religions were to blame, and who the Phasmatians supported in the conflict. The reporter made a point of noting that Fisher smiled before replying, although she interpreted it as "a sign of the inner peace that clearly radiates through the man." I know better. Unless Fisher had just had an unusually rewarding encounter with the toilet bowl, that smile could only have meant he'd seen that particular question coming, and was well-prepared for it.

"Those who seek to harm others are, in the end, only harming themselves," was his reported answer. "It is never a simple problem, for life is full of difficult choices, wrapped in emotion, and clouded by our own ignorance, and who among us can say they have never chosen incorrectly? But before anyone purposely seeks to hurt another, they should stop, and seek the light inside themselves, and ask whether their soul will be diminished by what they are about to do. The concentrated inner light of a thousand devout individuals who seek to do good instead of evil can cast the bright radiance of a wonderful new day upon even the darkest of worlds."

Later, the reporter had tried to embroil Fisher in the whole debate concerning evolution versus creation (the latter now parading under the name of "intelligent design"). "Which side is the Phasmatian Church on?" she had asked him.

"Why, both," he replied, and she noted there was a twinkle in his eye. "First of all, life on earth did not arise by accident. Those who suggest that a higher intelligence was behind our design are correct. We are the handiwork of The Universal Spirit, who planted the cosmic seed that has turned us into a divine oasis in the darkness. But everything the scientists say about dinosaurs, and evolution, is absolutely correct. They are merely observing and gleaning The Universal Spirit's physical methods. Faith and science are not mutually exclusive."

With so much rampant public interest and hard scrutiny, I became paranoid that the wheels would come off of the whole scheme. I was actually grateful for the first time that my name was not down anywhere as one of the Church's formal directors (although I had no delusions Fisher had cut me out in order to protect me). Any paper trail would merely show me to have been a paid contractor of the Church (or, if they went back far enough, a former co-worker who had loaned Fisher money). Beyond that, they had nothing on me, although I often found myself mentally rehearsing my testimony, just in case a subpoena should appear. I was not prepared to lie about direct facts, nor did I figure I would have to. I had, however, sketched out in mind, rather brilliantly I thought, a defense of Phasmatia itself. If they dared question my faith, I would finagle and obfuscate to the best of my abilities. ("No, Mister/Madam Prosecutor, I cannot prove to you the existence of a Universal Spirit, anymore than I can prove the existence of Allah or Brahma.") And therein lay the ultimate

defens e against any charges of fraud. As long as we professed
to believe, and stuck by our faith, then we were as legitimate as
the Catholic Church.

Anyone familiar with current events knows, of course, that a
challenge *did* arise, but not from any crusading attorneys general, or muckraking journalists. Within a week of the Church
filing its first corporate tax return, the Infernal Revenue Service
issued an official ruling that it did not consider the Phasmatians
a legitimate church, and refused to grant it tax-exempt status
under section 501(c)(3) of the IRS code. Interestingly enough,
nowhere on our site did it actually state that donations to the
Church were tax receiptable, and most people who gave did so
purely out of devotion and a belief in the cause, not for the tax
write-off. Still, with all the income they were raking in, a decision like that had huge financial implications for Fisher and his
accountants, but there was far more at stake than mere money.
In purely symbolic terms, having a government agency formally
declare that Phasmatia was not a true religion was a huge slap
in the spiritual face.

Stan showed me his site visitation statistics, where you could
actually see the exact day the news of the IRS ruling hit the real
world. Fewer new recruits abruptly began showing up at the site,
and the frequency and duration of visits by the regular visitors
began to nosedive dramatically. It appeared that Fisher had been
wrong in assuming Phasmatia met all the criteria of an established religion, as previously defined by the Supreme Court ruling. The IRS side-stepped that particular quagmire, and didn't
even try to challenge the beliefs and practices of the Church
itself. No, their ruling was based on one fact only—the religion
was practiced online, and therefore did not have the same validity to its congregation as did a bricks-and-mortar church.

Fisher stepped up to the challenge. Anyone who followed
the case would have to admit his avenue of counterattack was
brilliant. He avoided having the burden of proof placed on the

Church and its practices, and religion never even entered into the defence strategy. Instead, he attacked the basic IRS reasoning that an online community of any sort had less validity or significance than a traditional one in the real world.

The outpouring of support was fantastic. The blogosphere was ablaze with postings of protest, and so much email flooded the IRS that their server crashed. At least that's the official version. I happen to know Stan rented a zombie-net of a million computers from some Romanian hackers, and surreptitiously launched a denial-of-service attack, cleverly disguised as mass internet dissent. Other unsolicited champions entered the fray, from the ACLU to AOL, not to mention all the opportunistic politicians courting the youth vote. The dream team of lawyers that came out of the woodwork and volunteered to fight the ruling *pro bono* on behalf of the Phasmatians was even more impressive. (I have it on good authority that a couple of them actually paid Fisher to let them sit in on the case.)

None of that was as impressive as the marches, sit-ins, and protests staged by young people around the world, something unseen in their scope and fervor since the 1970s. I doubt if most of them truly felt their online culture was being threatened—I suspect to them it was a *cause célèbre* that allowed them to meet and mingle, and rail at the establishment. But if I thought Fisher's appearance on the Billy Reno show had been something, I was totally blown away by the video of him standing in front of a million marchers in Washington, D.C., and leading the chant, "My world is real too!" which is now as iconic as any piece of footage in humanity's news archives.

The IRS relented, as you undoubtedly know, and Phasmatia began to grow again at unprecedented rates. After coming to a roadblock with the landlord over more office space, the Church ended up acquiring its building outright, and breaking the leases of all the other tenants so it could take over the space completely. The old warehouse was systematically gutted and completely renovated, section by section, and Fisher soon took the entire top floor for himself. You only had to glance at the hard, suspicious look on the faces of Devon and his cadre of fellow bodyguards (not to mention the bulges of the not-so-concealed weapons under their jackets) as they stood by the private elevator and stairwell, and you got the message. Access to The Chosen One was now totally restricted.

You couldn't miss the bodyguards, and it wasn't just because most of them resembled a cross between a heavyweight wrestler and a commando. By now, almost all the Phasmatian workers were wearing special Church garb, which not only identified them as members of the Church, but also denoted their status within the organization. The Palace Guard, as I referred to them, had a distinct, black, quasi-military uniform of their own, complete with badges of rank, and topped off with calf-length black leather trench coats they each wore to a man.

It quickly became evident that, even among the Church faithful, the guards formed an elite and isolated group that was looked upon with awe. I'm not sure whether they began being referred to as monks because of their discipline and apparent celibacy, or whether that designation was actually handed down from on high by Fisher himself, but the name soon stuck, and eventually became official.

Once The Sacred Text was in print, I no longer had a specific anointed task at the Church. Still, I dutifully—and eagerly—came into the offices several evenings a week, and most weekends. I admit the generous side income Phasmatia provided was gilding my bank account, especially since I wasn't out drinking it away so often, but I wasn't just concerned about remaining on the Church payroll. There was an infectious atmosphere about the place—a heady mixture of spirituality, enthusiasm, and self-righteousness—and I wallowed in it. It felt utterly uplifting to watch Phasmatia spread all over the country, and in fact the planet, and to know I was instrumental in its success. I felt, dare I say it, born again.

So I decided to earn my paycheck by ministering to the cyber-flock. For hours on end I would wander around in the virtual world of Phasmatia and provide counseling to those who sought my help. And I was *good* at it. Among the scores of other online priests, I really stood out.

You might think it was because I'd literally written the book on Phasmatia, but that wasn't it. Hell, by now all sorts of hard-core devotees had read The Sacred Text from cover to cover, and there were lots of them who knew the actual details better than I did, and who could recite the writings practically word for word.

The problem with those now ministering online was that they were generally green recruits, given rapid battlefield promotions to the priesthood, so to speak, on account of Phasmatia's amazing growth. These newbies were super keen, but tended to follow the scripts to the letter, and were petrified of censure from their supervisors (who monitored all traffic) should they deviate from the party line. Basically, they were all too brainwashed to realize that there's such a thing as being *too* devout, and this intrinsically limited their effectiveness as spiritual counselors.

Don't get me wrong. These humans proved essential to our online religion. Yes, much of the web site's dialog with users was still being performed automatically by Stan's amazing software, but even though he had really refined and improved his code over time, its usefulness was still extremely limited. People will always prefer to deal with real live human beings, and they can quickly spot the difference.

So, there was now a burgeoning class of live Phasmatians who took over interaction from the computer at the second level, and a whole automated and highly regimented back-end process for tracking their activities. I, however, answered to no one, especially since good ol' Stan had tweaked a few system parameters to make my online interactions invisible to the pit bosses who watched relentlessly over the cubicles full of Church employees.

To emphasize the difference, I also coaxed Stan into letting me customize my on-screen persona. Despite variations in gender and race for the sake of political correctness, all the other priests and priestesses were very similar in their attire, and the way they presented themselves. Not me. My online character was a mysterious wanderer dubbed the Mage Errant, and although I steadfastly refused to wear Phasmatian garb or the pendant in the real world, I did so online, but with some theatrical flair. Nothing gaudy, mind you, like the outfit Fisher's avatar wore, with its shimmering gold robes and big-ass headpiece. I wore a long, simple cloak, exactly the same color gray as the basic priestly garb, only with a hood that shaded my face. When I chose to, though, I could make my eyes glow subtly from beneath the hood. The plain pendant around my neck was weathered and dull, in contrast to the shiny gold and silver of the other clergy, and I carried a staff. Think of me as a cross between Gandalf and Obi-Wan Kenobi, with a bit of John the Baptist thrown in.

It wasn't just a unique outfit that made me popular of course. I had a distinctly maverick viewpoint compared to the others, a sense of humor, plus an inner belief in preaching the spirit of the religion, instead of being literal minded. As a consequence, I became somewhat of a cult figure, and people began to deliberately seek me out.

One incident still stands out in my mind. I was approached for guidance by an online churchgoer called Naomi after I had just finished an impromptu sermon to her online congregation. I could tell just from the sizeable glow around her avatar that she was serious in her devotions, and so out of curiosity I dialed up her account information from my priestly control panel—something I tended not to do in general, since I preferred to deal with people at face value, and give them some anonymity.

The administrative display told me Naomi was an eighteen-year-old from Miami, and was a devout practitioner. She had been registered on the site for almost two years, and had charged hundreds of dollars in donations on her credit card. As a result of her generosity, plus other online contributions—such as leading prayer groups, recommending others to the Church, and doing volunteer work—she had registered an impressive 2,323 "points of light" in her Phasmatian profile. The POLs, as we called them, were an important gauge of how active a member was online. They were basically an incarnation of the karmic points Fisher and I had joked about at the beginning. We had quickly learned that it was important to keep score, so our followers could measure their progress… and compete amongst themselves for higher standing. Plus, we could identify the hot prospects for upselling to the next levels.

"May I speak with you, Mage?" she messaged me, as soon as I had finished pontificating to the group.

"Sure. What can I do you for?"

"Is it true that those who are pure in spirit go to The Universal Spirit when they die?"

"That's covered to death in the scripture, no pun intended…is that really all you wanted to ask me about?"

"Yes…well, no, not exactly. What I mean is, like, I've been really good, you know, a faithful Phasmatian…"

"Yes, I can see you've been very devout. Way to go, Naomi."

"Well, then, I just wanted to be sure I was covered…you know, in case I died."

"Why, are you sick? Have the doctors given you some bad news or something?"

"No, I'm healthy. But if I did die it wouldn't be bad, right? Because I'd become one with The Spirit, wouldn't I? I mean, I've got over 2,300 points."

In front of my computer I sighed heavily. Suddenly I understood. *"That depends, Naomi. One misguided act could wipe out those*

2,300 *points in a heartbeat. Say, for example, if you were to kill your-*
self."

"*There's nothing in The Sacred Text against suicide...I checked!!*"

She had me there. I had purposely not made killing yourself
a formal "thou shalt not." There were just too many extenuating
cases—like giving up your own life to save others, or euthanasia
for the terminally ill—that made it far from a simple black-and-
white proposition. That did not, however, excuse what Naomi
was contemplating. I guess every religion has grappled with that
one at some point. If you make the afterlife appear too rosy,
people will be in a hurry to get there.

"*Listen, Naomi. Have you ever heard the expression 'The letter of the
Law versus the spirit of the Law?' Now we're debating the letter of the
Spirit versus the spirit of The Spirit.*"

"*But the Text says that The Spirit longs to be reunited with that piece
of Her that's in all of us.*"

"*True, but it also says that it's our sacred responsibility to make the
light within us shine as brightly as possible. You're young. You've accomplished a hell of a lot, true, but just think of how much more you can do,
how many people you can still help, if you live a long and devout life.*"

"*But I don't want a long life!! I'm so unhappy. Phasmatia is all I
have. I want to leave this bad world behind and join The Universal
Spirit.*"

"*That wouldn't be right. Even though you think you would be joining
the light, you would really be adding to the darkness.*"

"*So, how many Points of Light would I need to get before it would be
okay?*"

"*Forget the fucking points! They're not real. You're the one who's real,
and so is the world outside of your computer. That's where you have to
live. You can't live in Phasmatia.*"

"*I don't want to live in the real world. It's too hard. Nobody under-
stands me. My parents hate me. The other kids all pick on me because
I'm ugly. In Phasmatia I can be beautiful.*"

"Don't you see, Naomi. That's the real darkness you have to face. The virtual world can teach you, and help show you the way, but it's only a simulation. It's like trying to learn to play a sport by playing Nintendo. And now you want to quit before you've really found out how far you can go. The real good you can do is in that dark, ugly real world out there. Well, show it what you've got! Give it some love. Give it some beauty. Give it some enlightenment. Give it some justice. There are so many ways you can contribute. And, trust me, what you accomplish in real life may not tally on a score sheet somewhere, but it'll add up inside you, where it really counts. Life is too short as it is, sweetie. Give it all you've got, and don't go looking to give up before the final buzzer."

"I don't know if I can."

"I know, Naomi. It's hard. Damned hard. But you've already shown that you have what it takes. That's what Phasmatia really means. Finding the strength to go on. Finding the courage to do the right thing. Finding the serenity to love yourself. You can do it."

"Okay. I'll try."

"Be strong, Naomi. The Spirit is already inside you. Don't let Her down."

And so it went. There were so many confused, hurting people out there, and I discovered within myself the capacity to heal and guide them. I had a talent. And I came to believe it was a God-given talent. Plus, I really enjoyed doing it. Working outside of the system with impunity, I moved freely, and with my own unique style. I could wisecrack and be as irreverent as I chose. I strove to put some phun in Phasmatia.

Don't get me wrong. This was not some lark for me. I had come to see first-hand and to believe very passionately in the benefits our religion could unleash on the world. With my own laid-back approach, I ultimately did more good than a hundred scripture-spouting drones. In fact, I'm the one who brought Hollywood icon Brock Harrow into the highest echelons of the Church.

Mind you, I didn't even realize I had a high-profile movie

star on the hook the first time we met online. Other than The
Chosen One himself, no character in that virtual world created
more excitement upon appearing than my Mage Errant, and
word would soon spread whenever I popped into a chat or worship session. It was no different the night I was asked to settle
a dispute within a Phasmatian circle that called itself the Lotus
Eaters. I did a quick look-up and learned that the group had its
origins in Los Angeles, but since some chapters had members
distributed on virtually every continent, that didn't necessarily
mean much. I popped into their virtual chapel, which was quite
elegant, but tastefully so, announced my presence, and waited
for the excitement generated by my arrival to subside.

"So, why have you summoned me, my little sinners?" I inquired.
Often in these situations, two or three of them would start typ-
ing simultaneously, but in this case, one figure, evidently the
leader by group consent, glided forward. His robes indicated
he was a second-level acolyte—meaning he had probably been
in the Church for about a year, and had begun some degree of
serious study. The fact that the persona was a tall, good-looking,
and muscular male meant nothing—it was one of Phasmatia's
most popular character designs, and the real person behind it
could just as easily be a skinny kid with acne, or a fat old woman
for that matter. I could have accessed the underlying information on him or other members of the group through my control
panel, but in this case I didn't bother.

"Hail to The Universal Spirit," the figure answered. *"We thank you
for taking the time to answer us."* Well, at least he was polite, and I
could tell from the sizeable aura about him that he was a devout
disciple. *"We have been meditating on the Nine Paths to Light, and
seek your guidance."*

The section in question referred to some everyday stratagems
for leading a good life, and I found the fact they were openly
discussing among themselves how to be better human beings
endearing.

"So, what exactly has your metaphysical knickers in a knot?" I typed, knowing that adopting a lighter tone would place this cyber-gathering at ease.

"It's the passage that says material wealth weighs down the spirit, and can drag it down towards the darkness," the supplicant told me.

The ice having been broken, so to speak, one of the others, evidently a female, if her buxomy, slim-wasted, Lara Croft-like persona was any indication, jumped in. *"Yes, we want to know whether this means we should give away all our possessions."*

I had a suspicion I knew what Fisher's answer would be if he'd been asked (and exactly to whom the possessions should be given). I vaguely recalled what I had been thinking when I wrote the passage in question, and that I had been influenced by Christ à la Matthew ("... it is easier for a camel to pass through the eye of a needle than it is for a rich man to enter the king-dom of heaven") and by Buddha, who, after all, forsook princely wealth to go live beneath the Bodhi Tree. Still, in general I tend to have a more pragmatic attitude towards these things.

"Only The Universal Spirit consists of pure light," I replied. *"The rest of us are forced to live at least partially in shadows. Even though our struggle is symbolically painted as black and white, there are no abso-lutes, and no one can therefore say absolutely that wealth in and of itself is evil. But rich people are usually transformed by their wealth—they become hedonists or misers, or come to believe the rules of decency and morality no longer apply to them. On the other hand, money is a power-ful tool, and used properly can effect much goodness in the world. For even a weapon that destroys can also be used to protect the weak and feed the hungry."*

"So, you're saying we should keep our money," the original leader asked after digesting my holy pedantry.

My virtual character had a library of pre-choreographed actions and gestures, which Stan had helped me assemble. With a click of my mouse I selected one of my favorite poses, which no other character in the virtual Phasmatian world was capable of performing. It can best be described as a floating, upside-down lotus position, and was designed to both disarm and impress my audience.

"It is good that you ask these questions," I counseled, *"for it shows that you earnestly seek the light. But perhaps you should ask yourself what exactly you will do with your poverty, just as you wonder what to do with your wealth. It's true that money cannot buy happiness, but poverty will give you a hefty down payment on misery. If you become poor, will you end up harming others in order to survive? Perhaps you will end up staining your soul with regret and longing and degradation. I cannot answer these questions for you...each of you must find your own way."* There were bows and hand claps from the gathering, and I could tell the Mage Errant had hit another home run.

Just as I was preparing to disappear in a cloud of virtual smoke, the leader of the group approached me, politely thanked me for my guidance, and requested a private audience on the side. I was feeling magnanimous and consented.

"I was wondering if you could arrange an audience with The Chosen One," he asked when we were in a one-on-one chat.

"Email a request and maybe his avatar will grace you with a visit...although I wouldn't hold my breath," I replied curtly.

"No, no, not like that...I want to come to New York and meet with Sky Fisher in person."

"I am not The Chosen One's secretary," I made my character's eyes glow with a jaundiced disapproval.

"My apologies if I offended you, Mage, but I feel I can be of great service to the Church. Perhaps if you knew who I really am. My name is Brock Harrow, the actor. I suppose you've heard of me."

Of course I had heard of him. Brock Harrow was a cinematic heavyweight, and undisputed king of the blockbuster action flick. I was instantly star-struck, and all my previous insider's holier-than-thou affectations vanished. If that had been the real world, I probably would have been gushing all over him and asking him to autograph my copy of The Sacred Text. As it was, I had to remind myself to stay in character.

"Pleased to meet you, brother Brock. I'm an admirer of your work," I told him.

"And I of yours," he replied, making my day. *"Phasmatia has changed my life. I was drifting into despair and self-destruction until I was reborn into the Light. Now I want to help fight the darkness that I see everywhere in the world."*

"You want to offer the Church the gleaming light of your star…so to speak."

"I couldn't have put it better myself," Harrow responded. *"I had been thinking of simply turning my back on worldly ways and going to live quietly and piously in the country, but you've convinced me that would actually be selfish, and I should use my position and my money to spread the message."*

"Bless you for that, brother," I messaged back, *"and my guess is Sky would be very interested in having you on board."*

"That's just the point. I tried contacting him, but he's impossible to reach in person. His press agent must have misunderstood, because I got a form letter back saying The Chosen One wasn't interested in doing any movie roles."

"Okay, I'll see what I can do," I told him. If it had been some pleb, I wouldn't have bothered, but the Hollywood A-List is as close to royalty as we have in this country.

"Are you close to The Chosen One?" Harrow asked. *"I know the virtual world is no indication, but I got the sense you were someone special."*

"Let's just say I was there in the beginning," I answered, not wanting to get into specifics.

"You were! What's your real name? Were you one of those first disciples when he returned from Mount Skylight possessed by The Universal Spirit?"

Oddly enough, faced with the chance to step out of the wings and share some of the glory, I was reluctant to do so, even to be on a first-name basis with a megastar. Perhaps it was because I had come to be disgusted with the way Fisher was hogging the limelight. *"Names don't matter, only deeds,"* I said. *"I'll speak to him. How can we reach you?"* Harrow gave me his personal cell number, and I ended the chat with a final thanks and blessing, and went looking for Fisher.

I had no expectations I'd be able to walk right in on the head honcho himself, and so, instead, went directly to the man-mountain of a monk who was on duty guarding the private elevator to the penthouse. I briefly explained the situation, handed over the phone number I'd written down, and went back to my workstation to answer a few more online queries.

I was just about to call it a night and was actually in the process of logging off my computer when the light behind me was eclipsed by something huge, and I looked up to see Devon standing there.

"He wants to see you," the head monk said, his body language making it clear it was not a request, but a summons. I bowed courteously, and together we rode up the stainless-steel-lined elevator to the penthouse, finally affording me a chance to see firsthand Fisher's newly renovated private quarters.

The dramatic way the top floor of the warehouse had been transformed made my mouth pop open and boggled my suppos-edly jaded mind. Most New York loft dwellers like the exposed brick and old beams that ancient warehouses afford, but none of that was visible in Fisher's space anymore. Nor was there any of the trendy post-modern neo-chic look you'd expect from some-one who, until recently, had been one of the ad industry's lead-ing creative directors. Instead, the place looked like a throwback to some Babylonian palace.

Everything was covered in stone. The walls were sheathed in glowing white marble with a slightly pinkish, swirling serpen-tine grain. The cream-colored granite floor was laid out in huge slabs, each the size of a billiard table, and polished to a shine so reflective it looked like a sheet of virgin ice. Even the ceiling had been covered in a mosaic of tiny stone tiles. It took me a minute to realize the colored pattern of the mosaic was not random, but depicted a sky at sunset, with most of the Technicolor glory from the depicted sinking sun taking place at the opposite end of the floor.

"This way," Devon rumbled, and I was led across the open foyer and into the rooms. I peeked in whenever I passed a doorway, unashamedly gawking at the opulence. The dining room held an ornately carved oak table that could seat twenty people, and the state-of-the-art kitchen that serviced it looked like it could hold an equal number of chefs. The undisputed centerpiece of the floor, however, was a large domed solarium, for which a huge part of the ceiling had been removed in order to accommodate it. In the middle was what I could only describe as a small mountain, at least thirty feet high. The natural stone structure was terraced and pocketed all over, and these indentations had been collectively landscaped with a variety of exotic tropical plants and flowers. Along one sheer stone face was a waterfall that tumbled down, only to disappear into a specially designed recess in the floor, so that you could walk right up and stick your hand into the cascading water.

I was ushered forward towards a door that evidently led to Fisher's private quarters, but when I tried to step inside Devon immediately turned around to bar my access. He pointed at a spot off to the side. Evidently I was meant to stand there and wait, but although I could not see directly into the room, I could hear heavy breathing and obscene grunting noises coming from inside.

At first I thought Fisher might be getting all hot and heavy with one of his nubile nuns, but then I heard a toilet flush, and I realized he had been wrestling through another of his supreme bouts of constipation. A few moments later he emerged, and judging from the sour look on his face, his pilgrimage to the porcelain shrine had been less than fruitful.

Given that we were, if not friends, at least old co-conspirators, I suppose I expected some cursory pleasantries, but he got right down to brass tacks.

"Is this for real?" he demanded imperiously, holding up the slip of paper I had sent up to him.

"I wouldn't have bothered you with it if it wasn't, knowing how valuable your time is, your holiness." My words were soaked in sarcasm, and although it may not seem the smartest of strategies to try to get a rise out of someone when he has a large and dangerous bodyguard beside him, prepared to break your neck on command, Fisher's whole arrogant attitude was starting to royally piss me off.

"So, how the hell did *you* get it?" he asked, his tone making it blatantly clear that someone as menial as me did not hobnob with movie stars.

"Up yours, asshole!" No sooner did the words leave my mouth when the back of Devon's hand smacked me across the face and almost knocked my head off. It had probably only been a glancing blow, meant to educate me without causing any permanent damage, but as I felt my lip to see if it was bleeding, I understood for the first time just how physically outclassed I was by the big bodyguard. To this day, I don't know whether it was a hired henchman's sadistic reflex, or an act of pure religious devotion, but clearly I wasn't allowed to disrespect The Chosen One in Devon's presence.

I'm proud to say I didn't cave in and immediately start blabbing everything he was demanding to know. With as much restraint as I could muster, I looked Fisher squarely in his cold hazel eyes and hissed, "Are you kidding me? Have you forgotten who I am…how this all started?" I must have leaned too close to Fisher for Devon's liking, because he stepped menacingly towards me, but Fisher's hand went up and stopped the bodyguard in mid-stride.

"That's alright, Devon," Fisher said. "Leave us alone for a minute, will you?" The hostile expression on the big man's face showed just how much he disapproved of the idea, but he complied and walked away.

"Come on," Fisher said quietly, "let's go sit in the Prayer Garden for a while." By that he was referring to the plant-filled solarium I had admired earlier. He led me there, and sat me down on a rock bench beneath the pleasantly gushing waterfall.

"So, really Brad, how did you manage to hook up with Brock Harrow?" he asked me, suddenly taking on a chummy tone worthy of a school girl at a pyjama party. Even though that infuriating superiority of his was gone, I had little doubt the amiability was contrived, and his casual, friendly manner was a manipulative façade. But I guess part of me was just dying to tell the story of my master stroke of recruiting, so I proceeded to recount the entire incident, without any embellishment, culminating with Harrow's desire to come to New York for a meeting.

Fisher's response shocked me. He seemed to discount Harrow altogether, and instead seized upon my online activities.

"You're a priest?" he demanded incredulously, his eyes instantly going down to take in the jeans and sweatshirt I was wearing. Even though the hairs instantly went up on the back of my neck and I intuitively knew I was treading on dangerous ground, I was genuinely puzzled by his surprise.

"Hell, Sky... I've been counseling people from the beginning. You know that. In fact, if memory serves me correctly, I was actually the very first Phasmatian priest... if you don't count those programmed characters of Stan's."

"Yes, I'm fully aware of your invaluable early contributions," Fisher said impatiently, giving a little flick of his hand like he was waving off a mosquito. "That is, after all, why we continue to generously recognize them every payday. I just didn't realize you were still one of the practicing priests. Who's your bishop?"

"My what?"

"You know, your supervisor ... the one who logs your activities, assigns your duties, and guides you in your devotions and study of The Sacred Text."

"Are you for real?" I laughed. "I *wrote* the freaking Sacred Text, remember? I sure as hell don't need some snot-nosed brainwashed recruit to tell me how to preach and help others. I work strictly alone, and I'm damned good at what I do. I *earn* that fucking paycheck our Church so generously provides."

"That's impossible," Fisher said flatly. "After the seminary everyone is assigned a bishop. There's no way ... " His words trailed off as the cold light of understanding flooded over him, and he simply said, "Stan."

I kept my mouth shut, even as a fountain of different emotions bubbled within me—concern for Stan, white hot anger at Fisher's incredibly obtuse haughtiness, and some degree of disorientation over the surreal turn of events.

"Devon," Fisher called out, and although it was only a few decibels louder than the apparently intimate conversation we had just been having, the big bodyguard was suddenly standing in the doorway of the solarium. I should have known he wouldn't trust me to be really alone with his charge. I imagine if I had reached menacingly for Fisher at any time, I would have been gunned down on the spot.

"My son, please be so kind as to have Stan Shiu brought up, will you?" A cellphone materialized in Devon's hand, numbers were keyed, instructions murmured, and a few short minutes later a confused-looking Stan was ushered in to join us.

Fisher had him take a seat on a rock beside me and stood to face us both. "Stan, how is it Brad here is able to counsel members of our flock without a supervisor? Did you arrange that?"

Stan shot me a dirty look before answering. "Gee, Sky, he has the same privileges he's always had ... you know, from when we started." It was somewhat of an obfuscation, and Fisher saw right through it.

"I thought I'd issued *specific* instructions on how I wanted the clergy's hierarchy to operate," Fisher said with the tone of a disappointed parent.

"Well, yeah, Sky, I did that for everyone else, but, shit, I didn't think that meant Brad too. It's not like he's some newbie, is it? I mean he already knows everything."

I hated seeing Stan on the hot seat, so I interceded. "What's the big deal, Sky? It's not like I'm gumming up the works or something ... in fact I'm filling in a gap between the automated routines, and the stuff the clergy are trying to do."

"How so?" Fisher asked, suddenly genuinely interested.

"Well, it's the human connect. That's the reason we put real people online in the first place, remember? Our users aren't stupid, you know. A lot of them are on the cusp of becoming true believers, they just need to be gently shown the way. But those fucking moronic priests are acting no better than the computer programs ... they're reciting canned scripts and regurgitating the scripture, and generally talking down to people. It can be a real turn-off, you know."

"And you have a better way?" Fisher inquired.

"Well, yeah, I do. I talk *to* people, not *at* them. I answer their questions, and I tell them the truth."

"You *what*?"

"Relax, I don't tell them, you know, that the whole thing was made up, or anything like that. But, I do tell them the Church— any church—is just a means to an end, and that they have to find the answer within themselves. It's the soft sell, know what I'm saying? And it really works." Fisher's reaction was still impossible to read, so I added, "Aw, man, you really should see it. I'm doing real good ... I'm really *helping* people."

"It's true, Sky, I've seen the logs and blogs," said Stan, seizing on my point—although in hindsight I wish he'd kept his mouth shut. "He's probably the most popular character we have online ... maybe even more popular than *you*."

Fisher turned crimson. "Phasmatia is not your private playground. If you have concrete suggestions on improving the software for our clergy, then I'm ordering you to work with Stan to implement them. But I don't want you performing the sacred duties of a priest." He gestured at my casual street attire, and practically spat out his next words. "Look at you ... you don't even dress respectfully. My priests and priestesses may not be as glib or slick as you are, but they're true believers. What's more, they've sworn a holy oath of devotion. If you want to join the clergy, then you're welcome to enroll in one of our seminaries and *earn* the right to wear the Phasmatian pendant."

He waved his hand dismissively, and Devon, who'd been lurking behind the waterfall the whole time, stomped into view, indicating our audience with the Big Cheese was over. I was too blown away by what I'd just heard to open my mouth, and Stan meanwhile was visibly shaking all over with rage. I knew he was searching for some supreme, scathing retort, so I grabbed my friend by the arm and pulled him towards the exit before he could say something he might regret. But as we were leaving, I couldn't help myself, and called over my shoulder. "Hey, Lou baby, which seminary did *you* go to?"

I had dinner with the van Vroonhovens again last night. Now, I want you to know I had been fully prepared to dine alone in my trailer (on Beatrix's leftovers) after a day of writing—after all, I didn't want to wear out my welcome with my new neighbors right away. But Andy stopped in again on his way back from deer hunting, just as the late afternoon sun was starting to dip below the horizon, and practically dragged me back to eat at the farmhouse. I confess it didn't take a lot of persuading.

I joked with Andy about his apparent lack of success in bagging a buck, and he revealed to me the ageless secret of the hunt—even if there are easier ways to get your meat, they don't give you quite the same perfect excuse for disappearing into the woods for a while, away from the scrutiny of the wife, as deer hunting does. According to Andy, he could easily have filled his legal limit in the first day or so, but then it would be back to doing chores for Beatrix for the remainder of the season. "You just watch me," he said with a wink. "I'll shoot me four or so in the last couple of days, and there'll be plenty of venison in the freezer." I believed him, although I didn't expect to be around to see it.

Mind you, it's not like Beatrix wasn't wise to her husband's

ways, as she confided to me that night over dessert while Andy
stepped out to fetch more firewood. "The deer stroll into that
field over there pretty much every day. Papa could sit on the
back porch and shoot them from his rocking chair if he wanted
to. But he likes to get away from me for a spell, and I don't
begrudge him none, especially after a long season tending to
the farm." She looked off into space after saying that, and you
could see the life she'd chosen play itself out in her eyes. "It's
a hard life, farming is, especially without the kids to help out
anymore," she mused sadly, "but we like it, at least while the
Good Lord still grants us our health. Don't know what's going
to happen to the farm after we're gone, though. None of the kids
seem interested in moving back here and taking it over. We kept
hoping they'd see the world outside isn't all it's cracked up to
be and they'd come home, but, well, you know..." She seemed
to catch herself being maudlin, and the girlish grin returned to
her ample cheeks. She shoved the apple cobbler my way. "Have
some more, Jerry."

Every time they used my phony name it made me feel guilty
that I was deceiving these people who had so generously invited
me into their home, so I tried hard not to pile any fresh lies
onto the ones I had already spread. I talked openly about my
job at the ad agency, and about my life as a single young professional in New York, although I surprised myself when their
affable questioning extracted a confession from me about the
increasing desire to finally settle down with a good woman, and
raise a family.

"New York City's no place to bring up kids, though," I admitted. "I'd like something a little more rural, although it can be
tough finding work."

"It's beautiful country around here, don't you think? I keep
hoping my daughter Hannah will find some nice young man and
move back home. She's around your own age, you know," Beatrix said, looking at me significantly, and then brushed off her

husband's mild rebuke. "Hush now, Papa. I'll speak my mind if I want to. I know young people today don't think much of meddlin' and matchmaking, but I can't help it if I've taken a liking to Jerry here, and can see he and Hannah are perfect for each other."

With that she patted my hand, and the guilt rose in me like a creek in the spring melt. I promised myself that when I finish writing this exposé (and assuming I find a way to get it onto the Net and don't get killed in the process) I'll come back here and come clean with the van Vroonhovens. And, hell, I'd actually like to meet their daughter. Everything they've told me about Hannah indicates she's an exceptional woman with her head screwed on straight. Besides, they showed me a photo, and Andy was right. She *is* kind of cute.

Back to my 411 on The Chosen One. After Fisher learned about the exploits of my virtual Phasmatian persona, I was banned from any further priestly activities, and my popular Mage Errant character simply disappeared from the virtual world. I thought I might be given the boot outright, but in fact, I was kept on the payroll, and formally assigned the task of writing down improved methods for preaching The Sacred Text, to be employed by both the automated interaction programs, and the human counselors.

Stan suffered more than I did. He was put on a short leash, and a couple of Fisher's goons were assigned the job of shadowing him and reporting on his activities. That was a bit of a joke, given that both monks were clearly technomorons who didn't comprehend the first thing about computer programming. Stan could easily have trashed the whole system right in front of the eyes of his unsuspecting wardens if he'd really wanted to.

Nonetheless, the message was clear—Stan was forbidden to do anything that had not first been sanctioned. The loss of freedom and trust visibly rankled him, and he began to make noises about quitting the Church and going back to his old job at Warren & McCaul. I knew, though, that he was just letting off steam, and would never leave the Church voluntarily. It wasn't just the fact he was making three times the salary with the Phasmatians. He had also built something truly original that was on the leading edge of technology, and for a hard-core geek like Stan, it was that challenge that really mattered. I doubt if Stan truly fathomed the massive social implications of what we'd unleashed on the world, but the thousands of cross-connected servers and the petabytes of ground-breaking code he'd developed were his babies, and Stan would never leave them to someone else. Nevertheless, having someone looking over his shoulder all the time, and questioning his every action, now after years of absolute freedom, chafed him badly, and his enmity against Fisher grew steadily.

We took to hitting the bars together again, and it was almost like the good old days. Until the monks had shown up to stand guard over him, Stan had seldom left work, and in fact kept a cot in the back of the machine room, between the racks of blade servers, where he had slept most nights. Now, he couldn't wait to get away from the prying eyes of his keepers, and so he and I would often spend our evenings back at good old Macbeth's, pounding back drinks and bitching about how things had ended up.

Although Fisher had slapped me down for my unauthorized online activities, he had no qualms about capitalizing on the connection I'd made there with Brock Harrow. The movie star had been invited to New York, and feted with great aplomb (all of which was given seemingly non-stop media coverage), and before long had become the Church's most visible convert. Notorious on the talk show circuit for his unabashed self-promotion, now it seemed all Harrow was willing to talk about was his newfound religion.

Especially influential was one interview he had with Billy Reno, where he revealed that he was both a Phasmatian *and* a practicing Presbyterian. Asked if this wasn't contradictory, Harrow opined that not only was there no conflict between the two, but in his view Jesus Christ had himself been a Phasmatian.

"You have to remember, Billy," he said with the most sincere face he could muster from his acting repertoire, "that Jesus didn't call himself a Christian. *That* label was applied much later, by others. He gave his religion *no* name. He was merely an itinerant preacher, charged by a higher power with the mission of saving souls. But if you compare the scriptures of Phasmatia and Christianity, you'll see that there's a tremendous similarity between the two. I believe God and The Universal Spirit are facets of the same ultimate deity, Billy, and it is others who apply the labels. From time to time, She infuses chosen souls with Her divine power to help spread the message to the masses. Sky Fisher is just the latest in a long line of such Saviors."

I didn't see the original interview myself, but caught it enough times in the rebroadcast excerpts on the news, and viewed the clips posted all over the web. I think what impressed the audience most was the surprising intelligence Harrow showed when he talked, totally going against his public airhead himbo image. After all, he was known strictly as a hammy action hero and a former pro football player. Few realized Harrow had played his college ball at Yale, and had graduated *summa cum laude* in economics.

It was a brilliant stroke for Phasmatia. Not only did Harrow's proclamation of metaphysical dual citizenship allow Christians (and Jews and Buddhists and Muslims) to flock to the new religion with a clear conscience, but it placed Sky Fisher on the same pedestal as Jesus himself. And, as you probably know, Brock Harrow's very vocal support for Phasmatia did not harm his career in the least—quite the contrary. *Variety* reported that Harrow's contracts now called for passing positive references to the Church to be added to the script of any movie he participated in, and offers were still pouring in.

Suddenly, Phasmatians were trendy, and other high-profile entertainment personalities quickly jumped onto the bandwagon. The Phasmatian pendant became the new must-have fashion accessory, and not just among the glitterati. While you could soon buy cheap knock-offs on practically any street corner in the civilized world, true trendoids made a point of sporting the genuine article (just as you would want a real Rolex or Prada bag, not an imitation) and that was available only one place—on our web site.

Despite being constantly shadowed by the monks, Stan still had full access to all statistics and financial records, and told me over drinks one night that sales of the pendant alone were soon topping fifty thousand a day. It made him bitter... made us *both* bitter. Even though Stan's salary now ran into six figures, and I was being paid more for my part-time involvement with the Church than my daytime gig at Warren & McCaul, the billions now being raked in by an enterprise we had started, but had no legal shares in, became a major sore point and a prime topic for our nightly booze-fueled gripefests.

It was no consolation to us that Fisher didn't draw a penny of salary or bonuses from the Church, and to the best of my knowledge still doesn't. But then he doesn't really have to, does he? Do you think the pope walks around with a credit card or a wad of cash in his cassock? But Stan had seen the financial accounts, and knew the real story. Fisher lived in opulent splendor worthy of a maharajah, including private jets and yachts and limos, a personal chef purloined from a five-star Parisian restaurant, and a half-dozen holy homes reserved for his exclusive use, but all technically owned by the Church.

Stan began to make noises about confronting Fisher and demanding an equitable level of control over Phasmatia, and I, Lord forgive me, encouraged him. Maybe you think we were just being greedy, but to us the money was just a way of measuring the inequality. Neither one of us had delusions of million-dollar payments being slipped into our bank accounts, for we fully understood the ramifications of Phasmatia's status as a religion. Nor were we holding out for the same material fringe benefits Fisher lavished on himself. To us, it was purely the principle of the thing. We had been robbed of what was rightfully ours, and were being disrespected and demeaned. I had felt this way for a long time, even before I had been banned from my virtual ministry, but frankly I would probably never have done anything about it by myself. But Stan, the normally quiet and accepting milquetoast minion, was now the one rising up in open rebellion, and despite a nagging feeling we were treading on dangerous ground, I encouraged him, and prodded him on.

It was the *Time* cover article that pushed Stan over the edge. One late afternoon, while I was still in my cubicle at Warren & McCaul, polishing up some copy for an insurance company's web campaign that I was going to present to the client the next day, I got a text message from Stan to meet him at Macbeth's ASAP.

"Have you seen this?" Stan growled as soon as I sat down, flinging down a magazine with enough force to make Bill, the unflappable bartender, jerk his head around in alarm. There was Fisher's haughty face beaming up at us from *Time*'s cover, under a giant headline that read "Religion Rising."

I shrugged, even though the sight of Fisher stealing the limelight made my stomach churn. "So what? You know how much the bastard loves publicity."

Stan flipped through the pages furiously until he came to the feature story, and spun the words around so they faced me. "Read what it says here," he ordered, an angry scarlet flush on his normally pale face as he pointed out a specific place.

The article itself was in a question-and-answer format, and I read the indicated passage aloud:

"Time: Did you have any help getting Phasmatia started?

"Fisher: You mean, other than The Universal Spirit? No, I knew this

sacred labor was mine alone, not that there was anyone willing to help me anyway. So I sold everything I owned, and built the web site. It was clearly the best way to spread the gospel in today's online world. The actual words, of course, were easy because they came directly from the Spirit. I was merely the humble vessel."

By the time I'd finished reading, my face was as red as Stan's. "The lying prick," I yelled, giving Bill his second start in as many minutes.

"That's it," said Stan. "That's the last straw. Fisher's out in L.A. today, but he's flying back to New York tonight. I've already set up an appointment for ten o'clock tomorrow morning."

"Ten? Oh man, Stan, I can't make that. I've got an important client meeting... there's no way I can blow them off."

"You don't have to. I'm going to see him alone. It'll be better that way... you two have never really gotten along anyway. I think I'll be able to talk some sense into him, but don't worry, pal, I'll make sure we both get what we deserve."

I should have been counseling caution, but my anger (and selfish delight that Stan would do the dirty work) caused me to urge my friend onward. "Do it, Stan. Cut that constipated asshole down to size. And if he refuses to give us the acknowledgement we deserve... " I held up the magazine to illustrate my point. "... tell him we'll make sure the press get the full story—the *real* story."

We spent a couple more hours taking turns insulting Fisher, and howling over the injustice he had perpetrated, but I made sure Stan left early so he wouldn't be hung over for his morning confrontation with Fisher. As he headed out the door I exhorted a promise to meet for a liquid lunch immediately after his meeting, so he could fill me in on the juicy details.

When Stan walked into the bar at the anointed hour the next day, I could tell instantly from his body language that things had not gone the way we'd wanted them to. It took ten minutes and a double shot of Jameson's just to settle him down enough to relate what had transpired. It wasn't anger affecting Stan this time, though, it was naked fear, although I didn't fully get it at the time. Now, as I sit here writing this, in constant dread of the assassins who are searching for me in order to snuff out my life, I better understand what Stan was feeling that day. To my discredit, though, I was short with him on that occasion, and annoyed with his emotional preambles.

"For Christ's sake, Stan, get a grip and tell me what happened!" I said. "Did he at least agree to give us more credit?"

"He's a fucking lunatic. I swear he's totally lost it. He believes he really is The Chosen One."

"He actually *said* that?"

Stan nodded. "When I told him we wanted the credit and shares we deserve for helping start the whole thing, he said, right to my face, that everything that has happened was a fulfillment of divine destiny, because The Universal Spirit has chosen to act through him alone, and has filled him full of holy powers."

"Hello... Looney Tunes!"

"You're telling me. But want to know what I said?" Stan half-smiled then, the first time since walking through the door that I could see a ghost of his usual, upbeat self. "I told him he was so full of shit, it's a wonder he's always so constipated."

I howled at that one. "Ooh, good one, Stan." I clinked his glass.

He accepted my toast, but the somber look was instantly back on his face. "I said flat out that there would have been nothing without me and you ... that if it hadn't been for your writing and my coding the whole thing would never have gotten off the ground, and he'd be back at some ad agency, kissing the clients' asses."

"Way to tell him off, Stan! So, what did the All-Exalted One have to say about *that*?"

"Get this. He called me a heretic ... said I wasn't a true believer, and that was why I didn't deserve to be a leader in the Church. That's when I lost it, and told him what you said, you know, about going to the press and blowing the cover off of the whole scam. And then it happened."

"What do you mean? What happened?"

"He called in that big bodyguard of his."

"You mean Devon? Oh shit, Stan, are you okay? What did that oversized goon do to you? Did he hurt you?"

"The bastard came in and I thought he was just going to throw me out. But then he grabbed me and twisted my arms behind my back, and Fisher starts going ballistic on me, spitting in my face, and screaming all sorts of crazy things at me about how I'd betrayed The Universal Spirit, and that he could see my soul turning black with sin before his very eyes. He said I'd grown into a cancer that needed to be cut out. And then he reaches under Devon's coat and pulls out this big fucking gun and sticks the damned thing right in my face."

As he spoke, I saw Stan's eyes begin to mist up, and I clued into the anguish it was causing him to relive the moment.

"I swear, Brad, I thought he was going to shoot me. His hand was shaking, and honest to God, I saw his finger starting to squeeze the trigger. I ... I ... I pissed my pants."

He dropped his gaze as he said it, clearly humiliated by what he'd done. My eyes lowered too, but out of curiosity, glancing down to his crotch to see if there was a pee stain, which there wasn't. That's when I noticed for the first time Stan was not wearing one of his usual pairs of bad-fitting, nerdy chinos. There had been something discordant about his appearance when he walked through the door, but I'd been so distracted by his obviously agitated state that I hadn't been able to put my finger on it. Now I could see Stan was wearing the charcoal-gray pants from a Phasmatian priest's outfit.

"It saved me, I think," Stan continued, "when I peed myself.

The psycho started to laugh out loud, and said it was a sign from The Spirit. He handed the gun back to Devon, and had me dragged into his private apartment ... have you seen that place?"

"I was up to his penthouse once ... you remember that time, when Fisher ended up siccing his watchdog monks on you ... but I've never been inside his actual inner sanctum, not since he renovated anyway," I said, remembering the palatial grandeur I'd witnessed that day.

"Well, his bathroom alone is bigger than your whole place," Stan said. "As we walk through the bedroom, I see there's two hot babes in his bed ... I mean, it's 10:30 in the morning and they're just lying around naked, like they're waiting for some-one to jump into the sack with them. And, get this, there's these strange rubber and plastic things on top of the sheets. I thought at first they were sex toys. It took me a while to realize one is an enema bag, and the other is like some kind of an oversized turkey baster for flushing out your asshole."

Part of me wanted Stan to tell me more about the hotties, and kinky goings-on in Fisher's bed, but I bit my tongue and let him continue his story.

"Devon tells me to take my clothes off and shoves me into the shower, which is big enough to wash a car in, and is totally done in marble, and after I'm done washing up, there's a fresh pair of underwear, still in its packaging, and dry clothes for me to put on. I'm led back out to Fisher's office, but I'm through with making demands. By now, I know I'm dealing with a mental case, and I just want to get out of there alive. But Fisher's all calm again, and he surprises me by apologizing. 'You're right, Stan,' he says, 'we couldn't have done this without you, and I'm sorry if you were made to feel like you were being left out.' Mind you, I figure he's just saying it, trying to get me to forget the fact that he just pulled a fucking gun on me. But even though I wanted to leave, part of me also wanted to stay, and hear what he had to say next."

Stan paused, and if it had been anyone else I would have figured it was for dramatic effect, but that's not Stan's style, and I
realized he was looking for another drink. I ordered a refill, and
he filled me in on the rest of the encounter.

"Fisher sent Devon out of the room, although I know the guy's
really just around the corner somewhere, ready to blow me away
if I step out of line. 'Here's what I'm going to do,' Fisher tells me.
'I'm going to forget about our little disagreement, and we need
never speak about it again. You can go back to work, and there
will be a nice bonus for you come payday ... call it compensation
for any past grievances. And I'm offering you the rank of bishop,
plus a permanent seat on the Governing Committee.'"

"He made you a director?" I exclaimed. "Well, that's great,
Stan, you deserve it." Then it hit me that something was missing.
"Um, what about me?" I asked.

"He wants you to come and talk with him." Stan reached into
his bag and pulled out an envelope. "And he wants you to sign
this."

"What is it?"

"A non-disclosure agreement."

As I scanned over the document, it was blatantly clear to me
that Fisher was trying to buy our silence, although I somehow
doubted he would really give us any meaningful control over
the Church. Nevertheless, he seemed to be negotiating with us,
so at least that was a baby step in the right direction. But Stan's
demeanor was far from a victorious one, and I sensed there was
more to the story. "Did you sign?" I asked.

Stan sighed. "I didn't feel I had a choice. I figured if I refused,
he'd kill me for sure. But here's the kicker. He comes out from
behind that oversized desk of his and stands in front of me and
orders me to get down on my knees. Then he throws his arms
high up in the air ... you know, just like his character does in the
online world ... and starts to rant. 'I am The Chosen One, Stan.
I am the voice and the eyes and the guiding hands of The Uni-

versal Spirit. Swear to me, Stan. Swear you will follow me and
obey me, without hesitation, and without question. Swear your
never-ending fealty, and I promise you will be saved, and will
bask in eternal blessed light.' When I hesitated, I could see him
starting to go ballistic again. 'Kiss my hand and swear it, Stan,
or my avenging angel will come to cast you down into the never-
ending darkness,' he yells at me, and behind me I hear Devon
come shuffling back into the room, so I did it ... I ... I kissed his
hand ... and I swore."

With that, Stan opened his overcoat, and I could see he wasn't
just wearing priest's pants. He had the complete outfit on, and
around his neck dangled a Phasmatian pendant, except this one
appeared to be solid gold, and had a big honking red gemstone
in the middle, indicating Stan's newly elevated status in the
Church hierarchy. Lord help me, I had to laugh.

"It's not funny," Stan said. "I feel like I just sold my soul to the
devil. And now there's this big ceremony they're going to hold
for me, with all those other hard-core fanatics. Plus, I've got all
these lines I'm supposed to memorize."

"Ah, yes ... the hallowed initiation rites of the bishop. It's quite
the elaborate ritual, although not one of my more inspired works,
I'm afraid."

"Do you think I should go through with it? Not that I really
have a choice."

"Sure you have a choice ... everyone has a choice."

"To do what? Walk away ... or more like run for my life? No.
Somebody's got to stop that bastard, and I've got a better chance
of doing it from the inside. I figure if I give him what he wants,
he'll ease up on me ... maybe get those goons of his to stop looking over my shoulder every second. If he does that, then I can rig
things so he won't be able to fuck with me ever again."

He looked up at me with soft brown puppy-dog eyes. Poor
Stan. Despite his amazing technical smarts, he'd always been
somewhat of a babe in the woods. I felt sorry for him.

"What about you?" he asked me. "What are you going to do?"

"That depends on what Fisher has to offer me."

"So you're going to go see him?"

I nodded, my mind already fast-forwarding to the encounter. "I'm going to see him, alright, but not on his turf... not if he's as dangerous as you say. I'm going to meet him in public, where that big ape of his won't be able to lay a hand on me." I held up the non-disclosure agreement. "But I'm not going to sign this, not without some serious concessions first. And I'm not going down on my knees for him either." It was a shitty thing to say, and Stan started to cry.

"I couldn't help it... I swear he would have killed me," he sobbed, and then turned his head, clearly embarrassed by his tears.

"Hey, Stan, it's okay, man, everything's okay. Things worked out, and you got what we wanted anyway, didn't you? Hey, you're a top dog now. It'll be cool. So go with the flow, dude. Go back there and take advantage of it. Like you said, he'll probably cut you some slack now. But, me, I'm not nearly as useful to him as you are... at least not anymore. I'm going to have to play things differently."

I loved Stan like a brother, but I considered him a bit of a wimp, and honestly thought he had overestimated the physical danger he had been in (even if I wasn't going to take the same chance myself). I swear to God, if I'd known how things were going to turn out, I would *never* have let him return to the Church. But, instead, I bought him another drink, filled his head with visions of the upscale lifestyle and power he'd enjoy as a Phasmatian bishop, and cheered him up. Yes, great friend that I was, I fed him full of naïve reassurances, put a smile back on his face, and sent him off on the path that would lead to his death.

Article updated Friday 7 November 21:39

It's nighttime now, and I want to record the evening's happenings while the events are fresh in my head. The weather improved today, or at least turned warmer, bringing with it rain from the south. As a consequence, most of the earlier snow was washed away, although the yard around my trailer has turned into a muddy quagmire that's difficult to plod through.

The good news, though, is that the roads are clear again, so after my day's writing, I decided to get my motorcycle out from under the tarp, push the sucker out to the gate, and cruise around for a bit. By my estimation, it will take another week or so to finish writing my exposé, but I wanted to start scouting around the county for a library or internet café where I'd be able to upload my stuff onto the web.

The rain was down to a light drizzle when I started out, but even so, after an hour I was good and soaked, especially from the waist down. So, when I spotted the neon beer ads of a roadhouse on I-90, I decided to stop in for a drink to warm myself up. There was plenty of room in the parking lot, but out of some fugitive's reflex, I rolled my motorcycle out of sight behind a big maple tree in the back before going in. I plopped myself at the bar, ordered a Sam Adams, and tried to get caught up on world events—at least as much as the small overhead TV with no volume would allow.

I suppose if I had been in Manhattan, say sitting at the bar in Macbeth's, I would have attracted some attention, what with four days' worth of beard, and the hunter-orange baseball cap I'd put on to cover up how mussed up my hair looked after taking off my motorcycle helmet. Here in the country, though, I blended right in, and the customers that wandered in scarcely gave me a glance. I ordered some buffalo wings, and busied myself with the crossword puzzle in a three-day-old *New York Times* someone had left behind on the bar. With my head down, I didn't even see the two Phasmatian monks come in—and more importantly they didn't see me.

When I glanced up and saw their reflection in the mirror behind the bar, I almost fell off my stool. The duo was sitting at a table having supper, although one of them never stopped studying a map in his lap. While my own arrival had gone virtually unnoticed, these two men in black were attracting a good deal of attention from the roadhouse's patrons. The Phasmatian religion, despite almost a billion followers worldwide, is still largely an urban phenomenon, and I doubt if the monks' like had ever been seen here in the boondocks, even though I was probably the only person in the room who fully understood the significance of their particular dark uniform.

I had to pee, but was afraid to get up from my seat in case I caught the pair's attention, so I squeezed my thighs together, and kept my back to them. Eventually the monks paid their bill and left, leaving the locals' tongues wagging in their wake. I hurried to the washroom and, as the tension and urine flowed out of me, tried to digest the significance of the encounter.

I had no direct proof the Phasmatian enforcers had been out looking for me. I-90 is a major interstate route and, for all I knew, these men might have been on their way from Albany to New York for a meeting, or training session, or something. I'm still fairly confident I did a good job covering my tracks during my exit from the city, but even if I had somehow left a trail back in Manhattan, surely it would have faded out once I'd gotten into the country after sunset.

That night, I had purposely headed towards my hometown of Poughkeepsie first, before circling upstate to the Shius' trailer. Mind you, there was never any question of returning to my boyhood home. Whatever emotional attachment I might have had to the place was long gone, buried with my father. My mother lives in Arizona now with her new husband, and although my sister and her two kids have taken over the family home, she and I aren't close, and we haven't communicated in a year or two—beyond the usual holiday and birthday cards. But the Phasmatians wouldn't necessarily know that, and should have no way of suspecting where I'd ended up.

Only Sky Fisher himself should be able to connect me with the trailer, and would he even remember? The one time we'd all been up here together for our notorious weekend, I had driven both ways, while Fisher and Stan drank and yakked away the whole time. Besides, the property is connected to the Shiu family, not to me.

In the end, I have decided my best bet is to stay holed up in the trailer. I was extra careful driving back here from the roadhouse, and even stopped a half-dozen times to see if I was being followed. I felt a deep pang of longing when I drove by the van Vroonhovens' driveway and saw the lights on inside their farmhouse. It was too late to go knocking on their door, though, and maybe that was for the best. I shouldn't get too close to those decent, guiltless folks. At best, I'll be leaving shortly anyway. At worst... well, I certainly wouldn't want them dragged into my mess.

Yesterday I wrote about how Stan had become a Phasmatian bishop. Do you want to know something I never told him, or any other living being for that matter? I was jealous. Don't get me wrong. I certainly didn't begrudge Stan the success he richly deserved for his amazing technical and organizational accomplishments, but the simple truth was that I secretly coveted his ecumenical title.

Ever since Fisher had forbidden my itinerant preaching as the Mage Errant, I had become increasingly depressed. I felt like I had been cut off from something I really loved, and perhaps the only thing in life I truly, passionately believed in. We could all speculate and debate until Doomsday what exactly about the Phasmatian religion has proved so appealing to the masses, and what precisely the tipping point was but, damn it, I think a good part of it had to do with *me*. Who would have thought Brad Evans was a genius?

Look, I don't downplay the vital importance of the internet, and Stan's technological wizardry was undeniably a huge part of spreading the word. I also don't think I can be accused of having been stingy with my praise for Sky Fisher, even if you know by now how much I hate the man. I freely admit his zeal and ideas were the creative wellspring from which all Phasmatia flowed. Kudos to the Fat Cat ... the Big Cheese ... Numero Uno. You're one in a million, Sky. (Actually more like one in seven billion.) May you burn in hell.

And I've heard it argued more than once that Phasmatia was simply lucky—that we were at the right place at the right time, nothing else—and managed to exploit the whole social network-ing wave just as it was beginning to crest. I have no easy retort for that, because any artist or entrepreneur who manages to beat the odds and climb out on top of the heap will tell you, although perhaps not freely, that luck plays a huge part in any successful endeavor.

But deep down in my heart, dare I say my soul, I know the pure, simple beauty of the Phasmatian dogma was a key ingredi-ent in why it caught on. There were times when I swear I could almost feel the hand of God guiding me in my work. No, I'm not saying God was actually *there*, whispering in my ear, or pushing the keys of my computer. But I feel like I finally cut through the mundane, distracting crap of everyday existence—what the Hindus call *maya*, the grand illusion—and glimpsed the higher order of things. I realize that may make me sound as bad as Sky Fisher. The difference is, he's a fraud who wants to rule people, and I honestly want to save them.

Even if it felt sometimes like I was sprinkling water in the des-ert, I know I was doing tremendous good, and that I changed many, many lives for the better through my online counseling and preaching. And changed my own life in the process. Once you've tasted that kind of soul-stirring rapture, it's hard to have to give it up.

So, whether or not you choose to believe me, the truth is that all I wanted for myself from any deal I hoped to broker with Sky Fisher was the right to return to my preaching without interfer-ence. He had made Stan a bishop, after all, without a single day spent in any seminary or priestly training program, so was it unreasonable to think I deserved equal treatment? Of course Stan had dropped to his knees, kissed Fisher's hand, and sworn eternal loyalty, and for me that was a deal breaker. I had told myself time and again that no amount of rationalization about the ends justifying the means could bring me to kowtow to that evil son of a bitch.

The day before Stan was scheduled to receive his installation rites as bishop, I phoned the Church offices and asked to speak to Fisher. Of course, I could have just walked over to the building and approached Devon directly about making an appointment. My access badge to Phasmatian headquarters still worked, but it wasn't the getting *in* that worried me. No, I had received a healthy dose of paranoia after Stan's last encounter with Fisher, and had made up my mind that any meeting with the High and Mighty had to take place in a very public place, where the presence of witnesses would preclude any attempts to threaten or attack me.

Predictably, even after I explained who was calling, I was unable to get past the call-center grunt who first answered the phone. He did politely promise to pass on my message, though, even after I'd unloaded an earful of curses and insults on the poor guy. It took three hours to get a response, which was not altogether unexpected, but I was surprised (and pleased) that it was Fisher himself who called me back.

"Brad, my prodigal son, where have you been keeping yourself?" Fisher quipped, sounding a bit like his old pre-Phasmatian self (although even then he never could quite get that irritating tone of superiority out of his voice). The fact he had noticed my absence was itself revealing.

"The agency's been keeping me busy, Sky. You remember what it was like, I'm sure."

"I don't know why you still bother with those hacks. Your true place is here with us. There are still great works to be done."

"Well, that's exactly what I wanted to talk to you about. How about getting together? I was hoping maybe tonight."

"Of course, of course ... Why don't you drop by and we'll chat," Fisher suggested so earnestly it suddenly made me feel like someone had squeezed my scrotum.

"Actually, I was kind of hoping you might meet me someplace around here," I replied, and the silence that manifested itself on the other end of the line told me my message had hit home. When Fisher spoke again any attempts at pleasantries had disappeared.

"So, what are you saying, Brad? You don't trust me?"

"Cut the crap, Sky. I read every word of that contract you had Stan pass on to me. I think it's more like *you* don't trust *me*."

"Well, can you blame me? All that talk about selling a tell-all story to the press. Don't tell me that was Stan's idea."

"Well, you've certainly come to terms with Stan. Now it's my turn."

"Is that what this is about? Are you trying to shake me down? I'm warning you, you son of a bitch, don't screw with me or you'll regret it."

"Relax, Sky. I'm willing to sign. And I don't want your money."

There was another silence while he chewed on that. "What *do* you want, then?" he finally asked.

"Meet me at Macbeth's tonight around eight and I'll tell you. But come alone. I don't want your muscle-bound bozos breathing down my neck."

Fisher actually laughed at that one. "I'm afraid Devon won't let me go out in public alone. He's protective that way. But tell you what. I'll order him to keep his distance, and you and I can have a nice, private little chat. How's that?"

"Okay by me. Eight o'clock then."

Sky Fisher's face was about as recognizable as any on this planet by then, so, not surprisingly, he drew a lot of attention when he walked into Macbeth's and joined me in a corner booth. That was actually a deliberate ploy on my part, figuring he wouldn't try strong-arming me while so many people were gawking at us. As it turned out, I was actually glad he'd brought Devon along, if only because the big bodyguard's presence discouraged any admirers or celebrity worshippers from approaching the booth and disturbing our little *tête à tête*, although several tried.

"Alright, here I am," Fisher said before his butt had even hit the seat, "so let's hear it."

"Join me in a drink, old pal?" I was determined not to let him intimidate me. I'd already pounded back a couple of bourbons, but was in the market for some more liquid courage before the negotiations began. Fisher shrugged assent, and I flagged down my waitress, enduring her verbal outpourings of admiration for Fisher before we could place our order.

"You've got half an hour," Fisher said, "so let's get down to brass tacks. You said you were willing to sign an agreement, and you claim you're not looking for money. So, what exactly *is* the price for your silence?"

"I want back into Phasmatia … I want to be the Mage Errant again, and I want to be able to preach and counsel in my own way."

He snorted. "We have a formal structure now, with rules and a set hierarchy. There's no place for loose cannons in the Church."

"I assure you my Church canon is as tight as yours, given that I wrote it." It took him a second, but he smiled. Ad men are suckers for a pun.

"I already told you," he said. "If you want to become a priest, you're welcome to enroll in the seminary."

"So, how come Stan gets to go straight to bishop, whereas I get treated like any schmuck off the street?" I was getting worked up a little now, although I kept my voice to a whisper so as not to make Devon edgy.

"Stan heads the Church's entire technology division, and that easily makes him the equivalent of a bishop. Besides, he has sworn a sacred oath of loyalty to me as Church leader. Are you willing to do the same?"

I started to tell him to screw off but bit back my words, and took a swallow of my Jack Daniels instead. After all, what was stopping me? All I had to do was utter some hollow words and I'd have what I had been telling myself I really wanted—a chance to do immeasurable good, not to mention all the fringe benefits that would come from assuming a high Phasmatian rank. Sure, I hated Fisher's guts, but I wasn't overly fond of my boss at the agency either, and that didn't stop me from groveling and eating shit at work every day, all for way less money than I would likely receive as a full-fledged Phasmatian bigwig. And hadn't I earned it?

"So, if I swear the oath, I'll be a bishop too?" I asked.

"I didn't say that, and I don't want you back online spreading your heresies ... but I'm sure we could find you an appropriate administrative position, with a good salary." His words reeked of that infuriating haughtiness of his, and I almost threw my drink in his face.

"You arrogant prick," I hissed. "Have you forgotten who the hell you're talking to? I helped make you who you are ... and I can bring the whole scam crashing down. What gives you the right to shut me out?"

"You're calling *me* arrogant? Why, you were never more than a simple scribe who acted as a vessel for The Universal Spirit under my guidance. You are merely my instrument, and should consider yourself blessed you were granted the unique privilege of serving me at such an important stage. As for your question as to what gives me the right, I should have thought that was obvious—The Universal Spirit did when She chose me."

"You mean on top of Mount Skylight, after you had meditated for seven days? Ha! Wait 'til I tell the world you were actually sitting stoned on a toilet, wrestling with severe constipation, trying to concoct a get-rich-quick internet scheme."

I deliberately said it loudly, hoping the people around us would overhear, but the music was turned up pretty loud, and Devon was the only one who caught it. He took a pronounced step towards me, and I could actually feel the shockwave from his approaching bulk radiate through Macbeth's old wooden floor, but just then divine intervention arrived in the form of a paparazzo running out of the crowd and trying to descend on Fisher. Devon's eyes flickered uncertainly from me, to the cameraman, and back to me, and I could see the bodyguard's poor peanut brain trying to make up its mind who was the greater threat. The unlucky paparazzo won out, and while Devon diplomatically used a series of bumps with his massive chest to usher the journalist back to a respectful distance, it afforded me a chance to resume my conversation unmolested.

When I turned to face him again, Fisher's face was beet red, and I could see my last jab had hit home, although I couldn't tell whether it was from challenging his megalomania, or bringing up his bowel problems. "Don't screw with us, Brad," Fisher said, "or you'll be sorry. I've been given the divine power, and I *will* use it to defend against the darkness."

There was something about the way he said it that suddenly made me realize this was not an issue of greed, or power lust. The crazy bastard actually believed his own lies. I was reminded of my own boyhood when my grandfather, who was eventually institutionalized with Alzheimer's, had been brought home one morning by the police. He had been found wandering the streets in his underwear, completely disoriented, barely certain what continent he was on, let alone how to get home. There had been prior clues for months, of course, as to grandpa's worsening condition, but whether out of naiveté, or just wishful thinking, the signs of dementia had been ignored by my family. That morning it hit home in cold, irrefutable form.

So it was with my abrupt crystalline revelation that Fisher was clearly and dangerously out of his freaking mind. True, Stan had already concluded as much after his own confrontation with Fisher, but although I had patronizingly played along when the encounter was described to me, I had privately felt it was all a wily power play on Fisher's part. If I had considered Fisher dangerous before, now I knew beyond any doubt he was capable of anything. My cocky scheme to blackmail him into letting me join the Church's upper echelons had clearly failed, but where earlier I was adamant I'd blow the whistle on the whole Phasmatian fraud if I was denied, at that particular moment I was only concerned for my own skin.

I reached into my inner pocket and pulled out the non-disclosure agreement, and spread it out on the table before me. Fisher's eyes narrowed in hard suspicion as he watched me. He knew me pretty well by then, I guess, and was probably expecting me to tear it into shreds, or pour my drink all over it in an angry gesture of defiance. Somewhere in the back of his ugly reptilian brain he was probably already plotting how he was going to dispose of me. I surprised us both by signing the document, without any accompanying petulant protests or sarcastic retorts, and sliding it across the table.

The insufferable Fisher smirk came over his face as he snatched up the contract, and I regretted my action immediately, even if I was already feeling supremely relieved. He held up the papers triumphantly and gestured for Devon to come fetch them. "Bravo, Brad," he lauded me. "Now that wasn't so hard, was it?"

"Now what?" I asked weakly. I had a sick feeling in my gut he was going to demand I drop to my knees and swear an oath of fealty, just as he had with Stan. Admittedly, Stan had had a gun to his head at the time (I now believed every word of his story) but I felt my life was no less in peril, even if we were in a public place. Fortunately, I was spared the humiliation. Having won the victory he had sought, Fisher was clearly feeling magnanimous.

"I told you the Church would take care of you, and I'm happy to have a chance to keep my word. Come talk to me tomorrow, and we'll take care of things." His face lit up as an idea surfaced. "Hey, I almost forgot—the anointing of the bishops is tomorrow night. Why don't you come and watch Stan's big moment. I think you'll find it illuminating and, who knows, perhaps it'll inspire you. Your turn may come yet."

Devon was standing over me, shifting his weight from side to side to indicate his restlessness, and Fisher picked up on the body language.

"Yes, yes, Devon, I know we have an appointment to get to." He rose, and clapped a friendly arm around my sagging shoulders. "Welcome back into the light, my son. The Sacred Text was right. 'Forgiveness is like a beacon turned onto the darkness of one's own soul.' I feel invigorated."

Somewhere amidst the fear, anger, and self-loathing was the old familiar part of me that started to form a derisive and pithy comeback about having my own scripture quoted at me, but I was feeling too depressed to utter it.

Fisher departed, tossing blessings to the onlookers in his wake, and I was left alone to ponder what had just transpired. Even in my self-absorbed state of mind, I couldn't help but notice people staring at me with wonder, including a red-headed hottie at the bar whose piqued interest in me was unmistakable, and who was clearly ripe for the plucking. I didn't care. I just wanted to go home and puke, and then take a hot shower to try to wash some of the filth off my crawling flesh.

The next morning I went into work at Warren & McCaul and started to draft a letter of resignation, but found I couldn't bring myself to quit, and in fact never did—until just last week when, as described earlier, I fled Manhattan to come hide here in the trailer. It wasn't that I was hedging my bets. I fully believed Fisher would keep his promise to find some lucrative full-time position with the Church, so there was no financial reason to keep my job. Something inside me, however, rebelled at the idea of placing myself completely under Fisher's control.

I spent the day wandering the online Phasmatian world under an assumed name, dropping in to chat rooms and virtual parishes to participate in the discussions and services. On two separate occasions I ran up against presiding priestesses whose words I disagreed with, and when I tried to correct them, found myself booted off the web site—a new administrative feature Stan had added to the system, no doubt at Fisher's instruction. Clearly there was now no room for dissent, real or virtual, in Phasmatia. I had a sudden moment of paranoia that the IP address from my sessions was being recorded, and could be traced back to War-ren & McCaul, and perhaps my very computer. I made a mental note to ask Stan about that.

I did, in fact, attend the anointing of the bishops that night, partly to avoid suspicion, partly out of curiosity, but mostly to provide some moral support for Stan. The ceremony was also taking place at the Phasmatians' new cathedral, their first foray out of the virtual world that had previously contained the reli-gion. I hadn't been in it yet, so I was quite curious to check out the sacred new erection. Granted, it was just a converted ware-house down the street from their headquarters, and didn't look anything like a traditional church building (let alone the grand gothic cathedrals of Catholicism), but the lobby prominently displayed scale models and architectural renderings of a new generation of temples that were being erected throughout the world, accompanied by a collection box to solicit donations to aid in their construction.

All these new temples had that one distinctive feature that

now make them as instantly recognizable as those of any other faith (or, given that they are mostly being built in malls these days, as recognizable as McDonald's golden arches or the Taco Bell logo.) The main roof of each is a large stained-glass pyramid, signifying a prism that focuses the light of The Universal Spirit onto the worshippers below, topped off by a prominent, crowning Phasmatian symbol.

As I studied the renderings for the new temples, something else caught my notice, and conjured up a whole new level of resentment. Their walls were all covered with paintings and mosaics featuring Sky Fisher in various poses of benediction or grace, the most common being his infusion by The Universal Spirit atop Mount Skylight. For the umpteenth time I cursed myself for being the one who'd suggested our religion needed a human figurehead, and for allowing Fisher to usurp that role.

A sound like wind chimes on acid filled the lobby, and people began to shuffle inside to the inner temple for the ceremony. Sure enough, the space had already been painted up in the new Phasmatian style, and for the next hour a dozen Fishers beamed down on me, and while his glowing face was clearly meant to show infinite love, somehow I felt like a fawn surrounded by a pack of snarling, blood-crazed wolves.

The service itself was beautiful, though, and I'm not just saying that because I had personally created the ceremony. My job, as I had seen it at the time, was to come up with something reverent and mystical, while still keeping it accessible to the everyman—a trait I strove for in all the Phasmatian writings. Still, to see my words actually enacted in the real world, complete with an accompanying band and choir, and with the scene lit by a thousand scented candles, was a mind blower. At the culmination of the service, the bishops (there were two women being anointed in addition to Stan) each came forward, and were presented by Fisher with a shimmering white satin cape as a symbol of their office.

I did, however, notice one disturbing alteration to the ceremony's finale from what I had originally conceived. The bishops were now required to prostrate themselves before Fisher, kiss the hem of The Chosen One's robe, and utter an oath of loyalty (which I had not written). What's more, the pledge was not just for loyalty in this incarnation, but in all others throughout eternity. My own artistic vision of the finale had been quite different, for although the idea of elevating bishops was intrinsically hierarchical, I always stressed the egalitarian nature of the Church. My underlying message had been that we all basked equally in the light of The Universal Spirit, and each of us could aspire to rise closer to the source. In fact, my version had actually ended with a big, clerical group hug. As I watched Stan perform the altered rite, I was actually relieved I'd been denied the right to be a bishop, if it meant having to publicly grovel at Fisher's feet.

There was a reception afterwards, and I hung around hoping to have a chance to congratulate Stan, and make sure he was coping with the demands of the day. But it was like trying to be alone with the groom at a wedding—he had guests to glad-hand, photos to pose for, and interviews to give to the Church's PR service. I was barely able to shake hands with Stan and whisper platitudes of encouragement before some Church minion whisked the newly anointed bishop off somewhere.

So, I settled for a half-dozen vodka martinis in quick succession, and took to mingling with the guests, many of whom were notable A-listers, but I had little in common with these folks. Soon, the booze and lingering resentment were starting to take effect, and I'm afraid I made a bit of an ass of myself, sniffing out any conversation related to Phasmatian dogma, and making a point of putting the speaker in his place. Or *her* place, in one particular case, and that's how I actually met Brock Harrow face to face.

Admittedly, it wasn't just the woman's beliefs that drew my attention to her. I mean, she was smoking hot—a statuesque blonde with a flawless face right off a magazine cover, and wearing a low-cut gown that showed off her considerable assets—but I quickly jumped on some statement or other she was making to her short, bald companion about touching the essence of The Universal Spirit, and started to berate her ignorance. A couple of minutes later a large hand plopped onto my shoulder and a familiar baritone voice said, "The Sacred Text also advises us to be wary of loud voices who preach from spirits and not the Spirit."

As a movie buff, I would have recognized Harrow's voice anywhere, but even if I hadn't, the sudden googly-eyed expression of adoration on the faces of the couple I was haranguing would have been a dead giveaway. I swiveled to look into the movie star's handsome, square-jawed face, and saw that he was not just posturing for the babe's benefit—he was genuinely pissed at me.

"Judge not another's words, but judge that fellow by the light that burns in his soul," I quoted by way of retort. Bowing chivalrously to the hottie, I apologized for my rudeness (although she was so utterly oblivious to me I could have been speaking Greek), and then turning back to a visibly disarmed Harrow, I commented, "I'm happy to see you managed to connect with Fisher." I took in his Armani tux and the diamond encrusted Rolex on his wrist and added, "And that you decided there was no need to give up your wealth after all."

You could see his brain working out the clues, and I took a sip of my martini while he tried to figure it out. Out of the corner of my eye I saw the blonde's pretty lips slump downward as the movie star ignored her completely and focused on me. "I'm afraid I don't look anything like my monkish persona," I said to be helpful, "and I regrettably can't free-float in space, but it's a pleasure to meet you in the real world."

Finally a flash of recognition lit his face, and he took the hand I offered and wrapped it in a bone-crushing grip. Almost immediately, a look of puzzlement spread across his brow.

"But The Chosen One told me you were dead," Harrow said. That irked me, and I was in no mood to be charitable—or reverent.

"Well, Fisher did kill off my virtual self, but the real me is clearly alive and well," I said with an ostentatious gesture, spilling my drink in the process, "... and apparently a little tipsy."

"Killed you off? What do you mean?" Harrow glanced at the blonde woman and her companion, and I suspected he was suddenly wondering if they should be privy to the conversation.

The woman mistook the look for interest, and stepped closer to gush all over him. "Oh, Mr. Harrow, I'm so pleased to meet you. I'm a huge fan. I bet I've seen *all* your movies. My name's Molly... Molly Hamilton." The little man beside her cleared his throat and, taking the hint, she introduced her companion. "And this is an old friend of mine, Abe Burlander... he's a big contributor to the Church."

The little man's exuberant smile added even more wrinkles to his face, and he practically knocked his date over in his eagerness to step forward and shake hands with the movie star. I recognized the name. Burlander was a heavy hitter in New York real estate and was worth hundreds of millions of dollars, but he was no different than any other star-struck fan when it came to meeting Hollywood royalty.

Figuring I had lost my audience, I started to wander away in search of a fresh drink and new ears to bend, but Harrow reached out and grabbed me by the hem of my jacket, pulling me back into the circle and making me stay put. It took him all of two minutes to skillfully disengage himself from the adoring duo without appearing rude. Once he'd finally managed to extricate himself from their admiration, he led me off to a secluded corner of the room where we could resume our conversation about Fisher's decision to kill off my virtual character.

"I told The Chosen One I considered the loss of the Mage Errant a blow to the spread of Phasmatia," Harrow told me earnestly. "He ... that is to say *you* helped a lot of people step towards the light. I don't understand why he would shut down your character ... or lie to me about it." I had hoped his Ivy League mind would take its own step towards illumination, but then his eyes narrowed into that steely squint you've seen on so many movie posters and he became suddenly suspicious. "No, I can't bring myself to question the word of The Chosen One. He is after all infused with the perfection of The Universal Spirit. You must be an imposter!"

Harrow was looking downright hostile now—a better-dressed and only slightly smaller Caucasian version of Devon himself. "Then how could I know about our conversation?" I asked. "Everyone else there was part of *your* group, and then it was just the two of us when you asked me to arrange an introduction with Fisher."

"Maybe you were eavesdropping on the chat. I know the web site says all conversations are private, but I'm sure there are ways a hacker could listen in."

I snorted at that one. "Don't believe what you read in the Privacy Statement. Stan—I should say *Bishop* Shiu—records every message, and tracks every online activity, and then Fisher's priesthood sifts through it every day for suspicious activities, or items of interest, using specialized search programs."

"So, you admit you could have read a transcript of the conversation afterwards."

"I could have ... if I had that sort of access, which I don't. But I swear I'm the one that talked to you that day. I'm the real Mage Errant. Fisher killed me off because he resents me, pure and simple."

"Resents you? Why would the Chosen One resent you?"

"Because my character was becoming more popular than his," I blurted, desperate to get things off my chest, "because he saw me as a threat to his power ... because I know the truth about Phasmatia, and he's afraid of what I might say."

"Truth? What truth?" Harrow asked. He looked more angry than curious, and despite the buzz I had on, and all the frustration and jealousy festering inside of me, a red flag went up in my brain.

Part of it stemmed from the gag order I'd signed the day before. I'd made an extra copy for myself when Stan first gave it to me, and had revisited the document's text a couple of times since putting my name to it. While I knew the document's chief purpose was to prevent me from taking my story to the media, the language in it was sufficiently general to legally block me from talking freely to anyone, including Church insiders. But the real hazard that suddenly popped up in my mind was that Harrow was a hard-core and loyal Phasmatian, and anything I said would likely find its way straight back to Fisher.

I sighed. "The truth is, Phasmatia no longer needs me. It's a child that has grown up and left behind its poor father to seek the bright lights of the big city. But I'll always love my baby." I caught myself staring at my empty glass. "And the truth is I need another drink. Hey, is this a party, or what?"

Harrow was still looking at me with a dissatisfied look, so I slapped him affably on the shoulder (which was like hitting a side of beef) and added, "I appreciate your kind words about the Mage Errant. I feel like I managed to do some good, and wish I had the chance to do some more. Tell that to the High and Mighty next time you chat with him, will you?"

Andy dropped by this afternoon about 3 p.m. and dragged me out to go deer hunting with him for a couple of hours. After a day cooped up in the trailer in front of my computer, I was happy to get out into the fresh air and stretch my legs. He took me up to a high ridge that separates his property from the Shius, and I was panting heavily by the time we got to the top. Old Andy, on the other hand, despite being twenty-odd years my senior, looked fresh as a daisy, but he took pity on his out-of-shape companion and we sat for a while on an outcropping of granite, soaking up the late day sun, and taking in the vista before us.

"How's the writing going?" he asked me.

"Pretty good. I feel inspired … should be finished in a few days."

"So, what is it you're writing, some kind of detective story or something?"

I had actually anticipated being asked that question eventually, and had concocted an elaborate little cover story about my fictional piece of fiction (which wasn't hard to do since, like any copywriter, I suppose, I'd long harbored aspirations of penning the Great American Novel). But now I found I couldn't bring myself to lie any further to this decent, good-natured man. Or maybe I was just feeling desperate. At any rate, I proceeded to spill my guts about the whole Phasmatian scam, and my part in it, and what I was hoping to accomplish with my exposé.

The sun had become entangled in the tops of the tree branches by the time I was done. Andy had sat impassively the whole time, except to offer me occasional sips from a thermos of coffee he had been carrying. He looked up at me when I had finally stopped talking and asked matter-of-factly, "They killed Stan?"

I nodded. "I'm absolutely certain of it ... no matter what the police report said. And I have no doubt they'll kill me too if they find me."

He shook his head sadly, presumably at the horror of the crime, although I worried at the time he might be indicating disapproval of me, or disbelief in my wild story. Standing up, he announced, as if we had just been jawing amiably about the weather the whole time, "Well, we should start heading back. It's getting late. Wouldn't do to get caught in the dark." He led me back to a fork in the trail where our paths diverged, his leading off to Beatrix and the familiar farmhouse, mine back to the isolation and uncertain future of my trailer refuge.

Andy paused there, taking off his DayGlo orange ball cap to scratch at his bald spot, and I stood by silently, hoping I hadn't irreparably destroyed our fledgling friendship. "Do you believe in God, Brad?" he asked, surprising me with the question.

Part of me wanted to humor the man, to tell him whatever would keep him placated and on my side, but I had been stripped bare of lies by that point, so I told him the truth.

"Yes ... yes I do, Andy, today more than ever before. But don't ask me whether He ... or She ... or It ... even knows, or cares, whether I exist, or if I think there's a life waiting for me after this one. But I do believe there's a higher power responsible for all this, and a piece of that deity resides inside me ... inside my soul ... and it ultimately matters, if only to me, whether I do good or evil in this world."

Andy snorted, but he wasn't deriding me. "Well, there you have it... if that don't just sum it all up, I reckon. Heck, I've been dragged to church against my will pretty much my whole life—first by my mama, then by Beatrix—and Lord knows some of the biggest frauds and most mean-spirited men I ever met have stood in the pulpit. But that don't mean the whole thing is a load of bull crap. And, heck, I'll take a devout Hindu, or Jew, or Muslim... or a Phasmatian when it comes right down to it... over a thieving and philandering Christian any day of the week. It's all about doin' the right thing, ain't it? Well, it seems to me Brad, you're trying to do just that."

He put his cap back on and started to head down his trail, but then he stopped and called back to me, "You'd better come to dinner tomorrow night, then. Beatrix'll know what to do."

I slept badly last night. A rainstorm rolled through from the south around midnight, and while it was great to see the last of the snow washed away this morning, the unfamiliar sounds of wind-driven water pouring from the trees and pounding on the trailer kept jerking me awake all night long. But after a decent breakfast and a few cups of strong coffee I'm feeling reinvigorated, and downright eager to keep plugging away at my writing. Plus, I have a dinner and heart-to-heart chat with the van Vroonhovens to look forward to tonight. So, back to my story ...

I didn't see Stan for three days after his elevation to bishop, and when we finally hooked up again at Macbeth's, he had an amazing, and somewhat disturbing, story to tell me. It turns out he had been invited to a private banquet later that evening in Fisher's penthouse, attended only by a dozen of the Church elite and some special guests (including Brock Harrow). Needless to say, I hadn't been invited, although I vaguely recall observing at the time, through my boozy haze, that a number of the party-goers left en masse.

Somewhere between dessert and liqueurs, to hear Stan tell it,

Fisher stood up and started rambling on about how celebrating the flesh is a celebration of The Universal Spirit. Before Stan knew it, Fisher had leapt up onto the big banquet table and stripped completely nude while inviting (commanding, really) everyone around him to do likewise. One of the newly anointed bishops was the first to comply, pulling off her ceremonial robe in one smooth motion, and then crawling buck naked across the table on her hands and knees to begin kissing and stroking Fisher's inner thighs.

Now, one thing you need to know about Stan is that he was one of the shyest and most self-conscious men I ever met—the consummate nerd in that respect. He was reluctant to open up an extra button on his shirt, or even wear a pair of shorts in summertime, let alone bare it all in front of a roomful of strangers.

"I'm sitting there, totally frozen," Stan recounted, "while all around me clothes are being stripped off, and tossed like bouquets into the middle of the table, where Sky and the priestesses are starting to get down and dirty, right in front of everyone. Drinks are spilling, dishes and cutlery are flying every which way, and all I can think about is how the hell to get out of there."

As for me, all I could think about was that Stan went to an orgy and I wasn't invited. Although his discomfort, even days after the event, was evident, I craved details. "So everybody else started screwing right there on the spot too? How about Brock Harrow? Did he get into it? Is he, like, you know, really hung?"

Stan grew angry. "I'm not a pervert like you. I wasn't ogling the action ... I told you, I was too embarrassed. It made me sick. I got down onto the floor and tried to hide under the dining table. It didn't do me any good."

"Why? What happened?"

"The bishop was on top, riding Sky like a pony, and as his head lolled over to the side he spotted me, and let out a crazy yell for someone to grab me and strip me naked. Before I knew it, there were wet and sweaty bodies all over me, and hands tearing at my clothes. They pulled my robes right off of me, tore off my underwear, and then hauled me to my feet so everybody could see me completely nude.

"'Bring him here,' Sky told them, and a bunch of them practically threw me right on top of the table. Then that lunatic starts ranting about how his hallowed flesh was the worldly manifestation of the ethereal spirit that permeates the universe, or some such crap, and then he screams out at the top of his lungs as he grabs his prick, 'I am the *Axis Mondo*...'"

"*Axis Mundi*," I corrected. "The cosmic point of connection, where the higher and lower realms join ... "

Stan's angry look cut me off, and I clammed up.

"Fine, Mr. Know-It-All, Axis *Mundi*. Then he grabs me by the hair and tries to stick his cock into my mouth ... "

Up to then, I'd been following the story with salacious interest, picturing myself in Stan's place, diving into a pile of writhing and willing female flesh to fulfill long-standing orgiastic fantasies (and frankly starting to get hard as I envisioned it all) and suddenly I feel like I've been kicked in my stomach by a mule. I was no longer sorry I hadn't been invited to the party.

"So I clamped my mouth shut and started thrashing my head from side to side, and I wouldn't let him do it," Stan continued, and you could tell from his little-boy expression he was desperate for me to believe him, "even though it was tearing out chunks of my hair. I swear I would have bit the fucking thing off if he'd stuck it in my mouth ... and I don't care if Devon would probably have killed me on the spot. But then these two other female guests climb up onto the table, their eyes all wild like they're in a freaking trance or something, and they both start trying to blow Sky at the same time, but my head's in the way, and they're banging me in the skull as they try to get at him. To top it all off, the bishop that Sky'd been screwing in the first place, and who's lying on the bottom of the pile, tries to crawl out from underneath and get into the action, and all of a sudden Sky falls over her and the whole lot of us just collapse into a heap and go crashing down onto the floor."

"So, was that the end of it? I mean, did you manage to get away from that freak show?"

Stan stuck his chin right down into his chest and took an audible gulp, and I felt my calamari appetizer resurface as I realized this story was not going to have a happy ending. "Aw shit, Stan ... what happened?"

"There's three chicks on top of him, like starving dogs on a bone, but Sky hasn't forgotten about me ... no, not that bastard, although now he's laughing like some freaking maniac. 'Anoint the bishop,' he yells, pointing at me, 'anoint him with your bodily fluids.' And so the three of them stopped what they were doing and came after me with a crazy look on their faces like you see on zombies in a B-movie. They ... they ..." He stopped, clearly finding it hard to utter his next words. "Brad ... they raped me," he finally said, and broke into tears.

There may be some of you reading this (assuming *anyone* ever gets to read it) who don't accept that a man can be raped by a woman, but I know the courts say it can happen, and I'm not talking about statutory rape or seduction of a minor, but about the full-out forced physical variety. More to the point, if you'd seen the traumatized, anguished look on Stan's face, you'd know the bare-assed truth. I could feel his pain and humiliation. Rape is not about sex ... it's about violence and power, regardless of who the perpetrator is.

I didn't actually want any more sordid details by this point, but Stan volunteered them, albeit hesitantly and in fits and starts, as if he needed to purge himself of that painful memory. He had been repeatedly yanked, mounted, smothered, and even pissed on by the three women while Fisher laughed and laughed—and the worst of it is that most of the other revelers had sexually satiated themselves by this point, so they apparently sat around in a big circle, sipping drinks, and watching what happened to Stan like it was just some sleazy nightclub act.

"I lay curled up on the floor afterwards," Stan said, "until the orgy got its second wind, and then when everyone else was preoccupied fucking and sucking one another again, I grabbed what was left of my robes and got the hell out of there."

It dawned on me at that point that Stan was still wearing Phasmatian garb—not the ornate ceremonial robes of a bishop, of course, but a priest's everyday suit nonetheless. His eyes followed mine, and then dropped down to stare at the floor. "Yeah, I went back to work the next day," he admitted. "We're in the middle of a major server upgrade...quadrupling our capacity, you know, trying to keep up with the growth."

What I had really been thinking, I'm sorry to say, is that Stan had secretly enjoyed the sexual experience, his professed shame and anguished expression notwithstanding. I mean, in all the years we had been partying together, I could recall only two occasions when he had actually been to bed with a woman, and both of them had been one-night stands with drunken skags. Now that he was a high-ranking member of an elite and trendy group that offered the promise of endless promiscuity and hedonism with beautiful, and willing, women, was it really so far-fetched to think he had been seduced by the prospect?

In hindsight, I almost wish he had given in to his baser instincts...at least he'd still be alive. Instead, he looked back up at me, an angry determination now etched on his once-boyish face, and said, "Want to know why I really went back? To finish what you and I agreed on...to cut that bastard down to size and expose him for the evil monster he really is. You don't have to worry about me. I won't let you down, Brad."

Let me down? Now it was my turn to feel ashamed. I had, in fact, no longer been plotting any dethroning of Sky Fisher. On some cowardly and self-serving level, I guess I had capitulated to the bastard (hadn't I even signed my name to that effect?) and although a white-hot hatred for him still smoldered inside me, I was now little more than another hanger-on. I had resigned myself to being permanently disenfranchised from a great enterprise I'd helped conceive, and jealously waiting around like a beggar for scraps of privilege from the High and Mighty. Plus, now that I realized what a madman he really was, quite frankly, Fisher scared the bejezzus out of me.

Stan glanced over his shoulder to make sure there was no one at the bar within earshot, and leaned in closer to me. "I think I've got a way to nail him," he said.

The eager look on his face was like a child telling his mother he'd just gotten a gold star on his spelling test. I was sorely tempted to tell him to forget about it, that we were out of our league, and should be worrying about covering our own asses. My conscience had been tweaked, though, and a little voice inside told me that if mild-mannered Stan, who had looked the beast squarely in its insidious eye, and had been royally chewed up in the process, was willing to stand and bravely put up a fight, then maybe it was time for me to grow a pair too.

"I thought you told me he was keeping his nose clean, tax-wise," I said.

"He is … and with all the new bricks-and-mortar churches we're opening up in the real world, the Church's tax-exempt status is completely solid."

"Then how are you figuring on bringing him down?"

"I've got the whole place bugged," Stan explained with a grin. When my puzzled expression showed that I didn't comprehend either the act or its significance, he continued. "Well, actually Sky has everything bugged—his monks have been wiring everything, floor by floor, for the past few months—but it all gets digitized and stored on *my* computer system. Every phone call, every email, every conversation in the boardrooms, hallways, bathrooms—I've got access to it all."

"He's got the bathrooms bugged? Why? Does he want to hear

what it sounds like to have a normal shit?" That one actually made Stan laugh. Fisher's chronic constipation was one of our private jokes, and we never tired of it. It was good to see my friend lightening up.

"Well, I don't have to tell you he's one sick and paranoid puppy," Stan continued, "so he wants to make sure people aren't plotting against him."

The thought did cross my mind that, at that very moment, Stan and I *were* in fact sitting there plotting against Fisher. As the old joke goes, just because someone's paranoid, it doesn't mean people aren't really out to get him.

"Okay, so he's got the place bugged. How does that help us?" I asked. "I mean, even if word got out that he's spying on his own people, those Phasmatians—especially the ones working at headquarters—are a pretty fanatical and loyal bunch. It wouldn't change a thing. They'd probably get off on the fact The Chosen One is watching over them."

"Yesterday, they even wired up his penthouse," Stan said, "this time with hidden video cameras, in addition to the usual microphones."

"Okay, okay... I get the picture. But I still don't see how any of that is going to help us take down Fisher. What are we going to do... post pictures on the web of him screwing some chick? The Phasmatians make no secret of their sexual freedom... we specifically agreed on that point when we came up with the idea. Hell, a sex video would probably just bring more recruits to the Church."

"He's ruthless... if anyone gets in his way, Fisher rolls right over them. I'm convinced he's had people threatened... or worse. Those monks of Devon's are always booking sudden trips to cities where one of our new churches has run into construction problems, or some legal roadblock, and lo and behold, the problem suddenly goes away. It's only a matter of time before we get the goods on Sky. You remember what I told you about him pulling a gun on me that time? Too bad that was just before the camera was installed in his private office, but shit like that has to be going on all the time. Sooner or later we'll get something we can nail him with."

The "sooner or later" part appealed to me, and I was starting to feel somewhat relieved that I was not going to have to follow through on my resolution of bravery anytime in the immediate future, but Stan quickly changed all that.

"There is another possibility," he said. "Go up to his apartment and get in an argument with Sky about something or other...that shouldn't be too hard for you. Get him to admit out loud we made the whole thing up, and it'll all get recorded."

"Oh, yeah, right. Maybe if you're really lucky, you'll get a tape of Devon blowing my fucking head off too!" But even as I said that, my conscience was throbbing, remembering the time I had egged Stan on to confront Fisher while I waited safely on the sidelines, even if we didn't fully know at the time what a raving psycho Fisher was.

To make matters worse, Stan didn't try to cajole me into doing it. "You're probably right, it's too dangerous," he agreed, and I had to study him for a moment or two to figure out whether he was being sincere, or was trying to manipulate me. There had been a time when I would never have suspected simple Stan of anything but outright sincerity and a naïve eagerness to please (which explains why he didn't get laid very often). But that seemed like some distant dream now, and as he sat before me then and there—the co-founder and bishop of a major religion who, having been cheated and violated in the process, was plotting the overthrow of one of the world's most powerful men—I wondered if I truly knew Stan anymore. Lord knows, he looked ten years older.

"Oh, crap... okay, I'll try to find an opportunity to meet with him," I said, "but I'm not making any promises as to what I can get him to admit. If he starts foaming at the mouth, I'm backing off to save my own skin, got it? Meanwhile, see if you can come up with anything incriminating in all those surveillance tapes... although I don't know how you plan to do that. There must be thousands of hours of recordings. It'll be like looking for the proverbial needle in a haystack."

"Millions of hours, actually, if you add up all the feeds," Stan said with a grin, "but I've got more processing power than you can imagine, including my very own private supercomputer. I'm going to let it do all the work." He went on to explain about speech recognition, and heuristic clustering, and semantic pattern matching, and other such technical gobbledygook, all of which went right over my head. None of it gave me the warm fuzzies that there was going to be any other way to nail Fisher than me going in there personally, and performing some kind of a sting for the benefit of the hidden cameras.

Stan went to work, and I didn't see very much of him for the next few weeks, mainly because he was happily ensconced in his latest technical challenge, but also because we felt it wise not to be seen collaborating together. As for me, I went to idleness, at least as far as any useful role within the Church went. I still continued to receive fat Phasmatian paychecks, but was given no specific assignment or title, and as far as I knew, did not have a designated supervisor or bishop I reported to.

Although I didn't really need the money anymore, I stuck with my job at Warren & McCaul. Somehow knowing I could quit at any time took the edge off of my copywriting grunt work, and I found myself almost enjoying it, although I did spend a tremendous amount of company time on the Phasmatian web site, wandering the virtual world, and participating in religious discussions.

I soon noticed disturbing changes in the online environment from what we had originally set up. For starters, images of Fisher were everywhere, from the first home page you landed on, to the walls of every virtual temple where you were directed to worship. Even The Universal Spirit, the supreme deity that was originally supposed to be at the core of the religion, now seemed to have taken a back seat to the earthly prophet. Citations of The Spirit were inevitably made only to validate and reinforce the authority and holiness of Fisher, who was being depicted now as a living deity himself.

It also became apparent to me how mercenary Phasmatia had become. Solicitations for donations and the peddling of Church-related merchandise were ubiquitous and constant, and I couldn't figure out for the life of me how the religion was continuing to sustain its exponential growth worldwide with such a greedy, heavy-handed approach.

Worst of all (at least to me) was the authoritarian control the priesthood now exerted over discussions and gatherings. Having been heavily involved in the creation of the original programs, I was quite adept at spotting the difference between computer-generated personae and those avatars that had a real person behind them. Priests and priestesses were everywhere now, and there was no longer any room for metaphysical debate or free-minded interpretation of the scriptures. Oh, the Powers That Be weren't so stupid as to kick new recruits out completely, but if you were diagnosed by the clergy as a potential troublemaker, you were neatly transported under some pretense or other to a specially designed virtual setting where the other participants were evidently all artificial, in effect quarantining your disruptive disease of dissent from the population at large. You could rant or question all you wanted, while the software humored you, peppered you with dogma, and tried to separate you from your money—usually with the promise that payment would grant you privileged access to the answers you were seeking or even, if you were prepared to fork out enough, a private audience with The Chosen One himself. Logging out of the web site was no help. Once the clergy had identified you as a heretical *persona non grata*, you were instantly diverted to one of the virtual isolation cells every time you signed back on.

Since I always registered under a pseudonym anyway, these *de facto* abductions were little more than an inconvenience, and I would quickly leave, obtain one of the internet's infinite supply of free email addresses, and come back to roam about under a different name. I soon discerned, however, that the priesthood I was butting heads with online was not an especially bright lot. I quickly found ways to appear eager and compliant, while still getting my sermons across to any other Church members I encountered. I nevertheless switched up my aliases on a regular basis, as I moved around frequently within the vast virtual Phasmatian world. It was frustratingly like playing hockey underwater, but I still felt like I was making a contribution in my own small way, and living up to my original, pure religious vision.

Stan would drop me occasional emails that hinted at some progress in his cyber snooping on Fisher's activities, although these communiqués were always cryptic and vague (apparently even though he controlled the computers and was theoretically capable of covering his own tracks, he still felt it prudent to be cautious). Then one day he emailed me to drop by and visit him. Although the wording innocuously suggested that two old buddies who hadn't seen each other for a while should get together, I could tell he had something he wanted to show me—if for no other reason than he asked for the meeting to take place at his Phasmatian offices, and not at Macbeth's.

Even though my key card still provided me with access to the headquarters building, and there was no reason why I shouldn't be there, I felt some anxiety when I arrived for my visit. Knowing there were microphones and hidden cameras all over the place was also disconcerting. Although Stan had assured me the transmissions were not actually monitored in real time, I still felt like Fisher was watching my every move. It also didn't help that everyone I encountered, including the non-clergy, was dressed in some form of Phasmatian garb, making me feel like a civilian who had just walked onto a military base.

Stan's rank of bishop entitled him to a new, spacious office, I noticed, complete with a massive carved wooden desk, behind which hung an impressive painting of Stan himself, sporting full ceremonial robes. I would have smiled at the sight of it, except for the twinge of envy that surfaced when I took it all in. Hell, the desk alone, which was twice the size of a billiard table, was bigger than my cubicle at Warren & McCaul.

Not surprisingly, Stan was not actually in his office, and from the looks of things, he seldom used it. I found him in the machine room amidst his beloved computers, which had visibly gone forth and multiplied in numbers since my last visit. Although he had a staff of hundreds now, he was happily crawling around on his hands and knees, pulling bundles of cables up through a spot where a panel had been removed in the raised floor.

"Want a beer?" he called out upon spotting me, and reached down into the floor to grab a couple of bottles. They were beautifully chilled—one of the fringe benefits of working in a cooled computer room. Stan indicated with a finger to his lips that we were not free to talk, so we sat around, drank our beers, and got him caught up on the latest office gossip back at the ad agency.

I saw the reason for his caution a few minutes later when two assistants, who had evidently been at the other end of the cable-pulling operation, showed up to begin plugging the ends of the wires into a box on a nearby rack. The fact that both were attractive young Asian women made me wonder whether Stan's cables were the only things of his being pulled by these women. I gave him a "you dog" wink, and when his face failed to redden, I concluded, expert Stanologist that I was, that there was nothing inappropriate going on between them.

"Go and configure the addresses," Stan instructed the duo, "and then you can call it a day."

"Yes, your Eminence," they replied in unison, and both shot me an inquiring look before leaving. At first I thought they might have been checking me out, before my ego gave way to reason and I surmised they had more likely been making mental note of the fact I was not wearing a Phasmatian uniform. My suspicion was confirmed when, once the door had clicked shut behind them, Stan quickly explained. "Fisher hand-picked them himself. He said it was a perk, but I call it bait. I'm pretty sure they report my every move back to him."

"No reason not to nibble at the bait a little ... just to keep the Fisher interested," I joked, although I was actually picturing myself lying naked, sandwiched between the sweet young things.

"At least they're good at their jobs, and it's a damned sight better than when I had Devon's two goons breathing down my neck ... remember?" Stan got up and gestured for me to follow him, and we moved further to the back of the server room where he had a computer workstation set up. In front of him, no less than eight large display screens formed a visual array worthy of a small movie theatre. From the empty Coke cans and crumpled-up candy bar wrappers in a nearby trash can, I could tell this was Stan's real office.

"You have to check this out," he said, lowering his voice and sitting down to start stabbing at the keyboard.

"There are no mikes or cameras in here?"

"There's a microphone right there," he said, pointing up at a sprinkler head above us. When my face blanched in shock, he chuckled and added, "Don't worry, right now I'm feeding it dummy input from a week-long recording of background sounds I made a while back. Of course, Sky knows you're here by now, so when I'm done showing you what I've discovered, I'll put the mike back online, and you and I can have another beer and sit around bitching about him ... he'd be suspicious if we didn't."

"So, what have you found?" I asked, finding myself whispering despite his assurances.

"Bits and pieces that add up to nasty business, but you tell me. Okay, here's the first clip ... it's from the washroom in the monks' quarters." He clicked with his mouse and a man's voice came onto the computer's speakers.

"Does the boss know yet?" the voice asked.

"He's out with the Big Fish at a Church opening in Chicago," another voice replied. "He'll be back tonight."

Stan paused the audio. "Big Fish is their nickname for Sky," he explained, "and of course 'the boss' is Devon." I nodded, and he continued the playback.

"He's going to be pissed," the first voice went on.

"Shit, what was I supposed to do? The bastard came at me with a pair of scissors ... look at this, six inches higher and he would have got me in the neck," the second monk said angrily.

There was a whistle from the first man. "That's nasty, alright ... you'd better have the doctor look at that. Still, you weren't supposed to kill him, just get him to sign the contract. If the cops get into this ... "

"They won't!" the second man said, still angry, although I thought I detected fear in the voice. "I took care of it ... it'll look like an accident, like he fell down the stairs and broke his neck." There was the sound of a toilet flushing, drowning out the rest of the conversation, and Stan clicked the recording off. He looked at me, clearly wanting to know my reaction.

"I always said those monks were little more than a bunch of street thugs, but it doesn't exactly incriminate Fisher, does it?" Stan shook his head, as if I had confirmed his own opinion.

"Okay, here's the next one," he said, clicking and scrolling away deftly with his mouse. Interestingly enough, none of what Stan was doing could be seen on his giant screen, and I suspected this was a security precaution on his part in case somebody walked in on us. "Again, it's audio only," he advised me.

The sound of grunts and groans came on the speakers, and eventually a male voice sighed, "Oh baby, that was terrific." The voice sounded familiar, and Stan, evidently reading my thoughts, said, "it's the same guy from the washroom … the one that was stabbed. His name's Tony."

On the recording a female voice giggled and said in a husky voice, "There's plenty more where that came from, big boy."

"Yeah, baby, later … but we have to be careful," Tony answered. "I can't let Devon find out. We're not supposed to be screwing around."

"What the hell's wrong with you guys?" the woman chided him. "I mean the Church is all about free love—that's one of the reasons I joined—but you dudes act like you're not even interested in sex." She giggled again. "Everyone in my department thinks you're all gay. If they only knew … "

Judging from the vehement nature of Tony's reply, she had evidently struck a nerve. "Hey, we're not gay! Shit, didn't I just show you I wasn't no faggot? We're soldiers. We're killers, baby. Devon says women make you soft, and he wants us to stay sharp … like a knife!"

"Killers? Come off it. You don't have to try to impress me, lover … I'm already impressed," the woman cooed, "and there's nothing wrong with being a security guard. Hey, I'm just a clerk, remember? Don't worry, I still think you're hot." There was an audible kiss as she demonstrated her sincerity.

"Hey! I'm no fucking security guard!" Tony retorted angrily, "I tell you I've done shit … shit you wouldn't believe."

"Oh yeah? Like what?"

"Like I blew up a mall in St. Louis last month … The Chosen One wanted to put a temple there and the owner wouldn't cooperate, so he sent us. You'd better believe we're getting the property cheap now."

"Holy shit, I read about that! That was *you*?"

"Yeah, me and a couple of the other guys. And that ain't nothing. You see this ring?"

"Uh huh."

"Well, let's just say this ain't no Boy Scout ring. To get one of these you have to prove you're willing to do anything to anybody. Nobody fucks around with the Phasmatians...not while we're around. Security guards! Ha!"

"Well, all I know is you and your big muscles make *me* feel secure," the woman answered seductively, "...and you're making me hot. You ready for more?" The conversation turned pornographic then, but to my disappointment Stan clicked off the playback.

I chewed on my lip and thought over what I had just heard. "Well, it's pretty damning, I'd say, but only as far as incriminating that particular monk. It suggests but doesn't conclusively prove Fisher had a hand in it."

Stan grunted agreement, and was already clicking away to bring up the next clip. This one had video, which popped up in a window at the bottom corner of the big screen, and I recognized Fisher's lavish apartment immediately. A few seconds later the High and Mighty himself walked into the frame, Devon at his side.

"I don't care how long he's been with us," Fisher was saying angrily. "This is the final straw."

"But Chosen One, it wasn't Tony's fault. The guy tried to kill him. It was, like, you know, a reflex...and we still might get the property."

"It's not his incompetence I'm talking about," Fisher replied testily, "and no doubt you have already reprimanded him for that. No, my anger comes from this..." Fisher went around his massive desk and began fiddling with a laptop computer that was sitting on top. Presently, sound began to flood the room—the exact same excerpt of Tony romping with the female Phasmatian that I had just heard. It finished playing, and you could see from the slouch in Devon's body that he found the evidence impossible to refute.

Fisher began to rave. "He vowed! He took an oath of secrecy!

I will not tolerate that sort of disloyalty! Do you hear me, Devon? I will not have it. It's too dangerous, and it can ruin everything. He's betrayed me, and I want you to take care of it *personally*!"

"Yes, Chosen One," Devon said meekly.

"Just so there's no misunderstanding, Devon, when I say I want it taken care of, I mean I want him *dead*."

"It's done. Should I, you know, make it look like a car crash or something?"

"No! I want to send an unmistakable message to the others. I want them to know exactly how and why he died. They need it demonstrated to them, loud and clear, that disloyalty will not be tolerated!"

"What about the girl?" Devon asked.

"What the hell do *you* think? But hers can look like an accident."

Devon gave a little nod, barely perceptible on the screen, and left. Fisher clearly still had unspent anger, because he began to shove papers off his desk and kick every piece of furniture in sight, all the while ranting about "the inexorable wrath of The Chosen One," and "the divine retribution of The Universal Spirit," and Stan let the bizarre spectacle play for a while before turning it off. He looked at me expectantly, although my mind was still reeling and I needed some time to gather my thoughts.

"How old is that last recording?" I asked.

"The day before yesterday."

"Well then, if Tony's body turns up—and assuming the cops rule it homicide—I'd say we've got him dead to rights." The emotions churning inside of me hardly matched the clinical nature of my evaluation. Mostly I was feeling sheer terror, primarily at the prospect of having to live up to my promise and act on this evidence. A big part of me was pulling for Tony's survival, but those hopes were dashed when Stan grabbed a copy of *The New York Post* from his desk and dropped it in front of me. There in a photo, smiling up at me and dressed in a full military dress uniform, was a man identified as Tony Crupi. Above the picture the headline read, "Ex-Paratrooper Found Shot in Central Park." I felt my stomach turn over, not from the grisly details of the execution, but from the utter dread of what I was now expected to do.

"Don't say anything right now," Stan whispered. "We've been off the air too long already. Think about it, and meanwhile, I'll see what else I can drag up." He fiddled with his computer and the last few seconds or so of Ipso Fatso's classic rock tune, "A Thousand Excuses," played itself out on the speakers.

"Wow, that guitar gets me every time," Stan said with a wink when the music had concluded. Even though we hadn't actually heard the famous solo riff in question, I clued in that we were now acting for the microphones, and were supposed to pretend we'd just been sitting around silently listening to the music for the last ten minutes. Presumably the song in its entirety would show up on the audio records to cover up our actual conversation.

"Damned straight. No one plays guitar like Christmas McZeal. Hey, did you hear Ipso Fatso might be getting back together for a concert tour?"

"No way! That would be awesome. If they come to New York we've got to get tickets." From there the conversation ambled back to the good old days at Warren & McCaul, and highlights from our nights of drunken stupidity. I sincerely hoped our audience would enjoy it when they listened to the playback.

Before I resume the story of how Stan Shiu and I conspired against Sky Fisher, I want to tell you about my dinner at the van Vroonhovens last night. I don't necessarily mean to treat this exposé like some sort of personal blog, but I think it will prove relevant if/when I manage to get it posted to the web.

When I showed up at the farmhouse, I was feeling a little bit apprehensive as to how I would be received, given what I'd confessed to Andy earlier about being a founder of Phasmatia—not to mention the nasty and dangerous intrigue I was caught up in, which had cost Stan his life, and now threatened mine. Of course, there was the good chance they'd just think I was some big-city psycho who was making it all up.

I needn't have worried. When I stepped through the door Beatrix rushed up and wrapped me in a humungous hug. "Hello, Brad," she said, using my real name, and the supportive smile she gave me almost brought tears to my eyes. And then her smile changed into something more impish, and she took me by the hand and led me into the kitchen. There, sitting at the table, was the van Vroonhoven's daughter, Hannah.

Although she's certainly not a dog, you couldn't call Hannah drop-dead gorgeous either. She probably wouldn't attract a lot of attention if she walked into Macbeth's on a Friday night. Her sandy-blonde hair was cut in a short, unimaginative bob, clearly for utility, not style, and her face was utterly devoid of make-up, with a slight ruddiness to it. She was carrying a few extra pounds, and I could see she was destined to end up looking just like her mother. Still, I liked her instantly.

"Hello, Brad," Hannah said, standing up to offer me a firm handshake that testified to the earlier years she had spent helping out on her parents' farm. "So, you're the holy ghost writer. Mama and Papa were just telling me all about you. They think I might be able to help you."

I give Andy and Beatrix a pained look. "Listen, I appreciate everything you're doing for me," I protested, "but I don't want you getting involved. This is way too dangerous. I only told Andy the truth because ... well, because I didn't want to lie to you anymore, but I wasn't trying to dump my problems into your lap. I couldn't live with myself if anything happened to you on my account."

The look the three exchanged among themselves indicated my answer was exactly what they had expected, and Hannah stepped forward and touched my arm.

"We want to help, and that's that," she said. "If you're in as much trouble as you say, then we can't very well turn our backs on you. It wouldn't be Christian ... or Phasmatian for that matter. After all, doesn't your Sacred Text say, 'Love of thy fellows is measured by what you give them, not what you take in return.'? Of course, you just ripped that off from the New Testament, but it's a credo worth living by, wouldn't you say?"

My eyes went down to her chest, not to ogle her assets, but to see if perchance a Phasmatian pendant was hanging there. She caught on immediately and gave a hearty, unabashed laugh that testified to a free and easy sense of humor.

"Relax, I'm not one of them, although the school where I teach is full of rabid Phasmatians who are always trying to convert me ... especially the idiot vice-principal, who's a real lech, and always hitting on me. I think he just uses the religion as an excuse to try to get laid."

"Hannah! What kind of way is that for a young lady to talk," Beatrix chided.

"Come off it, Mama, we both know I'm no lady, and I'm sure as hell not that young anymore," Hannah retorted, but came over to give her mother a peck on the cheek as a peace offering. She turned back to me and smiled. "So you made up that whole Sacred Text by yourself. What a hoot."

"Well, more like edited. As you say, I, um, borrowed most of it." I was blushing, and felt the need to change the subject. "You ... you say you think you might be able to help. How?"

"Well, Mama called me up and asked me to come down for Sunday dinner. They're blessedly cut off from the outside world here, so they want me to help you get your story out to the public." She wrapped an arm across her mother's shoulders. "Mind you, I know Mama well enough to know she also wanted me to meet *you*. She's always trying to set me up ... although it's usually with one of the local boys. Poor old girl just can't wait to have more grandchildren."

"Hannah, mind your mother!" Andy scolded.

"Yes, Father." Her tone, however, was far from compliant. "Are you hungry, Brad?" she asked me, and slipped her arm in mine.

Beatrix shepherded us to the dinner table, making sure Hannah and I sat beside each other. There was a meal of holiday proportions laid out for us, but the mood was far from festive. Despite my best efforts to initiate more convivial small talk, the subject of the conversation kept turning back to me and my predicament. In a farmer's life catastrophes are commonplace, and it was clear the van Vroonhoven family tackled their crises head on.

My story was recounted once more in detail, and I made a point of answering their questions as frankly as possible, even where it painted me in an unflattering light. Finally the discussion turned to the future, and how Hannah might assist me in getting my story out onto the web.

"If you tell me where you want it emailed or posted, I can do that for you," Hannah suggested. "I have a computer at home with a high-speed connection. Frankly, I'd love to wipe the smile off those smug Phasmatian faces."

"I'm not sure you should take that chance, Hannah," I said. "You certainly wouldn't want your email address associated with it, and even if you post it anonymously, believe me, they have ways of tracing the IP address it came from."

"Well, there are a bunch of computers in our library with web connections. Or I could go to an internet-café."

"Hannah, it's so sweet you want to help, and if I feel it's too dangerous for me to do it myself, I may take you up on it. Thank you. However, there is another problem."

"What's that?"

"I was in such a panic to get out of Manhattan, I forgot to bring along anything for transferring my files. Everything I've got—the files I downloaded from Stan, and what I'm writing now—it's all on my laptop. I guess I could drive out to the closest town that has an office supply store and buy a flash drive or a writable disc, but that can wait. The thing is, I'm not done writing yet."

"So, how much longer do you think you need to finish writing your story?" Andy asked. Even though he didn't know the first thing about computers, he had filtered out the technological chaff and gotten down to the core of the problem.

"I dunno… another few days I guess." (I haven't really been writing with any sort of firm completion date in mind and, as you've seen, I have a tendency to ramble. I think I've been using the writing to fend off my fears—a way to occupy my mind and keep my sanity while I hide.)

"Okay then," Andy declared, "Hannah will be back later in the week, and she can bring you any doohickey you need. Maybe by then you can figure out who you're going to send your story to."

And there he'd put his finger on the real problem. The Phasmatians have millions and millions of followers, and are prevalent in every avenue of American society. Tag onto that all the non-believers who could simply be bribed or threatened by an unscrupulous Sky Fisher. How am I going to ensure my story doesn't arrive onto the internet stillborn? I have to find a way of guaranteeing it won't be deleted as soon as it's posted.

More importantly, I have to find a way of making sure it doesn't lead the Phasmatians directly to me, and especially not to the van Vroonhovens. So far, I have felt it safe to write about them, even disclosing their geographical location, and using their real names, because I figured that once the truth is exposed Fisher and his evil henchmen wouldn't dare lay a hand on those good people. But what if this is intercepted before the public has a chance to read it? Aren't I just placing the van Vroonhovens in terrible jeopardy? Won't Devon and his killer monks come and silence the potential witnesses? Shit, maybe it was a mistake to include them in the story. I shouldn't be gambling with other people's lives. I'll have to think about that, and maybe the wisest move will be to go back and edit them out. But for now, I guess I have a deadline (God, how I've always hated deadlines) and will continue to move forward with this narrative.

After Beatrix's scrumptious feast, Hannah and I washed the dishes together, and then went out and sat on the verandah for a while, ostensibly to chat, although Hannah really just wanted to sneak a cigarette.

"My folks don't know I smoke," she whispered, "but then there's a lot of things I do they wouldn't approve of." I wondered whether I was supposed to take that as a hint. She glanced over her shoulder to check out the whereabouts of her parents through the living room window.

"If they come out, grab the cigarette from me and say it's yours," she instructed, with a cute, conspiratorial smile. Despite instantly liking Hannah, I was apprehensive that the attraction might not be mutual. After all, we had just met, and in my experience, the very fact her mother was trying to shove us together would normally have been a deal breaker for many women—not to mention the fact I had just confessed openly to being a former philandering drunk, and a major accomplice in one of the greatest frauds of modern times.

Hannah, though, appeared to think it was worth us getting to know each other anyway. She was easy to talk to, unlike those forced, awkward conversations I used to have when trying to pick up chicks in bars. Normally, you quickly find yourself inventorying all the little things about a woman you don't like, and which will drive you crazy over time, once the novelty of sex wears off. The opposite was true of Hannah. The more we talked, the more I admired her. She was really smart, yet didn't throw it in your face. She was also quite funny, but I liked the fact she didn't laugh at her own jokes. Most of all, she had inherited her folks' decency, which counterbalanced a healthy cynicism. I'm going to use a word here that one of my writing profs at Columbia had once railed against for half an hour. Hannah was really, really *nice*.

Oh, I know what you're probably thinking. A skirt-chasing New York City barfly like me, who's been hiding alone in a trailer for a week, fearing for his very life, would latch onto any backwoods pair of boobs he stumbled upon. Perhaps that's true of the old me, but I feel recent events have changed me somewhat. Maybe I was projecting my newfound affection and appreciation for the van Vroonhovens onto their daughter, but I like to think I was only practicing what I had preached—appreciating someone for their character, and not just their looks.

Eventually Hannah yawned and looked at her wristwatch.

"Shit, look at the time. Okay, one more cigarette, and we're call-ing it a night. I've got to be up at the crack of dawn tomorrow to drive back to Albany by 8:30. It may be heresy for a farmer's daughter, but I'm not much of a morning person. Maybe *that*'s why I left."

"So, you'd never come back here to live?"

"Oh, I don't know. There was a time when I swore I'd never move back. Now, I'm not so sure. I'm feeling the proverbial bio-logical clock a'ticking, I guess, and all things said, it's not a bad place to raise kids." She shot me an inquiring glance (at least that's how I interpreted it) and changed the subject.

After she finished her smoke, I accompanied her back inside to say my goodbyes to Andy and Beatrix.

Hannah saw me to the door. "Good night, Brad," she said, locking onto me with beautiful brown doe eyes. "It was really nice meeting you, and I'll see you again on the weekend. Thurs-day night, actually... I'm not working Friday."

She placed a hand on my arm. "Look, Brad, I know you don't want my family getting involved, but I'm going to bring you a flash drive and some CDRs. While I'm at it, I'm going to do some surfing... maybe help figure out a place for you to send your stuff." With that, she gave me a hug. Although it was clearly a casual, chaste embrace, it got me tingling nevertheless. Last night, my bedtime fantasies centered squarely and exclusively on Hannah.

Okay, back to my story for real this time, I promise. The very next day after I had met with Stan to hear the incriminating evidence he had gathered, I was shocked to receive an email at work from Sky Fisher, asking me to meet him that evening at the Phasmatian offices. It was a casual and innocuous enough note, apparently sent by him directly from his personal email, but it nonetheless threw me into a state of terror and indecision. Had

Fisher discovered our plot against him? Was he now setting me up for the kill? Should I run for my life?

I re-read the email a dozen times, searching for possible clues as to my state of peril. The curse of the wordsmith is to be able to find hidden meanings in everything, and soon even the very fact Fisher had signed the note with a friendly "Sky," and had requested rather than commanded my presence, was compounding my worries.

I vacillated about phoning Stan to ask whether he had gotten wind of anything, but the rising paranoia in me cautioned that, if our plot was indeed under suspicion, then I'd be playing right into the hands of any Phasmatian snoopers. Eventually my faith in Stan's technical ability to conceal our activities won out, along with the belief that if Fisher did want to dispose of me, he wouldn't do it in his private quarters. I reluctantly emailed back my consent to the meeting.

When Devon ushered me in to Fisher's office that evening, The Chosen One was clearly in good humor.

"Brad, baby," he called out jovially upon seeing me, and made the trek out from behind his massive desk to give me a hug, (which, in my skittish state, conjured up disturbing thoughts of a Mafioso's farewell embrace). "I bet you thought I'd forgotten all about you."

A few choice cutting retorts came to mind, but I was still wary enough not to want to antagonize Fisher. "I know you have much greater matters to worry about," I said, taking care to not let any sarcastic tones creep into my delivery.

"There's shitloads of work still to do, that's for sure ... and that's precisely what I wanted to talk to you about." Fisher guided me over to a leather sofa big enough to accommodate an entire basketball team, and motioned for me to sit down beside him.

"Listen, Brad ... I know you were really pissed when I told you I didn't want you preaching anymore," he said, and actually sounded sincere, "and I just wanted you to know I'm sorry I cut you off at the knees like that. But listen, old buddy, we have thousands of priests and priestesses out there who can do that sort of thing. You have a much more important role to play."

"I just wanted to help people."

"And you will, Brad, you will. Hey, where are my manners? You want a drink?" He turned and called out towards his private apartment. "Hey, Diane... bring us a couple of vodka martinis, will you?" It was at that moment, fear for my life having temporarily abated, that I remembered there were cameras secretly recording everything we said and did. Stan had thought it possible I'd be able to goad Fisher into saying something incriminating if I got him angry enough, but now I was wondering if I could accomplish the same through subtle guile, without risking the wrath of a homicidal maniac in the process.

"You know Sky, there's something I've been wanting to tell you for a long time," I started out casually, making sure I kept my tone friendly. "I know you, me, and Stan concocted this whole Phasmatian thing as a get-rich-quick scheme, but I really think we've accomplished something amazing and profound, beyond our wildest expectations... and you get the lion's share of the credit for that."

"We were merely instruments of The Universal Spirit. She chose us," Fisher said, waving his hands with a theatrical flourish.

"Oh come on Sky, it's just you and me—you can drop the act. We both know how it really started," I persisted.

"You see, Brad, this is your problem. It's precisely this lack of faith that makes you unsuitable to be a priest. If you truly believed, you would understand that we merely pulled aside the veil of shadows and allowed the Divine Light to shine through." He said it with that patronizing tone I despise so much, as if he was talking to a child, and I felt my anger rising. I had to bite back the urge to start screaming insults at him, and to demand what special faith Stan Shiu held to warrant a bishop's rank.

Fortunately, I was saved by the arrival of our drinks. Not surprisingly, the woman who served us was stunningly beautiful, and was dressed in a form-hugging mini-skirted variation on the Phasmatian priestess gown, just sheer enough to show the absence of undergarments beneath. It was clearly designed for allure, not for ecumenical utility.

"Will there be anything else?" she asked, and you'd have to be a moron not to catch the suggestive tone in her voice.

"No, thank you, Diane, dear," said Fisher. "Go tell the others to get ready for dinner. I won't be long." She smiled dreamily and spun away, clearly putting on a show as she left. It should have been arousing, but I was actually put off by her behavior. I'd written a lot about the concept of grace in The Sacred Text. The way Diane and the others were demeaning themselves was, well, *disgraceful*, on so many levels.

"To the Spirit," Fisher offered in the way of a toast, and I clinked glasses with him and took a restorative sip of my vodka.

It was obvious to me Fisher was either too deluded or too cagey to make any incriminating admissions about the past, so I figured I might as well find out what he had in mind for me. "So, what's this important role you have for me?"

"I want you to write a new chapter for The Sacred Text."

I couldn't resist a little jab. "You sure you want someone without the proper faith tampering with the holiest of books?"

He didn't rise to the bait. "We have both been chosen—me to lead, you to write. It is not for us to question the wisdom of The Universal Spirit."

"Oh yeah? What exactly did The Spirit have in mind? I thought we had pretty much covered it all already."

"I want you to write The Book of Miracles."

"The what?"

"The Book of Miracles. It's a detailed account of the miracles I've performed here on Earth ... or more accurately, the miracles The Universal Spirit has conducted through me. There are a lot of people out there questioning my divine powers. This will shut them up."

In hindsight, I can think of a hundred biting and witty comebacks I should have made to a line like that, but I'm ashamed to say I just sat there with my mouth hanging open in complete surprise. Finally, I managed to ask weakly, "What miracles?"

Fisher smiled smugly, as if he had been anticipating the question, and rose to go over to his desk. He returned with a half-dozen stapled sheets of paper and thrust them at me. I leafed through the pages and, sure enough, there was a detailed inventory of wondrous acts, neatly arranged in chronological order, with the exact time of day and place indicated, and a short descriptive title for each. The first dozen entries showed events that had purportedly taken place over the past year. They were essentially real-world manifestations of his online persona, and included appearing out of thin air, levitating, and being enveloped in a mighty halo of blinding white light. The remaining items in the list, however, showed dates in the future, meaning those particular miracles had yet to occur.

As near and dear as The Sacred Text was to me, I had no interest in the writing project Fisher was now proposing. The only part that had ever appealed to me when composing the original dogma was the moral code we were outlining, even if it had been purloined from existing sources. To me those instructions for leading a positive and happy life were real, and their potential for doing good in the world transcended the fraud we had been perpetrating. But I had never really been comfortable with penning the chapters that hinted at the supreme powers of The Chosen One, and certainly had no stomach for adding more lies that would only further fuel Sky Fisher's megalomania.

"You seem to already have it all neatly laid out here," I said, handing the papers back to him. "What do you need me for?"

"What do you mean what do we need you for? Don't be so

modest. We need the master's hand ... not just for consistency in the writing style, but because of the passion and persuasion that leaps from every page. You say you only want to help people ... well, here's your chance."

I remembered the hidden cameras. "How, by spreading lies?"

"They're not lies!" Fisher shouted, all his previous chummy civility having evaporated. "I have affidavits from people who have witnessed every one of those miracles!"

"Including the ones that haven't taken place yet? Now how's that possible?"

"Those miracles *will* take place, and the whole world will see them happen." Fisher pointed a finger at me, and I noticed it sported a mammoth ring encrusted with enough diamonds to feed a small country. "And, make no mistake about it, you *will* chronicle them, or feel my wrath."

Despite all my previous cockiness and bravado, Fisher's threat instantly hit home. Hell, I had found out exactly what he was capable of doing to anyone who defied him. I suppose I could easily have goaded him into killing me on camera, but I wasn't ready to make that kind of a sacrifice. I took back the papers and gave a little bow with my head. "As you will, oh Chosen One."

Any sane person would have detected the sarcasm in that last statement, but Fisher's face lit up in a huge smile of satisfaction. "Great. As you can see, the last of the miracles will have taken place by the end of the summer. I'd like to be in print by mid-October. Let me know when you have a draft ready." With that he gave a dismissive wave of his hand and jauntily headed into his private quarters, where hedonistic delights no doubt awaited him amongst his harem. *Victori spolia*—to the victor go the spoils.

I wandered back downstairs, passing a smirking Devon en route, who predictably had been lurking just out of sight, but clearly not out of earshot. His formidable physical presence only served to reinforce Fisher's threat, and I was shaking with a combination of anger and fear as I found my way to the server room and pounded on the door for Stan. There was no answer, and I had to bang another three or four times to gain entrance.

It was not my old pal who finally came to the door, however, but one of his female assistants, and I got the distinct impression from the aroused flush on her cheeks and the slightly askew apparel that she and Stan had been getting hot and heavy. My suspicions were confirmed when I caught a glimpse of the other Asian lovely's bare backside disappearing out of sight behind a rack of servers. At one time I would have been happy to know my geeky buddy was getting his wick waxed, but now the Church's whole climate of orgiastic excess was starting to grate on me.

"Let's go grab a drink," I said, when I was led back to Stan's little nest, where he was fussing theatrically with his computer and generally doing a bad job of acting nonchalant.

"Um, I'm kind of busy ... " He exchanged a furtive glance with the girl who'd ushered me in.

I snorted. "Yeah, I'll just bet you are. Well, have it your way, Romeo. I'll be over at Macbeth's getting drunk if you change your mind." Stan's assistant was hovering nearby, visibly irritated by the interruption and making it clear she resented my presence, so I added, "I'll be busy working on the special assignment Sky High and Mighty just gave me—personally. It appears we live in an age of miracles." That did the trick, awing the babe, and piquing Stan's curiosity.

"Give me half an hour or so ... I'll meet you there," he told me.

"No hurry, Your Eminence," I replied with as much sarcasm as I could muster. "I'm sure you three have a lot of important computer stuff to take care of ... the ol' input-output-input-output, and all that."

When Stan slid into the booth next to me, he immediately started defending his sordid little back room banging before I had a chance to say a word. "Look, don't worry about what was going on back there ... I figured it would take some of the heat off us if Sky knew I was getting cozy with his spies."

A trio of rapid-fire shots of tequila had put me in a more forgiving mood by then, so I wrapped a friendly arm around him. "Well, I'm just relieved to know you're sharing the sugar with them both ... wouldn't want one of them getting jealous. Say, you don't talk in your sleep, do you?"

I'd meant it as a joke, but Stan was earnest when he answered, "Oh I won't ever bring them home with me, but you know how it is ... they've been practically rubbing themselves against me for weeks while we've been working closely together. And, like I said, I don't want Fisher getting suspicious."

He caught the attention of our waitress and waved her over. I studied my friend closely as he placed his order, flirting with the server in the process. There was clearly a newfound confidence in him, which even manifested itself in the way he sat upright, and threw an arm across the back of his seat. The old Stan had generally slumped when he sat, as if he wanted to slide under the table and escape public scrutiny, and he'd always had some difficulty making eye contact with any woman. Now he owned the room. Was it the fact he was having regular sex with not one, but two attractive women, or was he starting to enjoy the status and privileges that came with the rank of a Phasmatian bishop? Either way, I didn't like it—although now I find myself eaten up with remorse over the mistrust I showed, and which urged him on to his doom.

"Just tell me you're still committed to taking down that psycho, Fisher," I said when we were alone again. "'Cause after what he just ordered me to do, I'm not sure we can wait any longer."

"Oh yeah ... tell me about your meeting. Did you get him to say anything we could use? I haven't had a chance to check the surveillance tapes. I was ... "

"Yeah, yeah, I know. You were busy."

"I was going to say I was being watched. What the hell's wrong with you, Brad?"

"Nothing, it's just that Fisher has me scared and angry. While you were busy humping your assistants, I was being threatened and forced to do that bastard's bidding."

"Listen dude," Stan said, "don't forget I'm the one that spends every day there under a microscope. But just because I take advantage of some of the fringe benefits don't think that means I'm not going to live up to our bargain. So, did he or didn't he say anything incriminating when you met with him?"

"Fuck no. Not only does he really think he's The Chosen One, now he thinks he's able to foretell the future." I pulled out the printout Fisher had given me, and proceeded to relate the details of the new Book of Miracles, including the wondrous deeds that were apparently yet to unfold.

Stan's face was screwed up in contemplation by the time I had finished. "Now I get it," he said softly.

"Get what? I don't understand."

"Well, he's been planning to hold these big public services over the next couple of weeks…a hundred thousand people packed into stadiums all over the country—Austin, L.A., Ann Arbor." He pointed at the dates on my list. "See? The upcoming miracles he wants you to write about each coincide with one of those appearances."

"That maniac can't really think he can perform miracles…or does he expect to get that many people to lie about what they saw?"

"Maybe a bit of both. But I suspect they won't be real miracles." Stan stared at the list of upcoming amazing events. "It all makes sense now."

"What makes sense? Come on Stan, spill."

"Well, healing the sick, that's pretty basic, right? I mean, traveling revival show preachers have been pulling that one for years.

"Hire some guys to pretend they're crippled or what not, and then Fisher lays his hands on them and, hallelujah, they come leaping out of their wheelchairs, or start shouting that they can see again."

"Yeah, yeah, sure, but those are just the opening acts. What about this stuff? Shimmering apparitions ... levitation ... oh yeah, and my personal favorite, Fisher appearing out of thin air on a shimmering golden throne."

"Fisher's been hiring all these theatrical effects consultants ... I thought he just wanted to put on a big show, but now I figure he wants them to help him stage his miracles. One of them is Simon Tarot."

"The Vegas magician? The guy that made a tractor trailer disappear in the middle of Times Square?"

"The very same. Of course, when he stages one of his stunts everyone knows it's a clever illusion. If Fisher pulls one off in the middle of a stadium packed with his loyal followers ... "

"Then it's a freaking miracle," I concluded, having caught up to Stan's train of thought.

"Exactly, especially with you to write all about it, and proclaim it as such. The crazy fuck wants the world to think he's some kind of living god."

I shook my head as I contemplated the distasteful task I was being forced to perform, but part of me was in awe. "You know, it's really quite brilliant. I mean, it's clear Fisher is a Grade A lunatic, but let's not forget he's also a world-class ad man. Phasmatia still gets most of its recruits via the web site, right?"

Stan nodded. "Everything goes through the web site."

"So, there in virtual reality, anything's possible and no one takes what they see too seriously. But once Fisher starts to blur his virtual persona with his real-world, miracle-performing self, then his appearances and actions online will no longer be like some kind of 3D game—people will feel like they're really communing with God." I held up my glass in a toast. "And you, my friend, who holds the keystrokes to the Kingdom of Heaven, will be the second most powerful man in the world."

"We have to stop him," Stan said softly. I guess I wanted to hear that, even if the coward in me, lurking somewhere in the pit of my stomach, gave a sudden lurch in protest. "The only question is," Stan went on, "do we go with what we have already, or do we wait and try to get some more evidence?"

"What if we could prove he was staging the miracles?" I suggested, hating myself instantly because I knew I was just stalling for time.

Stan's face lit up, though. "Hey, that's not a bad idea. You can ask to go along on the tour ... you know, to be there in person to witness the miracles so you can be inspired when you write about them."

I didn't want Stan to think he couldn't count on me, but frankly the idea held no appeal for me whatsoever. "Well, assuming Fisher lets me go along, and I can get that much time off work, what's the guarantee I'll uncover anything we can use against him? How would a technically illiterate guy like me tell all those lights, and lasers, and computers, and stuff apart? Besides, Simon Tarot stages his illusions in front of audiences and TV cameras all the time, and everyone knows it's a trick, but no one's ever been able to figure out how he does it. Couldn't you likely get more damning evidence from the surveillance recordings? Did Tarot meet with Fisher at his offices? Wouldn't you have them on video discussing the trick?"

I could tell Stan was disappointed with me. When he shook his head, I felt like it was as much a comment on my cowardice as to reinforce his answer. "No, they met at Tarot's private hotel suite in Vegas. Fisher flew down to catch the show, and to meet with Tarot afterwards." We both stared at each other for a few seconds, neither of us revealing our thoughts.

I relented. "Okay, okay. I'll ask if can attend his final rally, the one in Ann Arbor with the big Golden Throne miracle, and I'll try to get a backstage pass."

"I'll sneak a peak at the financial records, and see if Tarot's gotten any money," Stan added quickly, and I swear he was trying to hide a smile, "and I'll chat up the other bishops. Maybe they know something." His face grew more serious, and he leaned closer. "Who do we give this stuff to once we have it ... and how do we cover our asses?"

It was a damned good question, and something I'd been pondering over the past few days. We needed to find someone who was not in the Phasmatians' pocket, and who had the clout to bring Fisher to justice. That was theoretically doable. But making sure Fisher's suspicion—and wrath—didn't land on me and Stan afterwards was a thornier problem.

"How many people have access to those surveillance recordings?" I asked.

"Just Fisher and Devon ... the whole point was no one was supposed to know they were being snooped on."

"And you, of course," I added. "You set it up for them."

He nodded glumly, and then stuck his finger out at me. "And if his big miracle gets exposed as a fraud after you show up there to watch, he'll know it was you right away."

Well, duh, all the more reason for me not to go, I thought, but I said nothing. We ordered more drinks and went over things again, but it was unclear whether we were trying to talk ourselves into or out of taking the next big step. Finally, although we did agree that Stan should go ahead and compile a DVD with the evidence we had so far, and I would try to come up with the name of someone to send it to, we decided to bide our time, at least until after the Ann Arbor rally.

Since it was important to prevent Fisher from getting suspicious, I reluctantly turned my hand to drafting The Book of Miracles, as he had commanded. Although my heart wasn't in the writing, it didn't take long to regurgitate the events that had already been laid out so precisely for me, and so a few days later I emailed a preliminary version off for Fisher to review. Although I had promised Stan I would try to wrangle an invitation to the Ann Arbor rally, I had secretly been hoping to wrap up the writing well in advance of that date, and perhaps be excused from having to live up to my word.

Certainly, I had not been anticipating any editorial flak from Fisher, who had previously granted me almost total leeway in writing The Sacred Text. Of course, those had been the days when it was just the three of us working side by side, more or less as equals, to create the Phasmatian religion. Things had changed dramatically since then, and yet it still both surprised and angered me when, within a matter of hours of making the submission, I received a scathing phone call at work from the Big Man himself, condemning the quality of my work.

"It's absolute crap ... like some kind of bad high school journalism assignment," Fisher railed. "Have you forgotten who it is you're writing about? Where's the power? Where's the glory? This is meant to inspire people ... to make them fall down on their knees and shout 'Hallelujah!' Instead, it reads like something out of *The Midnight Inquirer*!"

I felt my temperature rise. "Whoa, hold on, Sky. I didn't think it was anywhere that bad. It may not have the same cosmological pizzazz as other juicy parts of the Text, where we're talking about, oh, I don't know, let's say the freaking universal battle between light and darkness for peoples' souls, but I thought it was *meant* to be more down to earth ... you know, more factual ... and therefore more believable."

"You moron, Brad! Down to earth? Where the hell did you get that? This is meant to raise me up to the highest level ... to make people worship me and be awed at the extent of my powers as manifested by these miracles."

"Gee, I guess you had to be there," I couldn't believe I heard myself saying. "Maybe if I actually witnessed one of your mighty miracles firsthand ... you know, got up close and personal with The Universal Spirit ... I'd be more inspired."

"Yes, yes, that's it. You're trying to write this while languishing in the shadows. We need to turn your pen into a mighty weapon blazoning with the great light of The Spirit. You should come and write here, right beside me, to receive inspiration, and you'll be foremost among the faithful when they witness my greatest miracles. Come to me, my disciple. Abandon that dark cesspool of greed and banality that you cling to, and come join the other faithful bowing at my feet."

The last thing I wanted to do was go join Fisher's retinue, where I'd be living 24/7 within arm's reach of Devon and his killer monks, and the mental image of me bowing before him made me want to puke. (Besides, I didn't hear anyone offering to, say, make me a bishop.) Still, I had come to recognize Fisher's megalomaniacal psychotic episodes, and so knew I had to tread carefully.

"Well sure, Sky, I'd be honored to witness your miracles, but I'm feeling kind of inspired right now," I lied, just to blow him off. "Actually, I have all the files open in front of me as we speak. Let me get cracking at a new draft right away, and I'll send it to you in a day or two. I promise you won't be disappointed."

There was a silence at the other end of the line, and I held my breath hoping he'd be placated with my compromise. When he spoke again I could tell he was still annoyed, but had at least stopped chewing the rug. "Okay, I'll trust you to do the job right this time, Brad, and I'll let you do it your way. Meanwhile, just see my secretary if you want something. I'll instruct her to make whatever arrangements you need."

I found my heart was beating wildly when I hung up the phone, but the writer in me was already sizing up what needed to be done, even if the thought of aggrandizing Fisher to the extreme sickened me. Fortunately, it was a relatively slack time for me at Warren & McCaul, so I spent the next couple of days working tirelessly on a rewrite of The Book of Miracles.

Those of you who have read it (and I'm told the new edition of The Sacred Text has again sold in the millions) will be familiar with the unabashedly flowery prose I produced. Personally, I thought telling it all from the perspective of The Universal Spirit Herself was a master stroke, so that every one of Fisher's miracles comes across as a cosmic act of devotion bestowed upon the Phasmatian followers, blurring the lines of separation between The Spirit and Her earthly conduit, The Chosen One. I just might burn in hell for that one.

Fisher absolutely loved the rewrite, and gushed with praise over it. I'm proud to say not a single word was altered, either by Fisher or any editor of the Phasmatian-owned publishing company. How many million-selling authors can say that? Plans were set in motion for a massive print run of The Sacred Text, its release scheduled to coincide with the climax in Ann Arbor, Michigan, of Fisher's traveling divine dog-and-pony extravaganza, which would even be broadcast on prime-time television

With the text finalized and frantically in production, and given that authorship was indirectly ascribed to The Universal Spirit and not some earthly witness who needed to put in an appearance for the record, there was technically no reason any-more for me to attend any of the Phasmatian rallies. But whether through lingering guilt at the promise I'd made to Stan, or just some morbid curiosity to see whether reality could live up to the literary epiphany I'd just concocted, I ultimately decided to go catch the big Michigan event anyway.

And I certainly went in style. My masterful rendition of The Book of Miracles had put me in Fisher's good graces, and he made a point of rewarding me. (I also think he was pleased to see me expressing such first-hand interest in the Phasmatian campaign, and wanted to encourage my finally getting subserviently into line. I wonder what he would have done if he knew my ulterior motive for catching the show was to try to publicly discredit his greatest of miracles.)

Since Fisher and his traveling phreak show were going from city to city by bus—Fisher's private, oversized coach was actually more like a luxury condo on wheels—along with twenty tractor-trailers full of road-show gear that would have made The Rolling Stones green with envy, I was given use of The High and Mighty's private jet. I flew from New York to Ann Arbor, and was taken by limousine to the show. I had an anxious moment when the limo driver turned out to be one of Devon's monks, but my concerns were alleviated when he looked me fiercely in the eye and proclaimed that he was ready to die to protect my sacred skin. I guess, despite my stubborn refusal to wear anything resembling a Phasmatian uniform, word must have spread that I was some kind of Church bigwig, and I was being given the royal treatment.

The limo was amply stocked with booze, and I was feeling pretty tight by the time we arrived at Michigan Stadium. When I was discharged in front of the teeming throng and ushered past the long line-up, I could see the heads turn in awe and puzzlement over who this mysterious big-shot was receiving the preferential treatment. Damn, it felt good, and as I write this now I wonder how differently things might have been if Sky Fisher had offered me a share of the power and status instead of grabbing it for himself. I know myself well enough to wonder if I'd still be doing what I now firmly believe to be the right thing by exposing the Phasmatian phraud.

When I was led to the backstage area, any sense of my own self-importance evaporated in the face of the real celebrities and VIPs I found there, including none other than the vice president of the United States herself. Between the cadre of Secret Service agents protecting the Veep, and all the movie stars and business tycoons pressing in to try to talk to her, it was somewhat of a chaotic scene, so I sidled over to the open bar instead. A few moments later, absorbed in watching how much vermouth made it into my martini, I was almost knocked over when someone slapped me on the back with forceful enthusiasm, and I turned to see Brock Harrow's grinning face.

"Well, well, if it isn't the Mage Errant himself," Harrow said loudly, and delivered a bone-crushing handshake. I was pleased that he remembered me, even if I thought I detected a hint of sarcasm in the salutation. "So, your holy wanderings have brought you forth here, to this momentous occasion. You clearly must be in The Chosen One's good graces again to warrant this kind of access."

"And I see *you* never left them," I countered, slightly irritated by Harrow's patronizing tone. "I'm surprised, however, you're not fawning over the vice president with all the others."

Harrow smiled. "Actually, we had lunch together this afternoon, so I figured I'd let the rest of them have their licks, so to speak. She may very well be running for president next year, you know, so all the hangers-on are hedging their bets. It would be a great coup for us if she won... Imagine, the first openly Phasmatian president."

The thought actually made me blanch, not because I objected to anyone who adhered to the moral code I'd set out in The Sacred Text running the country, but because I suddenly had this disturbing image of Fisher behind the seat of power pulling the strings of a presidential puppet, like some modern-day Rasputin. The very fact that a veteran politician would openly tout her Phasmatian beliefs showed just how far the religion had spread, and served as a stark reminder of the daunting challenge Stan and I faced in finding someone who would act on the evidence we had been gathering. But then again, standing right there in front of me was an insider who might be able to unwittingly help me with my dilemma.

"I don't imagine there are many politicians anymore who would be foolish enough to challenge the spread of Phasmatia," I said, reasonably certain Harrow wouldn't suspect I was fishing.

The movie star's face hardened into a frown and I knew instantly that I'd hit pay dirt. "You'd think so," he said, "but sadly it's not the case. We still have some very vocal opponents throughout the country—dangerous people with real power and influence."

I'm not very good at that kind of subterfuge, but I swallowed down a healthy dose of my martini and feigned shock as convincingly as I could. "No!" I exclaimed. "Like who?"

"Surely you've heard about Senator Lowry's investigation?"

"Max Lowry... from Rhode Island?"

Harrow nodded. "He's jockeying to have his Judicial Committee look into the Church's practices." My look of horror must have been really convincing because Harrow smiled and patted me reassuringly on the arm. "Oh, he won't find anything, of course, but the publicity might do us some harm... that is, if we don't get the whole thing shut down first. We've got some clout of our own on that committee." He supplemented the statement with a jerk of his head in the direction of the vice president. "And influence throughout the government, for that matter. Odds are the investigation will never convene... provided we can get Budd Durrell to keep his big nose out of it."

"You mean the gazillionaire who owns MediaROR?"

"The very same. He's been making noises about throwing his whole media empire against us. That's a lot of newspapers and TV stations from coast to coast."

"What's his beef?" I asked.

"Apparently his only daughter ran off and joined the Church, and now she doesn't want anything to do with him anymore. He took it real hard, and is taking it out on us... says we're corrupting the youth of America."

I was thrilled to have gotten such meaty inside information so expeditiously, and for the first time in weeks felt that maybe Stan and I might have a shot at taking down Fisher after all. These opponents of the Church were certainly no lightweights, and could potentially hold their own against the Phasmatian juggernaut. Still, as much as the prospect of that evil maniac Fisher twisting in the wind appealed to me, I experienced for the first time a twinge of regret at the realization that Phasmatia—the religion I had given birth to— would most likely be completely discredited and obliterated in the process.

Harrow was still looking at me curiously, and I didn't want him to regret having been so candid with me, so I offered up some scripture to lift his spirits (or perhaps it was to bolster my own). "Though the darkness be all around us, it can never eclipse the light of those who burn with true faith," I quoted.

Harrow flashed his impossibly white smile at me and wrapped me in a big man-hug. "May you walk in the light," he said. "As long as the Church has true believers like you, nothing will ever stand in our way. I don't understand why you're not playing a more visible role in our crusade."

I was disarmed by his flattery, and was on the verge of blurting out a scathing condemnation of Sky Fisher, when the stage lights dimmed and a mighty roar from the crowd washed over us, indicating the show was starting. Harrow gave me a final squeeze of the shoulder and hastened over to join the vice presidential retinue watching from the wings.

I procured another drink and went to stand on the fringe of the backstage onlookers, but my mind wasn't on the extravaganza unfolding in front of me. Instead, I found myself wondering if maybe there was some way to remove Fisher from his position as supreme Church leader without destroying the religion itself. And, yes, I even fantasized that perhaps I might ascend to the leadership. After all, who else knew the tenets of the faith better, or believed more in the powerful force of goodness that Phasmatia could unleash across the planet?

I was ultimately distracted from my musings not by the immaculately choreographed spectacle unfolding before me, but
by some frenzied machinations taking place off on the far side of
the stage. There, a crew of men and women, all attired in identical satin roadie jackets, were wrestling with a large array of glass
sheets and parabolic mirrors, hooking them up to an array of
thin cables which, I noticed for the first time, ran overhead.

Just then I glimpsed Fisher himself being ushered into the
middle of the setup, and I realized this was going to be the
technical means by which his illusion of a grand miracle would
be orchestrated. Although I had neglected to bring a camera
with me, I remembered there was one built into my cellphone. I
fished it out of my pocket and, discretely turning my head away
back towards the action on stage, held the device down low at
the end of my arm and busily snapped a series of pictures. Out
of the corner of my eye I could see Fisher disappear underneath
a sheet of some shimmering, reflective material. I had no way of
knowing how well the photos would turn out from that distance,
but I seemed to recall the salesman had talked me into paying
some stupid amount of money for multiple megapixels of imag-
ing resolution when I'd bought my cell.

I whisked the phone back into my pocket and looked around
to ensure no one had spotted my surreptitious photo taking.
Uncharacteristically, neither Devon nor any of his muscle-bound
monks were anywhere in the vicinity, and as I watched the hidden Fisher being winched up towards the rafters, I wondered if
the High and Mighty was concealing his base trickery even from
those closest to him. Hell, the lunatic would probably convince
himself afterwards that a miracle had actually taken place.

Out on the stage, a hundred-person Phasmatian choir was
in full voice, and I realized they had taken one of my favorite
passages from The Sacred Text and converted it into a hymn.
Despite the lingering adrenaline from my little act of espionage,
and a general feeling of disgust with the entire fraudulent spec-

tacle, I found myself being carried away by the beauty of the song, and blissfully started rocking back and forth in rhythm to the music. Out in the stadium, a hundred thousand souls were following suit, and I again found myself fantasizing about the possibility that I might be able to rescue Phasmatia from the evil false prophet Fisher, and guide it towards unimagined glory.

The choir seamlessly transitioned into a new hymn, and this one now evoked the passage in The Sacred Text where Sky Fisher had been bestowed with his holy powers by The Universal Spirit atop Mount Skylight. It struck me then how intrinsically The Chosen One was woven into the entire Phasmatian fabric, thanks largely to me, and how difficult it would be to unseat Fisher without destroying the entire religion in the process. In its online incarnation, where everything was just lines of computer code and programmable virtual characters, anything could be accomplished (with Stan's help, of course), but now that we had spilled out into the real world, Fisher *was* the Church. Was I being a fool to think I could ever supplant him?

The only way would be if Fisher died, and I then stepped in to carry on his holy message. I even found myself mentally tinkering with a new addendum to the scriptures. *The Chosen One, having achieved a state of perfect grace, was transfigured into a beacon of pure light that shone up into the heavens, and there his purified soul melded with the perfect goodness of The Universal Spirit for all eternity. But he left behind the word and the way for us all to follow, with a new shepherd to guide you through the darkness, and to watch over you.*

The more I thought about it, the more the idea carried serious weight. Christianity, Islam, Buddhism—they had all survived, in fact flourished, after the departure of the original founder. Surely Phasmatia could do the same. The thorny question, of course, was how to get rid of Fisher. What was I going to do, murder him? Even if I was somehow able to get past his bodyguards, did I have it in myself to pull the trigger (or plunge the dagger, or twist the strangling cord, or administer the poison)?

As much as I hated Fisher, and as easy as it might be to rational-ize the destruction of someone so evil, would I be any better than him if I committed murder? Could I lead others to the light with such a dark stain on my soul? Would God forgive me?

God? Where the hell had that come from? It was a sudden and sobering revelation to me that somewhere, somehow, I had actually come to believe in God. Almost as quickly as the notion crystallized, other seasoned mental forces leaped into the fray, raising all the classic arguments for atheism, and eloquently decrying any unknowable, ethereal deity. It was no use. I found myself stubbornly clinging to my newfound faith in God.

As if amplifying the thought that was burning in my skull, a booming voice echoed in my ear and proclaimed, "Life is light. Love life. Love the light." It was the ear-splitting response from the stadium crowd that made me realize the voice had not been God speaking directly to me, but was Sky Fisher beginning his onstage spectacle.

I turned to watch, and although I knew it was all a big hoax, and even had some sense of how it was being executed, I had to admit it was damned impressive. Amidst shooting lasers and ris-ing smoke, which I could tell had pragmatic as much as theatri-cal uses for the special effects team, Fisher and his golden throne seemed to fly together from a dozen different floating lights, like a multifaceted prism image in reverse, and solidify in the middle of the stage. The crowd absolutely loved it, and judging from the high-fives I saw the technical perpetrators giving themselves backstage, the illusion had gone off flawlessly, meaning that even the TV cameras recording it all out front wouldn't be able to detect the trickery.

Fisher proceeded to spout passages from The Sacred Text, which I couldn't help but notice all praised himself rather than paying tribute to The Universal Spirit, or preaching Phasmatian ethics. Not that there was any need to preach to that crowd. They had fallen completely silent, hanging on Fisher's every word, and the looks of utter awe and adoration on their faces was unmistakable. I had little doubt each and every one of them believed they had just witnessed an honest-to-God miracle, and were basking in the presence of holiness. The worst part was that I was a prime accomplice, having already written it all up, in gushing purple prose, as a divine apparition. At that very moment, millions of copies of my corroborating testimony were being cranked out by the Phasmatian presses.

There were a number of unnecessary pauses in the show, it seemed to me, when Fisher would stop speaking and wander down to the front row to glad-hand members of the audience. The worshippers obviously loved it, but I felt like it was breaking up the overall theatrical impact of what was otherwise, as much as I hated to admit it, a soul-stirring spectacle. It wasn't until I glimpsed one of the broadcast monitors that I realized these pauses were so a phone number and URL for donations could be superimposed on the television sets of those watching at home, urging them to pour money into the coffers of the Church.

Fisher's self-aggrandizing sermon lasted about a half-hour, and then the choir sang another hymn of tribute while Fisher just stood there, awash in a gazillion lumens of stage lighting, his arms raised up in a classic pose of benediction, like the statue of Christ on Sugarloaf Mountain. As the hymn concluded, there was a furor in the crowd as someone started fighting their way through the throng to try to get to the stage. For a second I thought that perhaps my prayers had been answered and a crazed gunman was out to kill The Chosen One, but when Fisher stepped to the front of the stage and ordered the audience to let the individual through, I suddenly knew exactly what was going on. After all, I had just finished writing about it. Fisher was about to restore sight to a blind man.

As disgusted as I was by the whole hoax being perpetrated before my eyes, I found myself unable to look away. It was like some bizarre form of *déjà vu* as the scene played itself out just as

I had described it, complete with the lines spoken by Fisher and the man allegedly being healed. Stan would tell me later that the man, blind since a fireworks accident at the age of ten, had just returned from a secret trip to India, taken under a false passport. There, surgeons had been discretely hired by the Phasmatian Church to perform a cornea transplant. Stan had heard this from another bishop, who'd gotten a little tipsy at an ecumenical council meeting one night, but no amount of digging through the financial records had been able to turn up hard proof of the scam.

Given that this particular miracle took place on prime time television, there were a couple of attempts afterwards by the media (especially those controlled by Budd Durrell) to expose it, but all they could uncover was that the man had indeed been blind for the past thirty years, and now could see again. No doubt Fisher had exercised this kind of caution with all his previous faith-healing miracles as well. Hallelujah! Praise be to The Chosen One. Bow down before His might.

When I returned from Ann Arbor, I got together with Stan at Macbeth's to show him the additional evidence I had gathered, and to plot our next move. That was when I first broached the subject with him about how we might expose Fisher without tearing down the whole Phasmatian Church in the process.

"Any chance we could get some of the other bishops to, you know, impeach him or something?" I asked. I had never had a sense that Stan cared about the social or spiritual possibilities of Phasmatia the way I did, but I thought that perhaps, given the privileges and power he had been afforded, he might have a selfish interest in not seeing his work destroyed. I was surprised by the anger my suggestion sparked.

"What the fuck are you talking about, Brad? Those other bishops are all devoted lackeys of his ... they'd go running straight to

Fisher the second we suggested anything to them. I thought we were in this together. Didn't we agree Fisher has to be stopped?"

"I *am* talking about stopping him, dammit! I just think the Church could do wonderful things…great things. We've changed a lot of lives, and we've helped a lot of people, but once we publicly expose Fisher, it'll destroy everything we've accomplished."

I could see Stan was unconvinced, so I looked him in the eye and delivered what I figured would be the *coup de grâce*. "They'll probably seize all the Church assets, you know, including your precious computers, and you'll be back on the street looking for a programming job. And do you think anyone will hire you? 'Hi, I'm Stan Shiu, and I helped perpetrate one of the biggest frauds in human history. Can I come work for you?'"

Stan's eyes narrowed into slits, like some comic book mutant trying to vaporize me with his death stare. "So, assuming we could push Fisher aside, who the hell would replace him?" he finally asked.

"Well, no one knows the scripture better than I do, and you must admit I was pretty popular with the worshippers when I played the Mage Errant," I said, trying hard to make it sound rational and not ambitious.

Stan snorted out half of his martini. "You, Brad? You're not a bishop. Hell, you're not even a friggin' priest! None of the others know you exist. No one would support a complete unknown."

Stan was right. What we were proposing was a palace revolt, and that could only be accomplished with the Church's current power elite. Even though I was one of the original founders of Phasmatia, Fisher had neatly hidden my seminal role from everyone. I was technically a nobody. And then I had an epiphany, and may God forgive me for it.

"What about *you*, Stan? Certainly no one deserves it more than you do. Hell, if you ask me, you have more right to the leadership than Fisher does."

Stan shook his head. "Like I said, the others are all loyal to Fisher. They're not going to just dump him and side with me." But I could tell my idea had potentially found some fertile ground.

"They will if the only other choice is to watch the Church go down in flames," I said. Already I was contemplating the New Order. Oh, sure, Stan had all the charisma of a day-old donut, and sadly knew virtually nothing about the actual tenets of our religion, but that was where I would come in. I could counsel him, and be the power behind the throne, guiding Phasmatia to newfound heights of greatness.

Exercising all my powers of persuasion, and with the help of several more martinis, I ultimately convinced a reluctant Stan that we should try to dethrone Fisher and seize control of the Church for ourselves. I swear to you, if I had known it was going to get Stan killed, I would have abandoned the whole scheme on the spot. At the time, though, I honestly felt that we could do it, and was enveloped in this silvery sense of righteousness, like we were exorcising an unspeakable evil, and realizing a divine destiny. Damn it, I actually felt like I was doing God's will, and I had never felt closer to Him than there, in that bar, plotting and scheming to bring holy salvation to humankind.

The plan was simple and, I was convinced, foolproof. Stan would privately approach the other bishops one at a time and reveal to them the hard evidence of Fisher's treacherous crimes. Their choice would then be clear—join with Stan in unseating Fisher (and in so doing keep their vaunted positions of privilege) or the whistle would be blown and they would go down with the rotting ship, ending up disgraced and ruined.

Ironically, the church status Fisher had worked so hard to achieve for Phasmatia would work against him, for he held no private shares, and technically commanded but one vote on the governing council. The bishops, as the legal directors of the non-profit corporation, could simply vote Fisher out of his leadership role (and completely off the board, for that matter) and banish him into exile. With the felony charges we could bring against him, I felt Fisher would quietly take the hefty cash settlement he'd be offered, along with an unsullied place in human history as the Phasmatian Messiah.

I unrelentingly pitched my divinely inspired, seemingly perfect plan to Stan, and even though he agreed to do it, my friend was not overjoyed at the prospect, and practically spit his final consent out at me. It was the beginning of a rift between us that would not be healed before Stan's death. I regret it immeasurably, and will carry that remorse to my grave.

I imagine he was afraid of what violence Fisher might do in retaliation, in spite of my assurances that The Chosen One would have no choice but to go quietly. To do so would be a rational act, however, and we both knew by then that Sky Fisher was a few bits short of a byte. And I'm pretty sure (classic shy guy that he was) Stan dreaded the distasteful political task of having to individually and surreptitiously blackmail and browbeat each of the other bishops into betrayal and submission.

What I think pained and pissed Stan off the most was the prospect of publicly assuming leadership of the Church. I had been appealing to Stan's ego during my arguments, naturally thinking that, like most human beings, he craved fame and power. I've had a lot of painful moments of introspection since then, and I think, above all, Stan absolutely feared the spotlight he was going to be pushed into, and blamed me for it. Why would he do it, then? If he hated the idea so much, why wouldn't he just say no? I believe now that he did what he did because of my convincing scare stories that his accumulation of hardware and software would be seized and dismantled. Stan acted to save his precious computers. Just like I acted to save my beloved Phasmatia.

***

I've been sticking to the keyboard pretty much non-stop for the past day or so, and I'm starting to get cabin fever. (Or is that trailer fever?) More importantly, writing the part about my conversation with Brock Harrow backstage at Sky Fisher's Ann Arbor show has given me an idea about who to send my story to. I'll need to do some research first, though. So I'm going to take a break from writing now, and go for a spin on my motorcycle. I passed through a couple of towns on the way here that seemed big enough to have a library. While I'm at it, I think I'll get a haircut, and buy some cologne. I want to look and smell my best when I see Hannah again.

Shit, shit, shit. There are fucking Phasmatians all over the countryside, and they're definitely looking for *me*. When I left the trailer earlier today, I retraced my route along Highway 5, which is the way I came in, until I got to the town of Little Falls. I vaguely remembered having passed through it on Hallowe'en Night when I drove up here, but everything sure looked different in the daytime. It's a beautiful little town, nestled in a big gorge on the Mohawk River and, I also discovered, right on the Erie Canal. I imagine it gets a lot more traffic in the summertime, especially from boaters, but it was still fairly busy for a Tuesday in November. More importantly, they had a library, and a mall where I could buy the things I was after.

I didn't want to lug around shopping bags, so I went to the library first. I have to say I was quite blown away by its architecture. Instead of the squat institutional buildings you usually find, this library was located in a beautiful old converted Victorian-style mansion, donated by a judge at the turn of the last century. Although they had a bank of brand new computers (compliments of Bill and Melinda Gates, and the local Rotarians, according to a sign) the machines were all occupied, so I moved to the reference book section and went to look things up the good old-fashioned way instead.

That turned out to be a stroke of luck for me. As I was out of sight in the back, perusing a thick copy of the latest congressional register, a woman in a Phasmatian uniform walked in. Although I knew from the cut and color of her garb she wasn't one of the monks (not to mention, the last I'd heard, Devon was keeping his outfit a male enclave), she was still clearly a Church insider of some sort, perhaps studying to be a priestess. I slunk all the way to the end of the racks, and hid behind my book, although I'd peep out occasionally to see what the woman was up to.

The Phasmatian strolled up to the front and started chatting up the man behind the counter. A piece of paper was produced, examined, and discussed, and evidently the woman elicited permission to post the item, because she was directed to the bulletin board. There she tacked up the paper and, after taking a quick survey of the room, left.

My heart was pounding madly, but I told myself not to panic, and to wait a little while before leaving my place of concealment. Needless to say, my curiosity was burning to see the contents of the leaflet the woman had put up, even though a sick feeling in the pit of my stomach gave me a pretty good hint. Sure enough, when I eventually sauntered over to check it out, trying to act only mildly interested, I saw my own photocopied face staring back at me. Evidently I was a disturbed nursing home resident who was off his meds and had gone missing while on a nature outing. As an act of charity, the Phasmatians, bless their kind souls, were trying to locate me and bring me home.

Even though I should have found solace in the fact I hadn't run into one of the murderous monks, I was shaking uncontrollably after I'd finished reading the handbill. What really had me rattled was that the general Phasmatian membership had been enrolled in the search, which meant that there were now thousands of people out looking for me. My guess was that the woman putting up the flyers probably believed the cover story, and in her mind was only trying to help me. But I had little doubt that, had she located me, she was under orders to call her superiors and not the local authorities, and it would be Devon's death squad that showed up to collect me.

The real burning question for me was how focused their manhunt was. Did they have information that specifically placed me here, in this part of the state, or were they blindly casting a wide net all over the country? In my mind I revisited my flight from Manhattan again and again, trying to think how I might have slipped up, or where I might have been spotted.

Although I had strictly paid cash that night while passing through White Plains, it was not unreasonable to think some store clerk or gas station attendant might have remembered seeing me. They likely know I was riding a motorcycle, and given that I'd bought the cans of paint at one of my stops, might even suspect the bike was now spray painted a crude black.

I'm convinced, however, that at that point my trail goes cold. I'd stuck to the back roads, at night, and hadn't stopped again until I reached the trailer. From White Plains I could have gone in any direction—up to my home town of Poughkeepsie, west through Pennsylvania, or off towards Connecticut and the East Coast. And even if I had traveled north, who's to say I wouldn't have been headed to Canada? No, if Sky Fisher really suspected that I'd gone to the Shius' trailer, then the Phasmatians would have been here days ago. The very fact that they are out posting handbills asking the public for information convinces me they don't know my exact whereabouts.

I abandoned my plans to go shopping at the local mall, though, and snuck out of town, purposely heading in the opposite direction from the trailer, and sticking to the back streets. I now had the unnerving feeling my motorcycle made me stand out, as all the locals I passed seemed to look up and stare at me as I rumbled by. I had this sudden desire to be driving a pickup truck like everyone else.

Every ten miles or so I'd pull over to the side of the road and hide behind a tree or something, watching to see if I was being followed. It was during one of these precautionary stops that I saw a van with the Phasmatian symbol on its side drive by. It was traveling in the opposite direction, so it wasn't tailing me, and I'd heard the killer monks used unmarked vehicles. Nevertheless I found myself trembling with fear at the very sight of it.

It took me the rest of the afternoon to swing around in a big circle and make my way back here to the trailer. I got lost a few times detouring down unfamiliar back roads, but other than spotting my own photocopied face tacked to a tree, and then again on a community center bulletin board, I saw no further signs of my pursuers.

I've been sitting in the dark for hours, clutching the borrowed deer rifle and listening for God-only-knows who or what to come knocking on the trailer door. Eventually my fear gave way to anger—as much at myself as any phantom Phasmatians lurking outside—and I turned on the lights, made myself some supper, and got back to writing. As I said before, if they knew where I was, they'd have come for me by now.

I'd dearly love to go visit my newfound friends, if only to feel human again and less like a hunted animal, but it seems to me now that I should stay away from the van Vroonhovens as much as possible, for fear of potentially dragging them into harm's way. It's also pretty clear that I really will need Hannah's help to get my story out. When I saw those internet terminals in the library in Little Falls, I thought for a minute that I'd be able to take care of that business myself, but now I'm afraid to visit any public places. First things first, though. I need to finish telling my story.

***

After his televised triumph in Ann Arbor, and the publication immediately thereafter of the revised Sacred Text, with its newly added Book of Miracles, Sky Fisher became the most talked-about person in America. Of course, I'm not telling you anything you don't already know. His picture began to appear everywhere, and supposedly rational and objective news organizations began to openly tout his possible divinity. Only Budd Durrell's MediaROR empire stood up in opposition, although I've read it personally cost Durrell billions of dollars in lost advertising and declining stock values when the disgruntled viewers revolted and jumped ship.

Fisher shrewdly seized the moment to attempt to bolster Phasmatia's international membership, and announced an ambitious world tour that was to include a heavily publicized swing through China. The fact that largely godless country single-handedly accounts for almost a seventh of the world's population jumped out at me, and I was positive Fisher's lust for power had now achieved global proportions.

Yet, while reviling his personal ambitions, I found myself admiring the brilliance of the move. China was a country on the rise, and yet its people were very much in a spiritual vacuum, unless you counted materialism as a new religion. If Phasmatia could gain a foothold there, it had real potential to dramatically transfigure the human condition. It was something, I told myself, that would bear focusing on once Fisher was removed and I held the reins of Phasmatia's future.

But as far as the actual plot to depose Fisher was going, I was totally in the dark. Stan shook off all my attempts to get him out for drinks, claiming that between his work and now his new secret project, he had no time to sleep, let alone socialize. I'm sure that was largely accurate, although I detected Stan's lingering anger at me, and could tell he was deliberately snubbing me. It started to eat me up inside.

I don't know whether it was purely remorse about the unfair

position into which I'd pushed Stan, or whether I was also feeling excluded from the new power structure that was presumably being hammered out behind the scenes, but I began to have second thoughts about the entire plot. One evening I literally picked up Stan and carried him away from his computers, forcing him to take a walk with me around the block—away from prying eyes and ears—so I could express my misgivings.

Stan looked awful. Bags were forming under his eyes, his skin was acquiring a jaundiced tint, and overall he looked middle-aged. But when I told him we should call off the plot against Fisher, and that I just wanted my old friendship with Stan back, he looked at me like I was some wacko who'd wandered up to him on the sidewalk, and give me a big derisive laugh.

"Are you fucking crazy, Brad? It's like we've cut down a giant tree and it's halfway to the ground, and then you rush in and want to try to stop it from falling. We're way past the point of no return now. I've already got a majority of the bishops committed, and the rest should be locked up in a couple of days."

A gleam came into his eyes, like the old days when he used to try to explain computer stuff to me, and I finally got to hear some details of what he had been up to.

"The first guy was hard, I mean *really* hard, to convince, and I swear I thought he was going to physically attack me," Stan told me. "But in the end it was just like you said ... show him the evidence and let him know there really isn't any choice. It got easier after that, especially when I could tell each new recruit that I already had other bishops on board."

I had been worried about the difficult position I'd placed Stan into, but it dawned on me then that Stan was actually enjoying his Machiavellian machinations. I never got to call him on it, but I think he had discovered, much to his delight, that people were as programmable as computers—something he should have known already after all those years working in an ad agency—and he was relishing the similar power it afforded the programmer.

I must have been looking at him quizzically, because Stan felt the need to reach over and give me a reassuring pat on the arm. "Don't worry, Brad, we'll get rid of that sonofabitch, and when we do, there'll be a permanent cushy spot for you with the Church ... maybe lecturing on The Sacred Text to the young priests or something. You'll finally be able to quit your job at Warren & McCaul."

He made a big show of looking down at his watch and appearing alarmed. "Holy crap! Listen buddy, I really have to get back. I'm meeting one of the other bishops in thirty minutes. You know how it is. But don't worry, you can expect some big news soon. Now just sit tight, and stop calling me five times a day. Promise?"

"Okay, okay, Stan. I promise."

His words about big news turned out to be prophetic, although not in the way he'd intended, I'm sure. He took off, and left me standing there, my mind blown by the words he had just spoken. Of course he had no way of knowing it, but his dismissive little speech about finding me a comfortable Phasmatian gig was almost a carbon copy of the one Fisher had given me earlier when he was trying to entice me to sign a non-disclosure agreement, and it rankled me to the very core.

I had worked side by side with those two men and both of them, especially my alleged best friend, Stan, should have understood exactly how much I had contributed to the substance and subsequent success of the religion. Instead, it appeared I was destined to be patronized, underappreciated, and excluded. I cursed them both and headed over, alone, to Macbeth's to get good and drunk. As it turned out, that was the last time I saw Stan alive.

I had little choice but to sit around and wait for the palace revolution to play itself out, and to hope I'd then be able to convince Stan I was entitled to an equal share of power, not just
some token stipend and low-level job. Although the suspense
was killing me, I nevertheless kept my word and left Stan alone,
not even phoning him. Still, I wanted to have some inkling of
how things were going, so I went down to hang out around the
Church's headquarters, and see if I could pick up any vibes or
gossip from the staff by osmosis.

Given that I didn't really know anyone there, it was a pointless
exercise. The fact that I didn't wear Phasmatian clothes worked
against me as well. Anyone I tried to strike up a conversation
with quickly looked me up and down and dismissed me as no
one of any real status. I actually found myself dropping Stan
and Fisher's names and recalling our past history, but I guess the
idea that I, a nondescript stranger in civilian clothes, had actually helped found the Church, was hard for the staffers to digest.
It didn't help that I mainly approached attractive young women,
who automatically assumed I was hitting on them—which I was.

Next to Stan, there *was* one other person there I knew quite well, and that was Sky Fisher. Knowing he spied on everyone, it didn't shock me that he could be aware of my presence in the building, of course, but I was taken by surprise when he summoned me up to the penthouse. Just my luck, though, there wasn't a single hottie nearby in the cafeteria to witness Devon approach me and ask if I could spare the time to visit with The Chosen One in his private quarters.

Even though Devon's invitation was polite and, in fact, deferential, I almost shit myself when I looked up to see him looming over me. My first reaction was to worry that Fisher had uncovered the plot against him, and was rounding up the conspirators. Only the rationalization that I was technically a small fish with no ecumenical authority or voting power sustained me, and helped keep my bowels in check when I was ushered into the presence of The High and Mighty.

But Fisher turned out to be in a relaxed and happy mood. He was evidently still riding the crest of his recent triumphs, and I was immediately set at ease. We cozied up on the couch, drinks in hand, and to my utter surprise, the Big Man actually wanted to consult me on religious matters.

"I guess you've heard about my China trip," he said. "What can you tell me about the state of their religious beliefs?"

The honest answer was not a lot, except for one *National Geographic* article I'd read back when I'd been researching The Sacred Text. But I didn't want to disappoint Fisher, and I was kind of enjoying this casual chat in the lap of luxury.

"Well, ever since the Communists took over, they've officially been an atheist country. There are pockets of Muslims, and Buddhists, and Christians... but these don't amount to more than five, maybe six per cent altogether. There's still a lingering mix of Taoism and paganism in the countryside, but again, it's a small minority. The real potential, of course, is in the cities, and the burgeoning middle class."

"Potential?" Fisher asked, and I could tell he already knew all this, and had been testing me. He looked mildly amused, but hadn't crossed the line to arrogant condescension yet.

"Well, presumably you're wondering how successfully Phasmatia might penetrate China. Am I right?" He held up his glass in salute, so I took a slight bow with my head and continued. "Well, given that I did borrow generously from Lao Tzu, a lot of it should at least sound vaguely familiar. People are people, no matter where you go, and the basic morality we evoke is archetypal. And, all indications are that there's a growing spirituality there, and I think we could fill it very nicely. But we're going to have to figure out how to get the government on side."

"How so?" Fisher asked. "I mean just because they're officially atheistic, do you think that means they'd physically ban us?"

"That's not it. Listen, Sky. China has, like over 220 million internet users—way more than all of North America. But the government controls the access to the web. Given that we're very much an online religion, it's crucial that we be allowed to get across the Great Firewall of China."

I could see I'd actually managed to impress Fisher. This was how it should have been all along. Me as an equal. Me receiving the respect I deserved.

"This isn't like getting a building permit for a factory, where you can always find a local official to bribe," I continued. "This is a decision made at the highest level. Now, one of the things they're sensitive to is outside criticism—especially over things like how they treat dissidents. So we don't show up and start publicly lambasting them."

"But wouldn't the rest of the world expect me to bring it up, especially given who I am?"

Given who you are? You mean a conniving murdering lunatic? The retort surfaced but I kept it to myself. "Do what every shrewd visiting politician does, Sky. Meet them in private, and then announce afterwards you had frank and fruitful discussions on a broad range of issues, including human rights…but stick to business. It would help if we had a plum to offer them. Maybe we could offshore the production of Phasmatian merchandise to China. We'd probably increase our profit margins by quite a bit in the process."

Fisher was grinning benevolently at me. He clearly liked what he was hearing. He kicked off his expensive-looking shoes and balled up on the couch, as if getting ready to take a nap. "I was thinking of inviting Stan along for the trip. What do you think, Brad? I mean, he is Chinese after all, and would look good beside me in a delegation, especially given that he is, you know, a bishop. Besides, he speaks it, right? He could be, like, a translator."

My heartbeat quickened when he mentioned Stan. Although there wasn't a single indication we were having anything other than a casual discussion, I was back to being paranoid that Fisher was playing with me in some way.

"Uh, Stan only speaks Cantonese. His parents came over from Hong Kong. Most of China uses Mandarin." I wondered if Fisher could see through my excuse, but even if this was all on the level, it was important that Stan remain Stateside to complete the recruiting for his *coup d'état*. "Besides, you know how crucial Stan is to the computer operations. Everything would fall apart without him here."

"There'd be some pain, I admit, but we'd muddle through in the end. No one's irreplaceable…not even Stan Shiu," Fisher said dreamily. His eyes were closed now, and it really did look like he was drifting towards sleep. "How about *you*, Brad? How would you like a trip to China?" he murmured softly. A smile came onto his lips, and his breathing deepened. Had he really just fallen asleep in the middle of making me a once-in-a-lifetime offer, or was this another part of some ploy?

I just sat there looking at him, trying to make sense of things. There was no way this was some kind of cat-and-mouse head-game, I decided. If Sky Fisher suspected a plot to depose him, he'd be ranting and striking out against anything that moved. I nudged him. "Sky? Are you awake, Sky?" He groaned a little, but his eyes stayed shut. Asleep, he looked harmless, almost childlike.

He was far from innocent, though, and I still loathed him. The idea sprang up that this would be the perfect moment to try to kill him, while he lay only inches away, helpless and unsuspecting. But, aside from the knowledge that I'd almost certainly be gunned down by Devon, even if I did succeed, I realized there was no need for murder. Soon, the plot Stan and I were hatching behind his back would finally bring down the High and Mighty, and good fucking riddance.

Then I had another thought, a much crazier one. Wasn't it morally wrong to hate Sky Fisher so strongly? Shouldn't I forgive him instead? After all, be you Phasmatian or Christian, forgiveness is a chief tenet. I looked down at him once more, and realized I'd never have it in me to forgive Fisher. I might have been feeling a little holier-than-thou lately, but I had a long way to go to sainthood.

One of Fisher's nuns materialized with a blanket in hand, and squeezed in between us so she could nestle up to her lord and master. "We've been keeping him up kind of late the last couple of nights," she giggled by way of explanation.

A large shadow swept over me, and I looked up to see Devon standing there. "We'll let him sleep," the bodyguard said, and there was a real tenderness in his voice. As he ushered me to the elevator, I studied the man, relishing the idea that his evil days too were numbered. What would Devon do after the bishops voted Fisher out? Would he follow his boss into exile? I suddenly found the idea disconcerting that a deposed Fisher might still command his deadly thugs. As the doors slid shut, I was actually contemplating whether, perhaps, it wasn't smarter for the Church to keep Devon and his monks on the payroll. What a fool I was to think he'd never come after me.

Most of the time, my copywriting job at Warren & McCaul wasn't especially challenging, and typically was contained easily within a comfortable nine-to-five window. After all, as we liked to tell our clients, it was all about quality, not quantity. That was probably the main reason I never quit, despite the honorarium that still arrived biweekly from the Phasmatian Church, and would in and of itself have been enough to live on, even in Manhattan.

Periodically, though, I'd be swept up in some huge project with impossibly tight deadlines and be forced to burn the candle at both ends. One such assignment landed on my plate that week, and took over virtually all my waking hours. If nothing else, it kept my mind off how Stan was progressing, but truth be told, the work was sufficiently grueling, banal, and distasteful—promoting, on behalf of a large pharmaceutical firm, a controversial drug with potentially deadly side effects—that for the first time in my career I was actually tempted to hand in my resignation.

The big dilemma I faced, however, was not knowing exactly where I would stand when the dust had settled downtown at Phasmatian headquarters. In theory, I should have been sitting pretty, but that was largely wishful thinking, and the reality was that the future was beyond my control. It didn't take a lot of imagination (and these days I was cursed with an overabundance of it) to imagine a scenario where I'd be left out in the cold, and would need to keep my day job. I felt utterly powerless, and this drove me crazy—although so did having to work double shifts at W&M prevaricating for some greedy and soulless pharma giant.

Even though I'd promised Stan I wouldn't bug him, after a full week of silence I finally broke down and sent him a friendly "Hey, buddy, what's up?" note, but received no reply. I actually took this as a personal affront, so the next day I tried Fisher. As an excuse for emailing him, I forwarded the link for an *Economist* article on religion in China. That at least got a reply, but it was an automated acknowledgement of my note, onto which was appended a piece of scripture from The Sacred Text, and not an example of my best work at that. No personal follow-up reply ever materialized. I concluded that Fisher had only been toying with me about accompanying him on his China trip.

With the kind of irony that only someone in the ad business can fully appreciate, after busting our buns to make the deadline (I'd even slept at my desk the past two nights), and one day before the pharmaceutical web site was supposed to open to the public, the entire project suddenly got put on hold by the client because of some thorny legal issues. I finally had my life back, and so had time again to try to find out what the hell was going on with the Phasmatian power struggle.

Despite being supremely busy at work, I'd been finding time to scan the media for possible signs of a change in regime. Most of the press continued to lionize Sky Fisher, and to play up his planned Eastern tour; so as far as I could tell the directors had not formally acted yet to remove him. Although I badly needed to change my clothes and get a decent night's sleep, and even though I knew Stan would be pissed at me, that evening after work I went down to the Phasmatian offices instead. I wandered up to the computer department, and banged on the door to the server room for like half an hour. When no one answered I tried calling Stan on both his internal extension and his cellphone, but all I got was voice mail. I left him a pair of testy messages and drifted down to the cafeteria for a cup of coffee, to try to figure out what I should do next.

Actually, by this point I was hoping the all-seeing eye of the almighty Fisher might spot me, as it had a week earlier, and grant me another audience with The Chosen One, but that didn't happen either. All around me the uniformed Phasmatian night workers came and went, but other than the inquisitive look many of them shot me as they sat down for their evening meals (probably as much for my rumpled, bleary-eyed, unshaven appearance as for the fact I wasn't wearing Church garb) it was like I didn't exist.

I toyed with the idea of demanding to see Fisher, even if it meant directly confronting Devon's goons, but oddly enough, there wasn't a single black-suited monk to be found anywhere in the building. There wasn't even one stationed by the elevator or at the stairs to the penthouse, although both were locked to me. In the end I just gave up and dragged my tired butt home.

When I opened the door to my apartment, I discovered my place had been ransacked. It wasn't the first time I'd been broken into since moving to New York, but something like that always affects you. All the things you've heard are true. At first it seems unreal, then there is a cascade of emotions—you feel violated, then enraged, then paranoid. The odd part was that after taking a quick inventory I found that nothing was actually missing. I'd been accumulating quite a few toys since having the bonus of a regular Phasmatian stipend on top of my W&M salary, but they were all still there—my plasma TV, Blu-ray player, X-Box, digital camera. I mean, the place had been thoroughly gone over, with drawers dumped, cupboards emptied, and even the mattress flipped, but everything of value was still present and accounted for.

I surmised that the perpetrator had been spooked while in the process of committing his crime, and had bolted empty-handed ... although he had politely closed the door behind him in the process. That led to the next mystery, which was how the thief had actually gotten in. My windows had unwieldy iron grates on them, which could only be unbolted from the inside to gain access to the fire escape in case of emergency. The burglar

therefore must have come in through the front door, although
there was absolutely no sign of forced entry. True, a skilled crimi-
nal could pick a lock, but that testified to a higher class of crook
than the ones usually doing apartment break-and-enters.

Despite my bone-numbing tiredness, I was too wired to sleep,
and spent a couple of hours putting things somewhat back in
place, the entire time cursing the bastard who had caused me
all that aggravation. Finally, with every extra latch, chain, and
deadbolt on my door fastened in place, and even the movie-
cliché chair slid under the doorknob, plus an aluminum baseball bat lying beside me, I hit the sack. Fatigue trumped nerves,
and I fell asleep immediately, although I remember my dreams
were a bizarre, anxiety-ridden lot in which Stan Shiu featured
prominently.

I backhanded the alarm clock into silence the next morning,
figuring two weeks of overtime had earned me the right to sleep
in that day, and finally rolled into work around eleven. There
was a weird vibe going through the office, and I picked up on it
immediately.

Now, I should explain that Warren & McCaul has a lot of
practicing Phasmatians in it—I imagine most ad agencies do.
The proliferation of young, spiritually bankrupt, techno-savvy,
creative types who are quick to embrace new trends perfectly
matches Phasmatia's main demographic. I wasn't connected to
any of them, though. The fact is, ever since Stan had quit the
agency, I really didn't have anyone at work that I was close to
anymore. It didn't help matters that I had once tried to convince a newbie in our department that I was a founding father
of Phasmatia, and word had quickly spread that I was some
deluded braggart. I had always figured that, eventually, I'd publicly receive my deserved high rank within the Church, and then
would come triumphantly back to the agency and, completely
vindicated, shut up the wagging tongues once and for all.

One of the most vocal converts was my department's senior graphic designer, a bossy firebrand named Britanny. She'd been heavily into the goth culture when she first joined our department. Now she wore a huge Phasmatian pendant around her neck, had a giant poster of Sky Fisher above her desk, and organized a regular Tuesday night worship group, which I'd heard was little more than a singles night for W&M's junior staff.

Looking at her damned poster of Fisher always made my stomach heave, but she also had a tendency to ridicule my design suggestions during team meetings, so we didn't really get along. As a result, I'd never talked to Britanny about my own connection with the Church.

On that day, though, Britanny rushed up to me the minute she spotted me getting off the elevator. She wrapped her arms around me, and there was a glistening of tears in her eyes.

"Brad, oh Brad, where have you been? Everyone's been looking for you!"

"What's going on?" I asked, suddenly worried that I'd slept through a last-minute resurrection of the pharmaceutical web site's launch. "I was told they'd put the project on hold. Besides, my copy's all finished and approved... or do they want more changes?"

She blinked a couple of times in confusion, and then shook her head vigorously. "No, no, you don't understand. It's Bishop Shiu. He's... he's dead."

Now it was my turn to try to make sense of things. Not only was the news itself dizzying in its significance, but I couldn't get a handle on why it had caused my peers at the office to go looking for me. A weak "what?" was all I could muster. I collapsed into the first chair I saw.

"Some people from the Church were here looking for you earlier," Britanny explained. "The Chosen One himself sent them. Can you believe it? It's so magnificent. He said he wanted them to console you. I think they were holy monks or something. They told us you and Bishop Shiu were extremely close ... I didn't know that. Why didn't you tell me?"

I looked up at her. A small crowd had now gathered in a semicircle behind Britanny, staring at me in barefaced awe. Evidently I had achieved Phasmatian fame after all. "How did it happen?" I asked. Somehow you always want to know the details.

"He was killed in a car crash last night in New Jersey," she told me. "I know he's one with The Universal Spirit now, but it's just so awful." She began to cry outright, fondling her pendant as she did so. A co-worker put his arm around Britanny, and started to mumble something. Another couple took up the chant, one of them reaching down to squeeze my hand. It took me a few seconds to realize they were reciting a prayer from The Sacred Text.

I somehow found it annoying to hear my own prose being recited at me, all the more so because things were starting to crystallize with frightening clarity—Stan's death, the break-in at my apartment, Fisher's henchmen coming to the office. I angrily shook off the consoling hand and headed for my cubicle. Plugging in my laptop, I went online to see if I could find any details of Stan's accident. Or rather his murder, because there was no doubt in my mind that Fisher had had him killed.

The story was all over the wires. Apparently somewhere around 8 p.m. a car had gone off the Palisades Parkway and plunged down the cliffs 400 feet before exploding in a fireball. The car's ownership had been traced from its VIN, although release of the victim's identity was awaiting an autopsy.

What the stories didn't say was how Fisher already happened to know that it was Stan who had been killed. I suppose a sympathetic state trooper might have notified the Phasmatians once the vehicle's ownership had been established, but I knew better. Clearly Fisher had gotten wind of the plot to depose him, and had ordered Stan killed. Even more chilling was the visit to my office that morning. That could only mean he suspected my involvement, and thought I might have copies of the damning evidence Stan had been using to try to sway the other bishops. It was clear to me my own life was now in jeopardy.

"Brad ... are you okay?" Britanny's voice said from behind me. "Is there anything I can get you? Do you want a coffee?"

"Please leave me alone. I just want to be by myself," I told her. What I really needed was time to think, and the last thing I wanted was that little Phasmatian nut bar clinging to me.

"Okay, whatever you say, Brad, but I'm here if you need me." She hesitated for a second, and then offered me a scrap of paper she'd been holding in her hand. "Those monks left their number. You should call them ... I'm sure they know exactly what to do at a time like this."

"Oh yeah, I'll just bet they do," I couldn't help snorting. When I reached for the piece of paper, Britanny hesitated.

"Or I could call them for you if you like," she said hopefully. I practically snatched the number from her hand, causing her to recoil with a look like I'd just slapped her in the face.

I realized it was wiser not to ruffle any feathers. "No, no thanks, Brit, I'll call them myself," I said, getting up to give her a placating hug. "Hey, listen, I really appreciate your concern. I'm just kind of stunned. You understand."

That soothed her, but it didn't get rid of her. "So you and Bishop Shiu were really close?" she asked.

"We were like brothers." *Yeah, like brothers, alright,* I was thinking. *Like Romulus and Remus. Like Cain and Abel. Like Höðr and Baldur. He's dead and it's because of me. I pushed him into it.*

"Well, I'm here if you need me," Britanny said. She wavered behind my chair. "Hey, I know this isn't a great time, and you might just want to be alone, but a bunch of us from the Church are having a Hallowe'en party tonight ... maybe you want to go. I mean, you know, if you're feeling up to it, that is. You wouldn't need a costume ... a lot of people don't bother." Her face had reddened while she talked to me, and I could tell it had taken nerve on her part to ask me out.

"Yeah sure, cool. Thanks. I think maybe it'll help me feel better." I gave her hand a final little squeeze before politely pushing her away. In fact, I had no intention of going to any Phasmatian shindig—or of being anywhere within a hundred miles of a Phasmatian for that matter. I was already formulating my exit strategy.

Britanny finally left me alone, and I plopped down to try to plan my next move. I needed to get far away from New York, that was clear. Admittedly, a piece of me also wanted to make sure Fisher was punished for what he had done to Stan, but I'll be honest—compared to the question of self-preservation, that was secondary. For the time being my cubicle was as safe a place as any to try to think things out, although I was having a hell of a time stringing two thoughts together. If Devon and his goons showed up, surely they wouldn't be so bold as to just kill me at my desk, and if I hollered for security, in theory I should be able to stop them from bodily dragging me out the door.

Sooner or later they'd learn I was here, though, and figure out a way to get me. I couldn't stay at work forever. Somehow I needed to find a way out of this mess. And as I chewed my lip and floundered in self-pity and indecision, something odd—you might even say miraculous—happened. Stan reached out to me from the dead.

As I had been working away, out of habit I toggled over to check my email. There were half a dozen work-related notes in my in-box, plus the usual pieces of spam that had slipped past the corporate filters, promising me a supersized penis and the ability to brandish it all night long. But there was also one additional piece of email that jumped out at me and utterly confused me. It was an automated note from the Phasmatian web site confirming a request to reset my personal password. First of all, I hadn't issued any such request ... in fact, I hadn't ventured online into Virtual Phasmatia in quite a while. More to the point, since my heretical online preaching had caused my work email to be blacklisted long ago, I'd been using anonymous Hotmail, Yahoo, and gmail accounts for several months.

My first inclination was to suspect a Phasmatian trap. At best, I figured the note was designed to help track me down by notifying them when the email had been opened. At worst, it might contain some spurious link that would download malware to my computer if I clicked on it. Stan had explained to me long ago how easy it was to infect an unsuspecting PC with a virus that would place it under outside control, even behind its corporate firewall.

Nevertheless, I stopped short of blowing the note away, and something told me to go ahead and open it. Stan might be dead now, but up until a day or so ago he was alive and in charge of the Phasmatian systems, so to my mind it was impossible anyone could have corrupted the web site without his knowledge.

The email's content seemed innocuous enough when I examined it. In response to a "forgot password" request I'd supposedly generated on the web site, an automated reminder had been sent to me. With hundreds of millions of registered users, the traffic in such requests and responses would be inanely commonplace. But when I saw the actual password that had been sent to me—"idiot"—that's when I realized that somehow the note must have come from Stan.

I guess that begs an explanation. Macbeth's, as I've mentioned countless times by now, was our favorite drinking hole. *Macbeth* also happens to be one of my favorite Shakespearean plays, and one drunken night, seemingly a lifetime ago, I had made the mistake of patronizing Stan, assuming that he, like so many other technogeeks, had led a one-sided educational life and so was woefully ignorant of the Bard's works. After I had completed my rather loud and overly pedantic lecture on the merits of the Scottish Tragedy, Stan had sighed and said simply, "idiot."

Taken aback by his apparent insult, when I had been working so hard to send a little culture and illumination his way, I was almost ready to drop the gloves. Stan simply smiled and elaborated, "'It is a tale told by an idiot, full of sound and fury, signifying nothing.' Act 5. Scene 5." When I just sat there dumbstruck, he added, "I told you I was a straight-A student all through high school. Do you think they don't teach Shakespeare in California?"

Thereafter, albeit only a handful of times over the years, whenever I was being especially overbearing, Stan would simply mouth "idiot" at me, and it served to instantly put me in my place.

So, it was totally clear to me that Stan was somehow behind the email I'd just received. I went to the Phasmatian web site, logged in with my Warren & McCaul email address, and then typed in "idiot" as the password. I was successfully granted access, but instead of the usual ornate Church entrance portal, crowded with scores of worshipping avatars, a stark virtual room appeared, consisting of nothing more than four plain white walls. My own on-screen character was in the middle and, much to my delight, I was being depicted as my long-lost Mage Errant persona, although the room was otherwise empty. While I was reacquainting myself with the Mage, making him dance and fly around the room, a system prompt popped up on the screen reading: "Turn on your sound, plug in your head phones, and press Enter."

I did as instructed, and suddenly Stan walked through the virtual wall, or rather a computerized representation of Stan did, one that was strikingly accurate in its detail.

"Hello, Brad," it said, speaking with Stan's actual voice. "I need to be sure it's really you. What did you give me for Christmas the year we first met?"

It was another test, and one that brought a smile to my lips as I remembered the occasion. I typed in "Brandi" and was rewarded by the sound of applause over the earphones. Only Stan or I would know the answer to that question, and that it did not refer to liquor, but rather the name of a buxom stripper who had given my friend his first-ever lap dance.

"Okay, Brad, listen and listen good," the Stan character instructed, and I could immediately detect the urgency and strain in his voice. "If you're hearing this, then the odds are that I'm dead. I'm going into a meeting shortly with the other bishops where we're going to formally vote on getting rid of Fisher, but I think he may have gotten wind of our plan. So, just in case, I've written this program that will contact you if I don't come back to cancel it within twenty-four hours."

I can't begin to do justice to what I was feeling at that moment—grief, remorse, anger, fear... and awe at Stan's ingenuity and grit. "But I'm not going to let that bastard get away with it," his avatar went on. "Since he hopefully hasn't gotten to you yet, or you wouldn't be hearing this, here's what I want you to do. I'm going to download all the dirt we've got on Fisher, and I want you to use it. Nail that prick, and nail him good. Forget about trying to seize control or save Phasmatia. We tried that, and look where it got me. So, the hell with Phasmatia, and the hell with Sky Fisher. We've unleashed a monster, Brad. Surely you can see that. You've got to put an end to it. You've got to do the right thing."

Stan's onscreen character disappeared, and off to the side a small window appeared showing a file transfer in progress. The download was substantial, and the indicator estimated it would take over forty minutes to complete. I found myself staring at that progress bar with tears in my eyes. After a few seconds I reached over to my keyboard and typed in: "Goodbye Stan. I'm sorry." In the virtual room nothing happened. My Mage character just stood there alone, motionless and impotent.

Sitting at my desk, waiting for the file transfer to complete, I was seized with mounting terror. Never in my comfortable yuppie life had I ever felt anything remotely like it before. Although I needed to come up with a plan, it was impossible to concentrate on anything, as my thoughts roiled and churned but failed to conjure up a solution to my dilemma.

Finally, even without thinking what I was doing, I sought help. I closed my eyes, folded my hands, and prayed to God for guidance and salvation. *If you will not save this lowly sinner, O Lord*, I implored, *then please at least have mercy on my soul. I believe you are the one, true Universal God. You can see into my heart, so therefore You know that with Phasmatia, I was in fact attempting to bring people closer to You. Everywhere Your children are confused and distraught as they have strayed from you, O Lord. I was only trying to help. I meant well. Forgive me if I have wronged You, and please watch over my soul.*

It occurred to me I was not praying to some new personalized representation of God, or the Phasmatian Universal Spirit. I was in fact praying to the same old Judeo-Christian God I'd been introduced to as a kid, and the only God I'd really ever known. You readers will, of course, say I only did it out of desperation. With the probability of death staring me in the face, you'll cynically assert that what I did was not an act of faith, but a last-minute cover-my-ass piece of liturgical legalese—a Hail Mary pass for the hereafter.

You may be right. After all, as the old saying goes, there are no atheists in the trenches. But it seems to me, unless you're some monk who has devoted your life to the singular task of trying to know and get closer to God, the vast majority of us can truly only glimpse Him/Her in moments of heightened awareness—be it rapture or extreme despair. All I can tell you is that prayer worked, inasmuch as God delivered forth a plan to help me live a little longer. Or, if you prefer, it calmed me down enough to allow me to think something up. And that was to escape here, to this very trailer where it all began, and to write down this tell-all confession.

I set Stan's posthumous file download to run in the background, and made myself busy. I decided to perform every action as if I was being watched. First, I sent out a couple of emails to create the impression I was settled in at work for the day. Then I confirmed my attendance at meetings for the coming week, like I wasn't planning to go anywhere. As an added precaution, I took out my cellphone, made sure it was powered on, and sent it via courier (but selecting ground transport, not air) to a client in Buffalo who I hated anyway. If I was lucky, the Phasmatians would give her a hard time when they tracked down my phone.

While the download was finishing up, I started poking around craigslist for a cheap motorcycle. I don't know why I thought a bike would be a good idea, what with November in New York only a day away. I guess somewhere in the back of my mind I considered it a more versatile means of escape, picturing myself darting along sidewalks, down concrete stairs, or into the woods to elude pursuing cars. I found the bike I've already described to you, phoned the guy in Soho to get more details, and arranged to come right over to check it out (although, barring a complete lemon, I actually planned to buy it on the spot).

I hadn't rolled in until 11 a.m., so I figured going out to lunch that soon might attract attention (or at least elicit comment). Instead, I entered a bogus meeting on my calendar (marked public so anyone could see the entry), slipped my laptop computer into my shoulder bag, and called out to the floor that I was heading down to the fourth floor (where all the conference rooms were). Nobody even blinked … well, except for Britanny, who gave me a wave and a perky little smile that was actually endearing in its obvious sincerity. I felt guilty to be deceiving her.

When I left the building I went straight to an ATM and hauled out the daily maximum cash advance on every bank account and credit card I could. Thank God I'd been getting progressively more paranoid over the past year, and had spread my money across a half-dozen different accounts. I'm just sorry I didn't have the surreptitious wherewithal to be able to create accounts under an assumed name.

I didn't make out too badly with the cash, and had over five thousand dollars stuffed into various pockets when I was done. My next stop was Bergdorf's, where I bought my Grim Reaper Hallowe'en costume. I suppose I thought I was being clever, reckoning that anyone watching me would think I was preparing for a party, meanwhile, I would be well disguised when I made my break for it. Of course, now that I've had some time to think about it, Death-on-a-motorcycle is pretty conspicuous on something like a traffic video feed, and I figure this is how the Phasmatians managed to track me down to this general part of the state.

There was one last piece of business I wanted to attend to before disappearing. Don't ask me to explain it, but I felt I needed to talk to Sky Fisher. I found a reasonably quiet phone booth, and went to call him. That's when I realized I had left his direct phone number in the address book of my cellular phone, which was at that very moment sitting in an envelope and awaiting pick-up for a trip to Buffalo. I remember smiling at my own stupidity, and then simply looked up the number for the Church offices in the phone book, and dialed the main switchboard.

"Brad Evans for Sky Fisher," was all I needed to say. I had little doubt my call would be made a priority, and sure enough, within thirty seconds, Sky Fisher came on the line with his oiliest, most pretentiously nonchalant voice.

"Brad? What a pleasure to hear from you, old buddy. Where are you?" No "how are you?" pleasantries, I couldn't help but notice. Straight down to brass tacks.

"I'm in Atlanta," I lied. "I had to fly down for a client briefing on a big campaign." There was a pause. Although calls from phone booths don't typically have a caller ID, I knew there were plenty of ways to trace the location of the call. That was okay; I didn't plan to be on the phone long.

"Atlanta, eh?" Fisher replied calmly. "I love Atlanta. Great city. How's the weather?" He was clearly stalling for time.

"Cut the crap, Sky," I said. "We need to talk."

"Sure, pal. Always love to talk with you. What about?"

"Don't get smart with me, cocksucker. I know where all the skeletons are buried, remember?"

"And you signed a non-disclosure agreement. I'll sue you for every penny you have."

"Get real, *Lou.* I'm talking about stuff that'll put you in jail."

"What destroys me destroys Phasmatia. You won't let that happen, will you, Brad? That's why you had Stan make his little power play, isn't it? You wanted the Church to survive. Well, without me there is no Church."

I was running out of time. "Okay, listen, I'm willing to talk about this. Meet me tonight at nine o'clock at Macbeth's. You can bring Devon, but nobody else, and he stays ten feet away at all times. You can wear costumes... that way nobody will recognize you. But don't fuck with me. I've made a copy of what I have, and if you try anything at all, it's going straight into the mail."

"Listen, you piece of shit..." his angry voice started to say, but I didn't hear the rest. I hung up, and left the phone booth.

Jogging over to Lexington to catch the subway, I headed straight for Soho, where I bought the motorcycle, paying cash. Then I donned my Grim Reaper get-up, and left New York. I had never intended to be at Macbeth's that night, although I had no doubt Devon's killer monks would show up to look for me. By the time they had unmasked every costumed reveler in the place and deduced I wasn't coming, I'd be long gone.

***

Well, that's it. I've already told you the rest, about how I got out of the city, and came here to the country. There is one more detail I want to add. Perhaps you may be skeptical that I've been telling the truth, figuring I'm just some disgruntled whistleblower concocting this story in retaliation for a perceived personal grievance. You may even have read this and, still unconvinced, gone and Googled the facts surrounding Stan Shiu's accident. If the verdict is in by the time you read this, it will have told you that his death was ruled an accident. Perhaps the autopsy will reveal alcohol in Stan's system. There may be some other forensic evidence that points at a mechanical failure, or other contributing factor. You will look at the reports and say to yourself that there is absolutely no evidence that Sky Fisher and the Phasmatian Church had any involvement in Stan's death.

I'll only add some additional pieces of privileged information, by way of clarification. First of all, Stan Shiu hated to drive. Yes, he owned a car, and that's the one they found destroyed at the bottom of the cliffs in New Jersey. Stan's parents gave him the car as a graduation present, and he kept it in a rented garage a few blocks from his apartment. But in the nine-odd years I was Stan's friend, I never saw or heard of him driving it even once. I know all this because I'm the only one who used it. I didn't mind chauffeuring Stan around, on those rare occasions when he would actually ask me to—he was my friend, after all. But I also got free use of the car the rest of the time, and I'll admit I got more use out of it than Stan ever did. It was a sweet deal. It was also one of the ways that Stan and I were tied in a symbiotic relationship.

On that occasion when Fisher, Stan, and I drove up here to the trailer, and brainstormed the creation of Phasmatia, I was behind the wheel both ways—even though I was pretty stoned, and my ass would have been grass if the cops had pulled me over. Fisher had never questioned why I was the one driving, but he knew the car was Stan's. He knew it because it came up in conversation (but not that Stan never drove it), and that murderous prick knew exactly where it was kept parked because Stan later hooked Fisher up with a parking space in the very same garage. So, you see, it was easy for Fisher to direct his monks to get the car, and to stage the accident.

But there are two missing details that probably will not have surfaced in the coroner's inquest. Firstly, no car keys would have been recovered at the accident scene. The car must have been hotwired, or a master key used. I know this, because the only set of keys to the car were in *my* pocket. Secondly, so averse was Stan to operating the vehicle, he didn't even have a valid driver's license anymore. These are facts, and can be checked. So, you'll understand why I say unequivocally that there is no way in hell Stan got behind the wheel of that car and drove it to New Jersey, and off the road to his death. That's how I know he was murdered.

Now that's admittedly only circumstantial evidence, but presumably, if you're reading this, you've seen the main body of evidence as well—the evidence Stan and I managed to collect, and which hopefully I've managed to upload in addition to this written account. It feels very strange to be trying to peer into the future, to picture perfect strangers reading these words and to speculate on how successful I will be in my exposé. Only time will tell.

I've been stuck to the keyboard now more or less non-stop for the past day or so in an attempt to get this story finished. It's time for me to sign off. Tomorrow, Hannah returns from Albany, and hopefully together we can figure out how to get this account, and the couple of gigabytes of accompanying audio and video evidence incriminating Sky Fisher, onto the net.

When I powered off my laptop almost a week ago, I assumed I was done writing this account, but it turns out my story was not quite over yet.

Thursday morning, after sleeping in, and then fixing myself a hearty breakfast with the remains of my food supply, I collected up all my stuff in preparation for leaving the trailer for good. Given that I'd arrived with just one knapsack on my back, packing took all of five minutes, and since it would be evening before Hannah came driving in from Albany, I found myself with time on my hands.

At that point I hadn't been out of the trailer in a couple of days, but after my close call in Little Falls, I was too scared to take my motorcycle out for a ride in broad daylight. And as badly as I would have welcomed the warmth and hospitality of the van Vroonhoven farmhouse, I also didn't want to drop in on them too early, especially since I couldn't shake the guilty feeling I was placing the family in jeopardy whenever I was at their place.

In the end, I grabbed my borrowed deer rifle, threw on my orange hunter's cap, and decided to go for a hike in the woods.

It wasn't a great day for it—with concrete gray skies and a cold steady drizzle that felt like all it needed was a slight breath of north wind to turn to snow—but I figured it was better than moping in the trailer and sleeping the day away. Besides, despite my concerns about endangering the van Vroonhovens in their home, I was kind of hoping I might nevertheless happen to run into Andy on the trail.

The walk was thoroughly enjoyable at first, as I took in the musty smell of the wet woods in greedy gulps, but within an hour, I was completely soaked from the waist down. Although my leather jacket kept out the weather pretty well, it was relatively short, and rain had been dripping off the end of it and down my pant legs, plus I had been brushing up against wet bushes as I hiked along. The jeans I was wearing were my only pair of pants, so I decided I should get back to the trailer to try to dry them out before the sun went down.

A fog had rolled in and the drizzle had morphed outright into rain, and I was shivering by the time I wound my way back down the last part of the path towards the clearing where the trailer was parked. As claustrophobic as my refuge had felt when I'd started out on my hike, now I was looking forward to its toasty coziness. My thoughts were preoccupying me somewhat at that point, between dwelling on the past and wondering what the future held for me, and I was pretty much walking with my head down. I didn't even see the deer—I'm fairly sure it was that same beautiful big buck I'd spotted a week ago—until it blew right past, almost knocking me over as it bounded by, its brown eyes wide with fear.

Now, despite the lack of an actual hunting license or, in fact, any real experience, it dawned on me that I should try to kill the critter. Maybe it was the magical power of the DayGlo orange cap I was sporting, or perhaps, somewhere in my mind, I thought it might impress country-bred Hannah to know I was not some dandified New Yorker, and could in fact bring home meat for the larder. I raised my rifle to try to get a shot off, only to discover that I'd left the safety on. By the time I had figured that out, it was too late, and the deer had vanished into the mist.

I stood watching the spot where the animal had gone out of sight, and that's when it occurred to me that something down the trail must really have startled the buck in order for it to come tearing by me in such a state. And whatever that something was, it had to be in the proximity of the trailer. I assumed it was probably Andy, or perhaps some other hunter, who had jumped the deer, but because I didn't want them shooting at me by mistake, I crept slowly up towards the clearing. The noise of the falling raindrops plunking off the branches helped mask the sound of my own footsteps squishing on the wet leaves.

I was just about to call out when up ahead someone spoke, causing me to freeze in my tracks.

"Whoa, did you see the size of that sucker? It must have been an eight-pointer."

"Since when do you get points for deer?" another voice replied. "I thought you just stuck the head on a wall or something."

"I'll stick *your* heads on a wall if you don't shut up," a third voice growled, and that one nearly made me pee my pants. I recognized it instantly as Devon's.

"Aw c'mon, Dev... there ain't nobody here. Can we at least go back in the car where it's dry?" the original speaker whined.

"I always knew you army guys were wimps," Voice Number Two chided. "Afraid of a little rain."

"Screw you! At least I ain't no street punk. We were dressed for it then... besides, I was air cavalry. We rode in style."

"I said, shut up!" Devon hissed. "Someone *was* here. The heat's still on in the trailer."

"It's probably just some hunters using this place for a camp," Voice Number One suggested, although Devon's rebuke had apparently hit home, and he was now speaking in a lower voice.

I could barely hear him, and stood there paralyzed with indecision. The coward in me wanted to go tearing off into the woods, just like the deer had done. The angry man in me wanted to stand up and start shooting, although my proficiency with the rifle had proven to be suspect, so the coward was exercising his veto. Ironically, a passage I'd penned for The Sacred Text came to mind, and spurred me on. *Even the humblest of us is regularly given a chance to be brave. Seize courage whenever and however it is offered to you.*

That actually made me smile. I removed my hunting cap, which after all was designed to be highly visible, tucked it out of sight inside my jacket, and getting down into the mud, crawled closer. Water was soaking me from both sides but at this point I hardly cared. I got close enough to where I could see into the clearing where the trailer stood. There's a reason they go deer hunting in November—all the bushes and deciduous trees are stripped of leaves, and there's less cover for the critters. Fortunately, I was able to find a great spot behind a large fallen log with a clump of small fir trees in front that concealed me beautifully.

"What makes you think he'd come here?" Voice Number Two asked, and I could see it belonged to a gargantuan biker type with shoulder-length sandy hair. The dude appeared to be even bigger than Devon.

"Because this land belongs to Bishop Shiu's parents," Devon answered, "and the girl said Evans was staying next to her family's farm."

The girl? Were they saying that Hannah had betrayed me? Lying there in the mud, soaked to the skin and shivering with cold and terror, the thought made me feel like bursting into tears, and yet I couldn't bring myself to believe it. Nothing could convince me that I was really that stupid or naïve. True, I had never been a terrific judge of character, especially when it came to the opposite sex, but then I don't think many people really are—we have a tendency to base our opinions on appearances, or our expectations, or to pigeon-hole those we meet into stereotypes.

No, I was convinced—I knew in my heart—that Hannah would not have deliberately betrayed me. As corny as it sounds, when I had looked into that girl's eyes I felt like I had looked right into her soul, and had found nothing there that wasn't decent and wise. I guess you could call it faith. I did not know yet how Devon had found his way here, but I could not let myself believe it was because Hannah had deliberately sold me out.

As bad as I felt, the next thing I heard made things even worse. "So, do we go back and get rid of the farmer and his wife now?" Voice Number One piped in. I could see now he was a nasty-looking little brute with a shaved head and a mess of a nose that looked like it had been at the losing end of several altercations. You know that chillingly cold and dead-eyed look you see on the murderers' photos pinned up on the post office wall? Well, this guy had it, and I could just tell he liked to hurt people. From the tone in his voice, he was clearly itching to make Andy and Beatrix his next victims.

"No, we wait until the girl gets home tonight, and then we deal with them all at once," Devon said. "If we don't get Evans before then, he's bound to show up at the farm tonight to meet the girl." His gaze fell on the tarp that hid my motorcycle, and I found myself wishing everything was still covered in snow. I tried to will him to ignore it, but instead, Devon walked over and yanked off the tarp.

"Well, well, what have we here?" he said. The smile on his face reminded me of the one Stan had had that time Brandi took off her top.

The giant biker-type had meanwhile been peering through the door into the trailer. "Hey, there's some stuff on the floor here ... looks like a knapsack or something," he announced. In a blink, the mammoth monk expertly used his elbow to smash in the window of the trailer door, unlocked it from the inside, and yanked out my bag.

Devon bellowed like a bull and ran over to deliver a violent slap across the back of his minion's head. "You fucking moron, Todd! Who the hell told you to do that? Now anyone'll be able to spot that broken window a mile away. Can't you see Evans' motorcycle is still here? That means he's probably out in the woods or something."

Todd seemed unfazed by the blow, and began ripping open my knapsack. "Hey, there's a computer in here," he said with a child's glee.

That got Devon's interest, and he snatched my PC. "The girl's email said he had a bunch of data he wanted to upload. Maybe we lucked out and it's all on here." He pensively surveyed the surrounding woods, and for an instant I was convinced his gaze had fallen on me. I fought hard not to flinch, or make any movement that would catch his eye. Devon's attention returned to his henchman. He violently yanked Todd by his long hair and jerked his head towards a spot not forty yards from me.

"Tell ya what you're gonna to do, Shit-For-Brains...you're gonna go hide there behind that tree in case Evans shows up. And whatever you do, don't kill him...we need to talk to him."

Todd did not find this idea appealing whatsoever. "You want me to go sit around in *this* rain?...Aw, Dev, ya gotta be kiddin'. Can't I just wait in the trailer and ambush him when he shows up?"

"Now who's a wimp?" the little shaved-head psychopath with the broken nose sneered.

"No, you can't wait in the trailer," Devon replied in a mocking voice, "because you're the one who broke the fucking window. As soon as Evans sees it, he'll bolt. I want you waiting outside where you can see him coming, and where you can nail him if he tries to run for it. Shoot him in the leg if you have to, *but don't kill him!* Got it?"

Todd muttered a string of expletives but obeyed, plunging through the brush until he reached the tree. I cautiously turned my head to track him, and watched as he wrapped himself up in his black leather trench coat, and plunked down out of sight.

"Let's get back to the house," Devon told the remaining monk. "You fucking guys are all trigger happy … call Jimmy and make it crystal clear I don't want him hurting the farmer or his wife before we get there."

I watched until their car pulled out, then lay my head down in the mud and weighed my options. As cold, wet, and miserable as I felt, I wanted nothing more than to lie there, almost wishing the mud would swallow me up. It seemed hopeless. Devon had my laptop, and with it all the incriminating evidence we'd collected on Sky Fisher. There were four killers on the loose, and they held Andy and Beatrix—simple, decent people who had extended me their friendship and hospitality, and had never harmed a soul in their life. Devon would certainly kill them, and Hannah too, whether she had willingly cooperated with the Phasmatians or not.

I replayed the monks' conversation in my head and considered what little I knew about Hannah having betrayed me. In some respects, the evidence was damning —they'd clearly learned from her exactly where I was, and that I had incriminating data to upload—but I still could not bring myself to pronounce her guilty. Again, I was reminded of a passage I'd penned in The Sacred Text. Although I had really only been ripping off the Bible's "judge not, lest ye yourself be judged" pronouncement, I had naturally had to reword it (so as not to make the plagiarism too obvious). I had ended up with: *Judge not in haste nor in ignorance. Mercy and prudence are the way towards the Light, not rage and blind impulse.*

Maybe Hannah had done it under duress, to save her hostage parents. No, that didn't make sense … there would have been no way for them to know about Andy and Beatrix beforehand

unless Hannah herself had directed them there. Devon had mentioned something about an email, though. It seemed logical she
might have emailed someone who was being spied on by the
Phasmatians—someone they considered a potential threat—and
her message had been intercepted. She *had* said she was going to
see about finding someone for me to send my exposé to, after all.

Although that nifty little piece of rationalization made my
achy-breaky heart feel somewhat better, it did nothing for the
miserable, rain-soaked, mud-covered rest of me. There was the
matter of some murderous monks that had to be dealt with first,
and the first of them, a giant of a man in his own right, was sitting only a few dozen yards away from me.

Seeing as my head was already bowed more or less, I prayed.
When I found I was asking the Lord for a way to let me kill Todd,
I balked a bit. *Geez, Louise, Brad,* I told myself, *you can't ask the
Judeo-Christian God—the God of "Thou shalt not kill" and "Turn the
other cheek"—to help you murder someone.* But I had been down that
road before, back when I was writing the tenets of Phasmatia.
The laws of the land allowed it, and the laws of Nature afforded
all creatures the right, so killing in self-preservation had to be
kosher. It was only logical—and I had taken great pride in making sure Phasmatian dogma always rang true.

Do it to save yourself, the Lord told me. *Do it to save Hannah.
Save the woman you love. Try not to kill him if you can, but if he attacks
you, nail the bastard.* Of course God didn't speak to me directly in
so many words. There was no burning bush (as much as I would
have welcomed the heat) or a booming John Huston-like voice,
but I knew, clearly and profoundly, that I *had* to act. I certainly
do believe God gave us the greatest gift of all—free will. It must
sadden Him terribly when we use it to do the wrong things. To
my mind, however, what I was about to do was not one of those.

Slowly, an inch at a time, I started crawling towards the tree
where Todd was waiting in ambush for me. As I painstakingly
inched along, I made sure I kept my deer rifle out of the mud.

The raindrops continued to splash all around me, and as miserably sodden as I was, I was thankful it was not a crisp, sunny day, when every rustling of the leaves would be heard clearly. Eventually I got close enough to see Todd's position. He was hunkered down with his back to the tree, and periodically glanced over his shoulder to check out the trailer, and its smashed window.

After another eternity, I worked my way around to where I had the best angle of attack, just slightly behind his off shoulder. Slowly I released the safety, and took a bead on him. Then I paused. Of course, he had to be armed, and we were for all intents and purposes combatants in a war—one I hadn't started, and in which I was acting in self-defense—but I couldn't bring myself to just pull the trigger and shoot him without warning. And hadn't Devon specifically instructed him not to kill me?

Silently cursing myself for a fool, I called out, "I've got you covered. Drop it!" I fully expected Todd to freeze and put his hands up, and in fact was already figuring out what the hell I was going to tie him up with, when the bastard leapt to his feet, whipped out this big-ass handgun, and fired a couple of rounds wildly in my general direction. It only took one shot to drop him, but then he was a huge target.

My bullet caught him at the base of the throat, and he was just lying there, with blood and air gurgling out. He looked up at me as I approached, and his wide-open eyes had that same exact frightened look I'd seen on the deer earlier, pleading with me not to let him die. I pulled out the orange hunter's cap I'd hidden in my jacket, and tried to stuff it into the wound as best I could. Then, not knowing what else to do, I started praying for forgiveness... for us both. A look came into Todd's eyes, somewhere between acceptance and gratitude, and then he died.

I'd never killed anything above the size of a squirrel before, let alone another human being, and as good as it was to be the one still alive, I suddenly became sick to my stomach. I crawled off to the side and hurled up the better part of the big breakfast

I'd made myself earlier, and afterwards found a pool of relatively clean rainwater and drank my fill.

Once my composure had been restored, I went through Todd's pockets. I took his gun, and a spare ammo clip I found stuck in his belt, but left his wallet, including $2K in hundred-dollar bills he had stuffed inside. (Don't ask me why, after I had just killed the man, I thought it was wrong to take his money.) Finally, although it was way too big for me, I put on his black leather trench coat, grateful for the extra warmth and protection it offered. I took one last look at the trailer, my sanctuary for the last week, and turned my back on it. There was nothing left for me there. The time for hiding was over.

I'll be honest, I had this brief fantastic vision of me riding in on my motorcycle, black leather jacket flapping behind me, with guns blazing. Aside from the tactical impracticality of such a frontal assault, I soon remembered that the keys to the motorcycle were hooked onto my knapsack … which meant that Devon now had them, in addition to my laptop. I was going to have to hike to the farmhouse … which was actually a good thing because it gave me a chance to try to work out a proper plan of action.

I'd walked about a quarter mile when suddenly I felt a tingling on the inside of the trench coat. In there was a small pocket I'd overlooked, holding a cellphone. When I fished it out and read the screen, there was a text message from Devon. It read: *In position at farm. Waiting for girl. Any sign of Evans?*

I thanked God that Devon hadn't phoned, because there was no way I could have imitated Todd's husky voice, but then I realized it had nothing to do with divine intervention. Todd had been lying in ambush for me, after all. It would have been too risky to phone him, and possibly give away his position. As I replied with a simple *No*, I contemplated how I could potentially use the text messaging to my advantage. I also wondered how long it would be before Devon recalled Todd from his post.

The text message had given me one piece of additional relevant information—Hannah had not arrived from Albany yet. I looked at my watch. That made perfect sense. The sun was just starting to dip behind the trees, and although I didn't know precisely at what time she'd be heading out after school, it was highly unlikely she would get here until after dark.

That still left a number of tactical decisions, the foremost being whether I should try to rescue Andy and Beatrix before their daughter got there. Yes, I decided. There was no point placing a third innocent party in jeopardy, especially one I held so dearly in my heart (any possible complicity on her part notwithstanding). Of course, that still left the not-so-trivial matter of how exactly I was going to take out three armed, experienced, and dangerous thugs. I wracked my brain, with nothing more than the plots from Hollywood action flicks to use as a source of ideas, but by the time I had hiked to the farmhouse I still had no definitive plan of attack.

Even though dusk had settled in, there were no lights on in the house, and I hovered at the edge of the woods trying to get a sense of where the three monks were positioned, and where they might be keeping their hostages. Although in all probability they were keeping a lookout at the front of the house, which faced the driveway leading to the main road, on the off chance someone might be watching the back window I opted to wait until it was completely dark before trying to get a look inside.

As I stared at the building, there was a brief moment of light inside as someone lit up a cigarette, and through the window I saw a glimpse of Andy and Beatrix sitting in chairs. There was one monk, the one who had lit up his smoke, standing behind them, and before the light went out, I was able to clearly discern a gun in his hand. The two farmers did not appear to be tied up, though, and were holding on to one another. Unfortunately, I had no idea where the other two abductors were standing. However, the momentary spark of light had given me an idea. If I texted Devon, perhaps I'd be able to spot the glow from his cellphone when he answered. Then I got an even better notion.

Shielding Todd's phone inside my borrowed trench coat, I composed my message. I was shivering badly by now, as the setting sun seemed to take every last joule of warmth with it, and I was having difficulty making my numbed fingers work. Finally I had managed to type out: *Got Evans. Come pick us up.* I pushed the Send key, then waited and watched.

Unfortunately, there was no telltale glow visible inside, so I still had no idea where Devon was standing, and in fact nothing seemed to happen at all. Suddenly the phone in my hands rang—its Ipso Fatso rock 'n' roll ring tone playing so loudly I was convinced they had to be able to hear it inside—and I almost jumped out of my soggy skin. Pressing the offending device hard against my stomach, I wrapped the coat over it, and prayed for the sound to stop, chiding my own stupidity the whole time. Idiot! If Todd had captured me, there was no longer a need to communicate silently via text messages.

The ringing stopped and I held my breath. A minute or so later, there was the sound of a door slamming on the far side of the house and two silhouetted figures came jogging around the side. I was so convinced I had given away my position and was about to be attacked that I raised the handgun I'd taken off Todd and starting fumbling with its safety in the dark. Instead of coming at me, however, the duo veered off to the left and ran into the barn.

In a few seconds, I heard a car engine start up, and the beam from its headlights came flying out and swiveled off towards the driveway. The monks must have parked their SUV in there to keep the vehicle out of sight. It looked to me that not answering the phone call had alarmed them, enough so that reinforcements were racing back to the trailer. In the darkness, I had not been able to discern which two, exactly, had gone driving off, and I found myself praying Devon was one of them. Regardless, that left only one guard inside to be dealt with. Plus, I appeared to still have the element of surprise on my side.

It was completely dark by now, and I knew the moment had come to act. This time I had the presence of mind to turn off the cellphone before I crept up to the house and peered cautiously through the window. Even though my eyes were getting accustomed to the absence of light, I still couldn't see anything inside … that is until, off to the right, I spotted a glowing cigarette ember being raised up and down a couple of times before falling straight downwards and fading out. I cursed the callous bastard. With murder and kidnapping on the monks' rap sheets, I don't know why it should have bothered me so to see a cigarette being crushed out on the ground, but I knew Beatrix took pride in keeping a clean house and I hated to see her pine plank floor being abused like that.

The window I was peering into belonged to the front parlor (as the van Vroonhovens had called it) so, recalling the layout of the farmhouse, I snuck around to the back door that led to the kitchen. Slowly, half an inch at a time, I opened its screen door, paranoid the sound of squeaking hinges might give me away and force me to bolt back into the woods. I needn't have worried. The hinges were kept immaculately oiled, which, given what I had come to know of Andy, was no surprise.

Next, I felt for the knob and turned it. The kitchen door swung open easily and silently. It, of course, was not locked. Here in the country they had no crime to worry about—unless you count the occasional invasion of murderous Phasmatian henchmen. My heart was pounding heavily, and I found I was grinding my teeth badly, so I took a couple of deep restorative breaths and practiced a calming exercise from The Sacred Text, which I'd lifted straight from the Upanishads.

I lowered myself to my knees and started to crawl across the floor, but had to stop after a couple of yards because I was getting tangled up in Todd's big overcoat, plus, it was making these noticeable creaking noises when I moved. So I stopped and wiggled out of the coat, and then once more started moving on hands and knees forward into the darkness, where memory told me a swinging door led out to the parlor. However, a new problem soon arose. I was holding that huge fucking pistol of Todd's in one hand, and it made crawling along rather awkward whenever I switched my weight to that side, especially since I was holding the gun up so it wouldn't bang against the ceramic tiles of the kitchen floor. Finally I stopped and stuck the pistol into the back of my waistband, where I felt the cold barrel nestle into the crack in my butt. I distinctly remember debating whether to put the safety on or off, and settled for off. As much as I preferred not to blow myself a new asshole, I wanted to be ready for action.

With both my hands free, crawling was much easier, and I soon reached the door to the parlor. On the other side, somewhere very close by, stood the man I had to incapacitate—but I had no idea how I was going to accomplish that. Flinging the door open for a full frontal assault seemed foolhardy, especially since I did not know exactly where my prospective victim was standing. Besides, even if I managed to pounce accurately, I had no confidence I would triumph in a hand-to-hand struggle in the dark. Furthermore, if any shooting broke out, there was a chance Andy or Beatrix could get hit in the exchange.

Even though time was working against me, I opted to continue a slow crawl towards the monk. Stealth and caution had gotten me this far. And as much as The Sacred Text has symbolically railed against it, here darkness was my ally. My plan was simply to get close enough undetected that I could stick my gun into the thug's side and order him to drop his weapon.

I took a deep breath, ever so slowly opened the door just a crack, and peeked in. Although I hadn't been able to see a damned thing when I'd looked through the window earlier, now

I could actually identify some fuzzy shapes within the room. I guess my eyes had acclimated to the darkness, and they were aided by one subtle source of light—a dying ember amidst the ashes in the fireplace.

I pushed the door open a little further and stuck my head out into the room. The monk's silhouette just stood there unmoving, like some black statue. Now I ever so tenuously worked my shoulders through the gap. I waited a second, and then crawled forward another inch.

Beneath me, one of the old floorboards gave the slightest of creaks, and I saw the monk's head swivel in the direction of the sound. I froze and held my breath, preparing to make a grab for the gun in my waistband if I detected any alarm. I could just make out the outline of the monk's head, craning to try to catch any additional sounds, and I was thankful the slight glow from the fireplace was backlighting him. Surely, with complete blackness behind me, and being down low on my knees, I was invisible.

The tension of the moment was shattered when Andy spoke up, addressing his captor. "Listen, mister. It's getting cold in here. Why don't you let me put on a fire."

The monk's head whipped back in Andy's direction. "Don't move. Just shut up and sit there like you were told," the Phasmatian commanded. I didn't recognize his voice, confirming my belief that this was Jimmy, the fourth monk who'd been guarding the couple all along.

"Damn you. My wife's getting cold … can't you see she's shivering?"

"It's alright, dear. You needn't worry about me … I'll be fine," Beatrix said.

"It's *not* alright," said Andy, still defiant. "I don't see why we shouldn't have a fire. It's bad enough we have to sit here in the total darkness while this madman points his gun at us, but there's not a single reason I can think of why we have to freeze to death."

Jimmy took a step forward. "I said shut up and don't move. You heard the boss. No fire—those were his orders."

"No they weren't! He said no lights. That's not the same thing. I'm sure he'll welcome a warm fire too when he comes back in from out of the rain."

"Yeah, well, a fire gives off light, don't it? So I say no fire, and that's that. Now, not another word out of you, or I'll crack open the old biddy's skull."

I took advantage of the verbal exchange to inch closer to the gunman, keeping my body as low as possible, with my weight widely distributed to try to avoid any further creaking of the floorboards. I was maybe two yards away when the talking stopped, and again I halted. I could see Jimmy's legs within striking distance now, and debated whether to try to lunge forward and tackle him. I'd never really had a good look at this particular thug, and although from my worm's-eye view he didn't look nearly in the same weight class as Devon or the late Todd, that didn't mean he'd be a pushover. Killer monks were not recruited for their winning personalities, after all.

Supporting my weight with my one arm, I reached around my back to retrieve the gun. It was a painstaking operation. I was close enough to hear Jimmy's breathing, which meant that any sound I made would be equally audible. My wet clothes pulled at me as I moved, and I was convinced the next move I made would be the one to give me away. I doubt if you can imagine just how difficult this was for me, and I know my words can't begin to do justice to the mixture of terror and concentration pounding in my brain. I was in agony from the tension of holding my body still and keeping my breath silent, while making the slow, tiny, controlled movements towards my goal.

By the time I had my hand on the pistol grip I was at the limits of my endurance. *Fuck it,* I thought, *I'll just shoot the bastard,* but still I lay there shaking and straining, trying to get up the nerve, and the stomach, to gun the man down in cold blood.

Although I'd learned my lesson with Todd and knew Jimmy was unlikely to surrender either (plus, there were Andy and Beatrix to consider), still something was holding me back—conscience or cowardice, take your pick.

Abruptly Jimmy's cellphone chirped, and I tensed up, realizing I had to hold still a little longer.

"Yo," he answered, and stood there listening. I was certain it was a call from Devon, and was guessing that, even in the dark, they had located Todd's body, and now knew I was still at large.

"Shit," Jimmy exclaimed at one point, his tone a mixture of sadness and anger, and my theory was confirmed. "Naw...no sign of him here." There were a few more words spoken at the other end, and Jimmy concluded with, "Okay, see you then," and flipped his phone closed.

And then, before I had a chance to make a move, Jimmy unexpectedly spun on his heels, took two steps towards the kitchen, and tripped over me. The collision certainly caught me off guard, but I was nowhere as surprised as Jimmy, and I heard a grunt of dismay as he crashed to the floor. Immediately I yanked out my gun, rolled over, stuck the barrel into the middle of the dark shape lying next to me, and screamed at the top of my lungs, "Freeze, scumbag, or I'll shoot you!"

Jimmy did not, in fact, freeze. I don't know what it is about those Phasmatian thugs that makes them want to fight to the end...maybe it's in their job description, or they all have a death wish or something. Probably they're just not afraid of a wimp like me. Instead of surrendering, Jimmy's elbow came out of the darkness and caught me in the side of the head. A searing pain went through my skull, but I kept my grip on the gun and managed to pull the trigger. In the light from the gun flash I could see a splatter of leather and blood as part of Jimmy's bicep exploded.

In the ensuing dark, I could hear Jimmy moaning and cursing, and for good measure I aimed in the vicinity of his head and pistol whipped him four or five times. "Andy, Beatrix ... it's me, Brad. Get the lights!" I called out. I was still pretty scared, mainly because I had no idea where Jimmy's gun was, and was paranoid he was about to plug me.

Light filled the room, and although the unfamiliar brightness added to the pain in my head and my dizziness, I was relieved to see Jimmy balled up on the floor, clutching his wounded arm and with his head lolled back and eyes closed. His pistol was on the ground next to him, and I struggled to my feet and scrambled over to grab it before he came to his senses.

Two pairs of arms suddenly wrapped themselves around me as I was enveloped by the van Vroonhovens. "Oh, Brad ... they said they'd captured you. We were so worried about you," Beatrix said. It was typical of that good-hearted woman that, even though she'd been a prisoner in deathly peril herself, and it was my fault, she was more concerned about me.

"It was a trick," I explained, "so I could come and rescue you."

Andy said nothing, but he gave an approving nod, and there was a tight-lipped smile on his face. Then he looked down at Jimmy on the floor and his smile disappeared. First he spit on the prone monk, and then he said to his wife, "Mother, this man's badly hurt. Get the first aid kit."

"Look, Andy, those other two killers are probably on their way back here right now," I protested.

Andy placed a hand on my shoulder, and I swear I could feel his calmness radiate into my body. "Beatrix will tend to the wounded man. You and I will take care of the rest." He went across the living room, fished some keys from out of his pocket, and unlocked an ornate wooden cabinet that stood in the corner. I saw that it was where he stored his firearms, and watched as he hauled out a couple of shotguns, and his own deer rifle.

He looked at me, standing there with a pistol in each hand like some B-movie tough guy. "Sorry. I left your other rifle out back," I said.

He nodded, as if it was the most natural thing in the world, and handed me the shotgun. "Better hang on to those handguns for the sheriff. You'll find this a lot handier in a scuffle anyway. There's a box of shells over there in the bottom of the cupboard. Then go and lock the door and pull all the blinds so they can't see in."

"Wouldn't it be better to just turn the lights off?"

"What? And risk you and me shooting each other in the dark? No, if they come smashing in through a window or something, I want to have a good target. Besides, Beatrix will need to keep an eye on *that* one. I'm going into the kitchen to call the sheriff. He'll put an end to this nonsense."

I felt a lump materialize in my throat and grabbed Andy by the arm. "Are you sure about that? I mean, the Phasmatians have all sorts of people in their pockets—I've seen it with my own eyes—and I just don't trust any cops."

Andy frowned and shook his head. "Son, this ain't New York City. I've known Sheriff Gus Martinssen my whole life, and he sits in front of me in church every Sunday. Now, I don't rightly know if he truly believes in God, but I sure as hell know he don't believe in no Phasmatian mumbo jumbo. And I ain't never heard once of him taking no bribe. We can trust him, and that's a fact."

It was really something else that was bothering me, and I had to come clean. "The truth is, Andy, I ... I killed one of them, back at the trailer."

"Well? Was it self-defense?"

"Yeah, I swear to God. The bastard tried to shoot me."

"Well then, it seems to me you're better off taking your chances with Sheriff Martinssen than trying to face that bunch of luna-tics alone. You say you want the world to know the truth about that Fisher guy ... well, I reckon this is as good a way as any to start, especially since we have to explain all this shooting and goings on anyway. Now quit your jawin' before those bad guys show up and plug us through the window where we stand. Let's lock up, hunker down, and wait for the cavalry."

Beatrix came back into the room carrying a towel, ice pack, scissors, and a small wicker basket. As she approached Jimmy, who was still lying on the floor with his eyes closed, Andy counseled her, "Best be careful of that one, Mother... he might be playing possum."

"Just let him try something," Beatrix said, brandishing the scissors like a dagger. "I'd sure like a chance to show this no-good so-and-so just what I think of him pointing a gun at me and holding me prisoner in my own house. I'd teach him a thing or two, believe you me."

Jimmy did in fact open his eyes at hearing that, but took one look at the scissors and the determined face behind them, and did not try anything. He meekly allowed Beatrix to prop him up and help him out of his leather trench coat so she could bandage up his arm. Still, I made a point of letting him have a good look at the shotgun in my hand, which I kept pointed in the general vicinity of his crotch the whole time I went about pulling down all the blinds. Finally, I locked the front door, and then, for good measure, pulled an end table in front of it, and stacked a couple of chairs on top of that.

Andy came back into the room shaking his head. "Gus and both his deputies are clear over the side of the county... some kind of a big explosion and fire going on over there, or some such catastrophe. No ambulance available either. The dispatch gal said she'd call it in, but couldn't say for sure how long they'd be."

The concern on my face must have been blatant. Despite my initial misgivings, I'd actually warmed up to the idea of the sheriff's help. Now it appeared we might have to face Devon by ourselves after all, and the paranoiac in me wasn't so sure that fire demanding the sheriff's attention was just a coincidence.

Andy had been thinking along the same lines. "I reckon we'd best turn down the lights after all ... maybe keep one candle goin' so we can see who's at the other end of the rifle barrel. And open up the front door." He noticed for the first time the impromptu barricade I'd erected in front of the door, and despite the tenseness of the situation actually chuckled. "That was a good idea, blocking the door like that, but now it seems to me we'd better let them walk right in, and see if we can't surprise them ... you know, instead of letting them see we're on the loose in here, and maybe ending up getting caught in a fire of our own."

He went over to his wife and gave her a kiss—not a little peck on the cheek, but a full-blown kiss on the lips. "Here, Mother," he said, handing her his deer rifle and retaining the other shotgun for himself. "I'll feel better knowing you have this." The thought occurred to me that, tactically speaking, she'd be better off with the shotgun, which depended a little less on accuracy, but I didn't want to openly question Andy's decision.

I must say I was inspired by the unflappable pluck of the man. Here was a simple, peace-loving man who'd dedicated his life to raising crops and children. Despite the fact he'd suddenly found himself involved in kidnapping and mayhem, and was now preparing to face gun-toting murderers, he was going about his business as calmly as if he was heading out to plow the fields. It was living proof that grace comes from within.

I remembered what he had told me about faith during our first dinner conversation. Andy believed that many people took up religion in the hope of gaining some advantage in life from their devotion. If their prayers weren't answered, or they felt themselves getting the short end of the cosmic stick, their faith wavered. "Now, me, I'm a farmer," Andy had explained, "and that's a blessing and a curse in its own right. I don't pretend to know God's divine plan, so I don't go blaming him for every hailstorm or infestation that destroys my crops. Then again, I don't really believe priests know God's divine plan either, so I always take anything the preacher orders me to do with a grain of salt too. In the end, all I know is we got to be good, we got to be strong, and we got to hang on to our faith."

So, hunkered down behind a couch, facing the prospect of my death for what seemed like the nth time that day, I fought hard to sustain the newfound faith that had been flickering inside of me. But I didn't want to confront God, whoever She or He might be, as a quivering coward begging for his life, and failing that, his soul. So, instead, I prayed for strength. I prayed for grace. I prayed that no innocent people would suffer because of what I had done, or might yet do.

Off in the corner, Jimmy moaned and said, "Man, it hurts like hell. I need a doctor." After bandaging his wound, Beatrix had made him crawl into a far corner, and had used the rest of the medical tape to bind his ankles and wrists before covering him up with his black leather trench coat. Now she sat between Andy and me, clutching the rifle, and I had little doubt she was prepared to use it. Still, when the wounded man complained, even in the dim candlelight I could make out the soft look of compassion that came onto her face.

"Be quiet," I hissed at Jimmy, "and we'll make sure you get help soon. But if you try to warn your pals when they walk through that door, I'll make sure you're the first to go." The monk fell silent, short of an occasional grunt of pain. Shoot a man once, and he has plenty of reason to believe you'll do it again.

It seemed like an eternity, but finally we heard tires crunching the gravel of the van Vroonhovens' driveway, and the arc from a set of headlights swept across the inside of the window blinds before going black.

"Make sure they're both inside the door before calling out. Don't shoot... give 'em a chance to surrender first," Andy whispered, and I could sense the strain in his voice. Something told me that Devon, of all people, wouldn't go quietly, and there'd be shotgun blasts, and two more dead monks splattered across poor Beatrix's living room wall before it was over, but I held my tongue.

The door started to open and I tensed.

"Mama? Papa?" a voice called out, and Hannah stepped into the room.

"Don't shoot!" I shouted in alarm, and suddenly from behind her a black-leather-clad arm wrapped itself around her neck, and then I could see Devon there, bringing his pistol to Hannah's head.

"That's right, don't shoot" he said, grinning like a maniac, "or I'll blow blondie's brains out." He pushed a little further into the room, making sure Hannah was shielding him, and surveyed the three of us behind our chesterfield fort, with our guns all pointed at him.

"Hello, Brad," he said affably. "Man, you've led us on one hell of a chase."

"Let her go," I said.

"Yeah, right, so you can plug me like you did Todd? I got a better idea. You put your guns down, and I'll let girlie here live."

"Like you let Stan live?" I countered. "Give it up, Devon. It's over. The police are on their way."

Devon's grin grew wider. "I don't think so. The cops are a little … preoccupied at the moment, and we planted enough little surprises to keep them busy for quite a while yet."

Off in the corner Jimmy groaned again, and Devon seemed to notice him for the first time. His smile vanished, and he tightened his grip around Hannah's neck.

"You've turned into one royal pain in the ass, Brad. Well, it ends here. I'm not fucking around with you anymore. Come with me, *now*, and I'll let the rest of these people live. Otherwise, what happens will all be on your head."

Something had been bothering me through the whole exchange (I mean other than the fact death was staring me in the face and a girl I was fond of had a gun to her head). I had this feeling something else was going on—that Devon had some kind of trick up his sleeve. Then, behind us at the door leading to the kitchen, a floorboard creaked, and I suddenly realized too late we hadn't yet laid eyes on Devon's other henchman, the broken-nosed little sadist I'd seen back at the trailer. He'd been sneaking up on us from the rear the whole time.

Two gun blasts in quick succession shook the room as I whirled around in a panic. I was just in time to see the crazed little monk collapse to the floor, a gun in his hand and a strange surprised look on his face. Although it was dim and the black of his outfit masked the bloody mess somewhat, I could see the entire front of him had been blown away by a shotgun blast.

I spun my head back towards the front door, and Devon wasn't there anymore. At least he wasn't standing there holding Hannah. She was looking down in anger, and I could see Devon had been shot dead, a gaping mess of a bullet hole square in the center of his forehead.

I don't really remember much after that, except that I ran over and took Hannah in my arms, and we clung to each other tight, and trembled, until the sheriff arrived almost an hour later. It wasn't until after I'd given the sheriff my statement that I found out exactly what had happened. Andy, more familiar with the sounds of his own house than I was, had also heard the little monk sneaking in through the kitchen and had let him have it with both barrels the instant he stepped into the room with gun raised. That was hardly the surprising bit. At that same moment Hannah had kicked Devon in the shin with all her might. The big monk had jerked backwards in pain and Beatrix, the sweet, good-humored farm wife, had taken him out with a pinpoint head shot a SWAT sniper would have been proud of.

I think the sheriff must have relished the shock on my face when he told me this. "I guess that big fella picked on the wrong mother's daughter," he chuckled.

"I can't believe she took a chance like that," I said. "She might have hit Hannah."

"Who? Beatrix? Hell, they say that woman can take a squirrel's eye out at fifty yards. Grew up the only girl in a family of six kids over in Schoharie County, you know. Her daddy was mad about hunting, and she had a gun in her hand by the time she was six." We both glanced across the room to where Beatrix was serving coffee and pie to some deputies and state troopers. "You'd never know it to look at her, would you?" the sheriff mused. "You know what she told me?"

"What's that?"

"That she knew God was guiding her hand."

Now there was a conundrum worthy of any religious text.

"Andy tells me you're a church-going man, sheriff," I said. "Do you believe that? Do you think God would help one person kill another?"

"I may go to church on Sunday, but I go to work every day, and even out here in the sticks I've seen some bloody awful things. But I've also seen some pretty damned wonderful things too ... some might even call them miracles. I guess I like to think that if God was going to choose, he'd land on the side of someone decent, like Beatrix."

He got up and put a hand on my shoulder. "Bloody mess, this was, bloody mess. I know the D.A. is going to want to talk to you, but I believe your story and I figure he will too. Man, I sure hope that evidence you have is as good as you say it is. I'd like to see that Fisher fellow pay for all this. I'll bet he's sitting by the phone waiting to hear they've done you in. What I wouldn't give to see his face when he finds out it's all gone south."

That gave me an idea. "Then why don't we tell him?"

"What do you mean?"

"Do you have Devon's cellphone? I bet he's got Fisher on speed dial. I'd love to give the bastard a call and tell him personally to go fuck himself."

"I dunno ... technically that phone's evidence."

"Then let's use it for some *real* evidence ... I'll put him on speaker, you can turn on that pocket recorder of yours, and maybe we can get him to say something incriminating."

I hope I don't get the sheriff in trouble by writing this, but he grinned and agreed. I took Devon's cellphone and scrolled through its directory, but Fisher's name was not there. I frowned and almost handed the phone back, then I had a thought and checked again. Sure enough, there was an entry for "Big Fish." I dialed the number and hit the key to switch it to the phone's speaker. The sheriff turned on his recorder and pressed his head up close to mine.

Fisher picked up on the third ring. "It's about fucking time, Devon. Tell me that pain in the ass has been dealt with once and for all."

"No," I answered, trying my best to imitate Devon's bass tone. The long pause told me my ruse had failed.

"Brad? Is that you?" Fisher asked. I swear he almost sounded happy to hear me.

"Yup ... your favorite pain in the ass."

"Where's Devon?"

"Dead, along with all his posse. Actually, that's not quite accurate. One of them ... Jimmy ... he's shot up, but alive."

"I don't believe you."

"I'm calling on his phone, aren't I?"

"True, but you may have just stolen the phone from him somehow. I find it hard to believe you single-handedly took out all my men."

"I don't give a flying fuck what you believe ... you can read all about it in tomorrow's news."

"Do you think it ends here? There are plenty more hired guns where those came from. You can't stop me, Brad. I *will* find you. I did it once, and I'll do it again. That stupid school teacher friend of yours thought she could contact her congressman for help, but we were secretly watching his email. You see, the Church is everywhere."

"Surely you must know by now it won't be as easy with me as it was with Stan. Why'd you do it anyway, Sky? Why'd you have to kill him?"

"You know damned well why. Did you really think I was going to let that little gook geek take my church away from me? He had to die."

"It was his church—and my church—as much as yours."

"Do you really believe that? You two were never anything more than pawns. Oh, you were useful—very useful at times—but this was *my* destiny, Brad, not yours. Everything that has happened was pre-ordained. I am The Chosen One, and the world has not yet begun to feel my might. You ... you're an insect, and just like a puny insect, I will swat you. No, that's too good for you ... too quick. The next monks I'm sending after you will have orders to make you suffer, *really* suffer, before they kill you."

"'Fear not the power of the tyrant, for he can only harm the vessel. Only you alone can extinguish the divine light that burns within you,'" I quoted. "Recognize that, Sky? No, probably not ... you were always too busy selling the scripture, or smacking down people with it, to really read it. Well, you're about to find out that the bite from the wrong insect can kill you. See you in court, you evil, twisted, murderous bastard."

My hand was trembling as I pressed the End button. I looked over at the sheriff. "How'd I do?"

He nodded reassuringly. "That was good ... real good. I'm not saying I didn't believe you before, but there's no doubt in my mind now. And the D.A. is absolutely going to love it."

He got up and put a hand on my shoulder. "C'mon, son, it's time to go."

I blanched. "You're not putting me in jail after what you just heard?"

He chuckled and shook his head. "No. Like I said, I believe

you. But you're a material witness now, and from the sound of things, there's going to be more people coming after you. We're going to find you someplace safe, where the law can guard you around the clock."

And that they did. In fact, given that the interest in the case ran all the way up to the federal level, I have several U.S. marshals outside my door as I write this. (I'm not allowed to tell you how many, or where I am.) I was able to convince the sheriff to let me keep my laptop, though—after I burned him a copy of all the evidence Stan and I had collected. The best part is that, unlike the Shius' trailer, my current hiding spot has a high-speed internet connection. No, wait, that's not true. It's the second-best part. The *best* part is that Hannah is also here under witness protection, and I get to see her every day. I've got to tell you, that woman is really growing on me. It's too early to tell, and certainly not the best circumstances for some good old-fashioned courting, but who knows? Maybe, in time, and once all this is behind us, we might even get married in that little Protestant church in her home town, and take over Andy's farm.

Well, that's it. Despite how things ended up, I'm finally putting this out onto the web anyway. I may have started writing this for my life, but now I feel I have to publish it for my soul. I have a good feeling, call it faith, it will be read and believed.

But before I click the Upload button, I leave you with this final entreaty. If you are one of the many people who have found in Phasmatia something that was previously missing from your spiritual life, please do not give up your faith because of what you read here. I know that's asking a lot, especially given who's doing the asking. I can just see you now, screaming at your computer, and calling me a fraud. And what else can I say but "guilty as charged."

Stop for a minute, though, and think about what you have

discovered—what you have *felt* in your very being. Isn't that knowledge, that goodness, worth hanging onto? It is not the means that matters, but rather the end. So what if we made up the part about Sky Fisher being The Chosen One? The rest of it, the rules for leading a better and more fulfilled life, and the pathway to God, are not made up. They are an amalgam of the most profound and sacred traditions of humanity, and I submit that they are in fact the ultimate truths of our existence. And they are many. They are varied. An Australian aborigine meditating in the bush has as much access to God (maybe more) as does an imam in Mecca or a cardinal conducting High Mass, despite the lamentable exclusionist stance many religions take. Yet even VIP membership in a long-standing and acknowledged religion doesn't guarantee you a place in heaven if you're not an active practitioner. That's like buying a new workout outfit and joining an exclusive fitness club, and then figuring you never have to actually exercise.

Maybe Phasmatia is like one of those cryptic Zen Buddhist koans... *"What is the sound of one hand clapping?"* and all that. When you get it, you get it. It doesn't matter how you got there. Each one of us is the medium for our own salvation. Given the diffused, confused, and cynical age we live in, perhaps getting there via a dot-com scheme conceived by a bunch of greedy advertising hacks is a perfect metaphor for our times. Stranger things have happened. After all, God does move in mysterious ways.

Credits

Heartfelt thanks to: Elsa Franklin, for her conviction and tenacity; my editor, Dominic Farrell, for his stalwart craftsmanship; Jim Miller for his sage advice and invaluable criticism; Sonia Holiad for her keen eye and thoughtful suggestions; and Cheryl Cooper for opening the door. Thanks also to my faithful early reviewers, Laura DiCesare, Peter Jagla, and Brian Bell. Special thanks to those priests who taught me firsthand about hypocrisy and intolerance, and to Zee, Abe, L.T., Jay, Sid, and Mo for trying to show us the way.

A few Phasmatians were harmed in the writing of this novel, but they deserved it.

Dan Dowhal, a writer and digital media producer, was born and raised in Toronto's culturally feisty Queen West neighbourhood and lives and works there to this day. Endowed with a pathologically self-expressive nature, Dan's precocious childhood included writing plays, performing on stage, and being paraded around public-speaking competitions.

His writing deftly balances left- and right-brain characteristics, a quality partly explained by his schooling as an engineer, work as a computer programmer, and a later return to academia to earn a journalism degree from Ryerson University. While at Ryerson his penchant for writing bloomed, and he received the A.O. Tate Award for reporting, and was elected editor-in-chief of *The Eyeopener* student newspaper.

Re-entering the working world, Dan Dowhal's rare blend of talents was recognized by IBM and the company snapped him up, leading to a prolonged stint with Big Blue as a writer, manager, and research scientist. Then, in the Nineties, Dan and his two brothers founded The Learning Edge Corp., a producer of interactive digital content, where he continues today as the company's chief writer, editor, and creative director.

Dan is currently a board member of Interactive Ontario, the trade organization representing the province's games, eLearning, mobile, web, and social media producers, and chairs IO's eLearning Committee.

With the turn of the millennium, Dan finally stopped trying to fight the voices in his head and embraced a conversion to fiction with pent-up energy and ideas. His novels to date include *Skyfisher* and *Flam Grub*, and he is just warming up.

Away from the keyboard, Dan shifts gears to chase balls, pucks, and flying discs. If his writing in *Skyfisher* gives the lowdown on the high and mighty, the author also engages high and low experience in his own life, currently learning to fly airplanes and lay stones. For a complete change of pace, he retreats to his northern cabin beside Algonquin Park where he walks in the woods and talks to trees.

Interview with the author

A number of recent news stories address the internet's effect on religion and the relationship between the two. Did one of those specific incidents spark this novel?

DAN DOWHAL: The original concept actually came to me quite a while ago, after reading about Rev. Jim Jones and the Jonestown massacre. At that time the internet was barely a fetus. The story was always meant to be, first and foremost, a study in power and mass manipulation. By the time this idea pushed its way to the top of my pile, screaming to be written, the world, and me personally, had been dramatically and irrevocably transformed by the internet revolution. So that ended up playing a huge part in the book.

Your character Sky Fisher leads a protest march against the government's decision to deny Phasmatians status as a church on the grounds that the Phasmatian religion exists only on the internet, to which he counters, "My world is real, too!" Do you think on-line communities are much different from ones that exist in the "real" world?

DOWHAL: In the way they transcend space and time, and facilitate access to information, online communities are radically different. Once we get beyond the technology, however, those communities, like all others, are still populated by self-interested individuals who have trouble getting beyond their stomachs, groins, and egos. People are people, for better or for worse.

 Can't something like Second Life offer a "real" experience?

DOWHAL: All virtual reality scenarios can stimulate a palpable and profound emotional response from their users—that's why VR has come into use as a tool for treating phobias, for example. But even though I understand the need to periodically escape from it, I do think a lot of online users need to immerse themselves more completely into their first life.

Another character in your book, Brad, says many positive things about the role of religion in general and the good which people can gain from the world's various religions, but doesn't your book also offer a pointed critique of religion, and in particular, of unthinking devotion to a religious leader or a religious text?

DOWHAL: I also can't abide unthinking devotion to a political leader spouting clichéd slogans, but I still have faith in democracy. Or unthinking devotion to a professor regurgitating hackneyed truisms, but I still believe in education. There's a danger in becoming too cynical, isn't there? Every one of us has the capacity to open our minds to larger possibilities. If, as a writer, I can make the reader stop and think, then I will have done my job.

What role do you see religion playing in the world today?

DOWHAL: Religion's job is not necessarily to play a role in the world outside, but to transform the individual within. As a consequence, the world can benefit from more enlightened, tolerant, caring, and motivated individuals. Unfortunately, as we've seen all too often, it all suffers from the destructive power of misguided zealots.

 Does the negative outweigh the positive?

DOWHAL: If you look around at all the ignorance, selfishness, and intolerance out there, it sure seems that way sometimes. But I choose to think it balances out—it's all a question of where you place the fulcrum.

 Do you think people respond in an unthinking or uncritical way to what they find on the internet, just as they might be gullible to religious messages?

DOWHAL: Gosh, you mean the Queen isn't carrying Elvis's alien baby? I think anyone with a modicum of intelligence quickly learns to separate the wheat from the chaff, although there sure is enough bile and crap out there. People generally believe what they want to anyway. The internet represents the democratization of information, and in a democracy, while you can't always agree with what's being said, you have to grant the right to an opinion.

When your characters Brad, Stan, and Fisher set out to design the Phasmatian religion, they deliberately target a younger demographic than traditional religions usually appeal to, successfully tapping into a real spiritual void amongst the young which the Phasmatian site helps to fill. Where is the line between virtual and real? Do you think younger people today feel a spiritual hunger?

DOWHAL: More like a spiritual vacuum, and it didn't start with the current generation. But I'll be honest, I don't really know where it's all heading. In my novel, I was just speculating, not prognosticating. It's a complex question, and it's always dangerous to generalize. I do find it disturbing that so many kids today have a tendency to lead very shallow lives, despite the amount of information they consume, and to follow others blindly. I also find it hard to believe, as some people claim, that humanity has evolved beyond the need for religion, or at least a spiritual life.

Is Skyfisher *really a blueprint? Could some new religion arise in cyberspace to attract a significant number of adherents?*

DOWHAL: Everything in the book is grounded in technical fact, so I think it's certainly possible. It would depend to a large extent on how any new religion was packaged and presented. However, you would never be able to make it catch on. The beauty of viral trends, much to the chagrin of ad agencies, is that you can ride the wave, but you can't really cause it … or predict it, for that matter.

In the character Sky Fisher, a megalomaniac craving adulation and power, you certainly demonstrate how power tends to corrupt and how absolute power can corrupt someone absolutely. Yet he remains a perplexing character, at times seeming to have lost his grip on reality but still able to function and control a complex organization. Is this a larger warning on your part?

DOWHAL: What I was striving for, most of all, was to tell a good story. An engaging villain helps in that regard, especially if he resonates with the reader. Tyrants, petty and otherwise, have been with us from the beginning, and there's certainly no shortage of them today. Still, that just creates an opportunity for the heroes, including the reluctant ones.